A SMALL INDISCRETION

This Large Print Book carries the
Seal of Approval of N.A.V.H.

A SMALL INDISCRETION

JAN ELLISON

THORNDIKE PRESS
A part of Gale, Cengage Learning

GALE
CENGAGE Learning

Farmington Hills, Mich • San Francisco • New York • Waterville, Maine
Meriden, Conn • Mason, Ohio • Chicago

GALE
CENGAGE Learning·

LIBRARY OF CONGRESS CATALOGING-IN-PUBLICATION DATA

Ellison, Jan.
    A small indiscretion / Jan Ellison. — Large print edition.
        pages cm — (Thorndike Press large print basic.)
        ISBN 978-1-4104-7867-2 (hardcover) — ISBN 1-4104-7867-X (hardcover)
        1. Mothers and sons— Fiction. 2. Traffic accidents— Fiction. 3. Large type books. I. Title.
    PS3605.L47534S63 2015
    813'.6— dc23   2015004807

Published in 2015 by arrangement with Random House LLC, a Penguin Random House Company

Printed in Mexico
1 2 3 4 5 6 7 19 18 17 16 15

For my husband, David,
and for my mother

In memory of
Andrew Miles Krantz,
who arrived early and left too soon
November 19, 1983–June 24, 2005

Nothing looks so like innocence
as an indiscretion.

— OSCAR WILDE

London, the year I turned twenty.

I wore a winter coat, the first I'd ever owned — a man's coat purchased at a secondhand store. I wore it every day, along with a silk scarf tied around my neck, imagining I looked arty or sophisticated. Each scarf cost a pound, and I bought them from an Indian woman who kept a stall in the tube station at Victoria, where I caught my train to work. They were thin, crinkled things, not the sort of scarves that ought to be worn to work in an office or that offered any protection against the cold. But I could not resist them, their weightlessness and soft, faint colors. The money I spent on them, and the habit I adopted of wearing a different one each day, seems to me now a haphazard indulgence, an attempt to prove that I was the kind of girl capable of throwing herself headlong into an affair with her boss — a married man twice her age — and escaping without consequence.

"Church," he said, the morning I arrived at the address the woman at the agency had printed out on a card. "Malcolm Church."

He extended his hand, and right away I was struck by a certain contradiction in him — the impressive height and mass of him in opposition to his stooped shoulders, his hesitant manner, his unwieldy arms and legs. He had a square face and round brown eyes and brown hair streaked with gray, but his features were mostly overwhelmed by his size, so that all I remembered afterward was the pleasing sensation of feeling small, by comparison, even at five feet eight. He had a strange way of talking, his head tucked into his neck and his eyes fixed in the empty space beyond, as if something were suspended there, ripe fruit or a glimmer of light, as if he were not quite brave enough, or perhaps too polite, to look a person in the eye.

He asked me how long I was available. I told him I planned to be in London three months, but that my work permit was good for six, through March of next year. I'd intended to claim I was available indefinitely, since the position was listed as full-time permanent, and I was entirely out of money and badly needed the job, but something had stopped me. Not a sense of right and wrong or fear of getting caught, but a hard center of self-importance I had not lived long enough to shed, the notion that I would offer myself on my own terms or not at all. And I was buoyed up by my typing speed — eighty words per minute — about which he never even inquired.

"That'll be fine," Malcolm said, staring intently over my shoulder as he proceeded to explain that his work was in structural engineering, and that he was currently preparing a bid for the new Docklands Light Rail station at Canary Wharf. The London Docklands, he explained, was an area in east and southeast London whose docks had once been part of the Port of London. The area had fallen into disarray, and in the seventies, the government had put forward plans for commercial and residential redevelopment. Malcolm had been involved in the early phases of the project. Now he was hoping to work on the renovation of the original rail station.

There would be dictation and word processing, he said, a little research and generally helping to set up the office and assemble the bid. The office was a single room upstairs from a sandwich shop near Bond Street, with two desks, industrial gray carpet and two folding metal chairs. On one desk was an unusual photograph of a woman and a baby, a posed black-and-white image with a startling play of silver light and shadow set against a background of trees and sky. A single smudge of pink had been hand-painted over the baby's lips. It was Malcolm's family — his wife, Louise, who would feature so prominently in my thoughts, and their infant daughter, Daisy, who was by then ten years old and away at the boarding school in the north that Louise had attended when she was Daisy's age. I was to learn later that the photograph had been taken by a young man named Patrick Ardghal, the son of an old family friend of Malcolm's, who was living in the cottage out back of Malcolm and Louise's house in Richmond. He'd taken the photo a decade earlier, when he was in art school.

In the photo Louise had blond hair and a fine straight nose and a smile with a hint of impatience in it, perhaps not with the baby per se, but with the general condition of motherhood into which Louise had finally plunged. It had taken them seven years to conceive their daughter, Malcolm told me later. By the time they became parents they had already been married a decade, and Louise had not wanted another child. She didn't have the temperament for it, Malcolm said. It overwhelmed and exhausted her and the delivery had nearly killed her, the baby, Daisy, having inherited from her father a rather large head.

I moved from a youth hostel in Earl's Court to a boardinghouse in Victoria. The building was five stories high, made of gray stone, on a block not far from the tube station. My room was ten feet square with bright-blue walls, a laminate desk and a hard, narrow bed covered in a thin white spread. There were bathrooms down the hall. There were no showers, only a single tub and a hose you attached to the faucet for washing your hair. There was no lock on the room with the bathtub, so I made a habit of propping a chair in front of the door for privacy. The chair, as I recall, did not stop Patrick Ardghal. Nothing much stopped Patrick when he had an idea in his mind. He simply shoved the door hard, and I welcomed him, I suppose, as I always did, and he undressed and climbed in. Our wet bodies were awkwardly entangled long enough to please him — then he left, as he always did, taking my heart with him.

My rent was sixty pounds a week, including breakfast and dinner. The meals were served buffet-style in the dining room downstairs. There were eggs and toast and stewed tomatoes for breakfast, meat pie or fish and chips or baked ham for dinner. It was a source of solidarity among the other boarders to complain about the food but I could not in good conscience join in. I loved those meals, the bounty and efficiency of them, the thick gravies, the custards and puddings and soft, fat rolls. It seemed a small miracle to me, to have so much available and to be paying for it all with my own wages. It pleased me, too, each time I handed over a pound coin in exchange for a scarf, and when I purchased, at the second-hand shop in Notting Hill, the winter coat, a full-length single-breasted gray tweed with covered buttons and a wide collar that could be turned up against the cold. I wore my coat and scarf and descended the escalator into the bowels of Victoria Station, emerging again into the dense, unyielding energy of city life feeling brisk, and stylish, and superior to the person I'd been when I'd left home. I was taken over by a sense of liberation and possibility. Any false steps I made now would be mine alone. Any foolish moves would be private business that had no bearing on the hopes and dreams of others, and that would not later be a source of remorse or reckoning or pain.

What a shock to discover, some twenty years later, that exactly the opposite was true. To learn, in the aftermath, that I hadn't known the half of it. To stand in my San Francisco kitchen last June and slip my finger through the flap of a white envelope, and to find a black-and-white photograph of myself in that tweed coat, standing on the chalk down of the White Cliffs of Dover, waiting to board a ferry to Paris.

It was a photograph innocent enough to anyone unacquainted with its history, its treacherous biological imperatives, its call for reparations left unpaid. It had been solarized, just as the photo of Louise and the baby on Malcolm's desk had been. It had been subjected to a light source in the darkroom, causing a reversal of dark and light. My form, and Malcolm's, along with the inch of air between us, were bathed in silver light that brightened at the edges like a halo. Louise and Patrick, on the other side of the photo, were deep in shadow. The scarf I was wearing had been hand-colored a blunt red. It was tied around my neck like a choker, like a noose. But it wasn't me who was about to hang.

15

PART I

ONE

It's not always wise to assume that just because the surface of the world appears undisturbed, life is where you left it.

Monday morning, September 5, 2011. Twenty minutes after eight. I was doing the breakfast dishes when the phone rang. I wiped one hand on a dishcloth and picked up on the second ring. I spoke a quiet hello. You were sleeping directly upstairs in your sister's room, and after the commotion of the night before, I didn't want the noise to wake you.

There was static on the line. I was about to launch into my "national-do-not-call-list" speech when a stranger spoke your name.

"Are you related to a Robert Jonathan Gunnlaugsson?"

"Yes," I said, "Robbie's my son."

There was a brief silence, into which I said what I believed — that you were still asleep. You couldn't come to the phone.

19

I heard voices in the background, then a contusion of words — automobile accident, broken rib cage, possible brain injury, blunt renal trauma. I began to shake. I called for your father. I thrust the phone at him as if it were burning my hand.

He grabbed a pencil and pad off the kitchen counter and made a few notes. "Get a helicopter to take him to the trauma center at Stanford," he barked into the phone. "We'll be there in an hour."

I ran upstairs. Part of me was certain I would find you where I'd left you, on top of Polly's bed, her decorative pillow, shaped like a ballet shoe, still cradling your head.

I flung open the door to her room. I stepped toward the bed. But you weren't in it. Your truck was in the driveway, Robbie, but you were nowhere in the house. We learned later that you'd been riding in the passenger seat of an old Volvo sedan when it flipped just north of Santa Cruz and expelled you into a ravine. The driver's seat belt had held, but yours had not.

Jonathan and I battled our way through the San Francisco traffic and sped thirty miles south on the highway, out of the fog and into the sunlight. We reached the peninsula and took the off-ramp and argued over the

20

route in voices clipped with panic. We made our way through that alien topography — the university, with its low, wide sandstone buildings and flat expanses of sky and lawn, the shopping center, with its vats of flowers and its acres of parking lot, the hospital inside its immaculate suburbia — that sunlit peninsula pressed between the green bay and a bank of hills the color of straw that five months later your father would begin to call home. We drove up the hospital's main drive and circled the extravagant brick fountain, an oasis of shaped trees growing in its center.

I was the one who'd counted your drinks the night before. I was the one who'd somehow incited a riot, then, in the aftermath, set about making sure my three children were safe for the night under the same roof. I was the one who'd moved a sleeping Polly in with Clara so you could have Polly's bed. If I had not made you stay, if I had not altered that sliver of fate, if I had not plucked that single wing from that single butterfly, you wouldn't have ended up in that car. You'd have said your goodbyes and driven across the Bay Bridge to Berkeley and fallen into bed and slept until noon. You'd have returned to the lab a day later to carry on with your investigations in particle physics, along with the pursuit of other elusive truths.

At the main entrance to the hospital were two dogs — eyes half closed, chins flat on the ground in a posture of patient defeat. That was the attitude to avoid. The task at hand — my task — was not to wait patiently but to act. To undo the twist of fate. To be vigilant and merciless in advocating for your medical care. To accept nothing less than a full recovery. To ask every question. To overturn every stone.

Did I suspect, that first morning, that there were some stones better left buried in the dust? That I might wish for the results of certain biological interrogations to be kept hidden, not only from you and from your father, but from myself? I don't think I did. Denial, as any addict in recovery will tell you, is not defined as knowing something and pretending you don't; it is failing to see it at all.

There was no parking at the hospital that morning. Up and around we went, three, four, five levels, then down again, your father taking the corners hard and fast. When we ascended and emerged a second time onto the top level and into the onslaught of the September sun, a car just ahead of us was pulling out of its spot. Jonathan kept his foot on the brake and undid his seat belt and reached into the back for his jacket and his wallet. I dug in my purse for my sunglasses. In that momentary lapse, a car angled into the spot from the other direction.

"What the fuck," your father said.

He thrust the car into neutral and leapt out. He was not so different from when I'd met him. He was as windblown and rugged, as blue-eyed and broad-shouldered and good-looking as he had always been. He still had a full head of dirty-blond hair that made him seem younger than forty-seven, as did his calm, positive, compact energy, his effortless refusal to bend to the mood of the day. So it was shocking to watch him now, storming toward the offending vehicle like an animal protecting its young — vicious, and angry, and so unlike himself, but in a way, beautiful.

He stood up close to the driver's side window and the car door opened a crack, whacking his shin. A leg reached toward the ground. Your father could not see the leg, since he was almost on top of it, but I could see that it was thick and squat and encased in knee-high nylons, the ankles swollen with fluid, the calves mottled with varicose veins.

The shoes were flat and white with rubber soles. The foot, and the leg, were attached to a woman to whom your father said, "My son was airlifted here, and this is my fucking parking spot."

The woman hauled herself out of the front seat. Her face wrinkled with the effort and her small, old eyes leaked and blinked in the sun. Your father took a step back. He stood for a moment, shoved his hands in his pockets, and crossed the parking lot toward me, the rage fading and his face becoming again the mask it had been since I'd returned from London and, four days before, made my foolish confession — a mask I no longer had a right to question or remove.

We exited the structure and pulled into a handicapped spot in front of the emergency room entrance and ran. I held my sunglasses in my left hand and clutched my purse with my right. I had forgotten my sweater. Your father flung his windbreaker over his shoulder and the zipper stung my cheek, the beginnings of retribution, perhaps, for a past that had long ago laid down the invisible blueprint of our future.

When we returned to the car at midnight, there was a ticket tucked under the windshield wiper.

"Two hundred and seventy dollars," Jonathan said. He didn't tear the ticket up but dropped it on the ground and crushed it beneath his foot, the way he might have snubbed out a cigarette. By then, a serious traumatic brain injury had been ruled out. But you had a concussion, a punctured lung, four broken ribs and a chipped right kneecap. And, most threatening, a severed renal artery that had potentially compromised your kidney — the only one, it turns out, you had.

They say the human body can lose 50 percent of its body parts and survive. But it depends on which parts, and which body. Renal agenesis. They don't call it a disease; they call it a condition. The condition of being born with only one kidney, occurring in roughly one in two thousand people. Most never know the condition exists, because the single kidney grows large enough to accommodate the body's needs.

What was it that hit you? Not a tree. Not the hard ground. Not a rock jutting up from the ravine. But something manufactured, plastic or glass or steel, some man-made, hard edge of the car that caught the curve of your body as you flew, piercing you on impact.

When we arrived at the hospital, you were in a medically induced coma, which I was made to understand was a sort of freezing of you, a fabricated reprieve from your own body that would allow your internal organs to rest. We had been informed that while your body was in that state, there was not much we could do. The coma might be necessary for a few days, or a few weeks, or even a few months. It was too soon to tell.

We called my mother. She said your sisters were sound asleep. She said that my father, whom I hadn't seen in more than twenty years, had indeed finally arrived from Maine. She said the two of them would hold down the fort. Jonathan and I drove up and down El Camino Real until we found a room in a motel close to the hospital, the Mermaid Inn, a pink stucco affliction squeezed between a Starbucks and an independent bookstore. Aside from its proximity to you, and the coffee that could be procured next door, the single feature that can be put forward in that motel room's defense was the price — sixty-three dollars a night.

Two

People say a mother is only as happy as her least happy child. But what if the state of that child's happiness has become a mystery? What if that child is no longer a child but a young man who has removed himself to a great distance and encased himself in a great silence? In June of last year, you arrived home from Northwestern for the summer, and a photo arrived in our mailbox. That September, the car flipped. Between those bookends was a family whose happiness might still be intact if only I'd been able to see the threats to it more clearly.

Kids are resilient. That's another thing people say. But what choice do they have? Polly is only six. Six-year-olds cry. Yet I worry that she cries more, this winter, than she used to. I worry about Clara, too. I wonder whether it's normal for a nine-year-old to spend so much time alone in her room making pencil drawings in a sketch pad. I wonder how much is simply their budding natures, and how much the result of our family's new arrangement, in which you are absent, and your father and I live in separate houses, and your sisters are passed between us like a restaurant dessert.

This morning, Polly sat at the kitchen table trying to write a story, squeezing the pencil hard between her fingers. She'd printed her name and the date at the top, writing the month as "Marsh" and making the 7 for the day, and both 2's in 2012 backward. If you'd done that, I'd have whisked you off to a reading specialist. But she's only in kindergarten. I've learned to wait that kind of thing out. And the whispers of small worries are silenced now, mostly, by the volume of the worry over you.

"How do you spell *gonna*?" Polly asked the room at large.

"*Gonna* isn't a word," Clara said.

"Yes, it is," Polly said.

"No, it's not," Clara insisted.

I poured them both Cheerios and started to make their lunches. Polly puzzled over the letters on the cereal box.

"There's no *Z* on this whole box," she said. "So why have it?"

"Actually, there's lots of *Z* words," Clara said. "Like zipper, zip, zebra."

"But Polly's right," I said. "It's one of the less frequently used letters. That's why in Scrabble, it's worth a lot of points."

"How many points?" Clara said.

"I don't know, exactly." I cut the sandwiches I'd made in half and slipped them into plastic bags.

"Actually," Polly said, "can I have a hot dog in my lunch? Daddy puts hot dogs in our lunches instead of sandwiches and they're much, much better."

It was a Tuesday, the last week of May, nearly ten months ago now. My favorite day of the week, because your father took the girls to school so I could get to the store early. I'd been working all morning on a series of lights made from vintage kitchen implements — stovetop toasters, copper colanders, antique silver spoons that I'd drilled and wired, then fitted with gorgeous halogen lights. I turned off all the other lights in the store and sat down to admire my work.

Fourteen years since I started the store. Fifteen since you entered first grade and I found myself a part-time job at a lighting store at the west end of Twenty-fourth Street, near Castro, between our house and your school. The original store sold contemporary lamps and chandeliers and sconces from designers all over the world, but the merchandise was too stuffy for a San Francisco neighborhood like Noe Valley, and within a year, the shop closed. Your father, who had listened to my complaints about the buyer's taste for months, encouraged me to take over the lease and start my own store, and I did. When we reopened, the shop had a new name, the Salvaged Light, and a new look, and one-of-a-kind fixtures that I bought from local artisans and sometimes made myself. It pleased me then, and still did fourteen years later. The reuse of discarded metal and crushed rock and old wood. The marriage of whimsy and beauty. The intersection of junk and utility. The transformation of dead stuff into brilliantly lit life. For a moment, I wished to sit alone in the silence and never compromise the store's perfection by allowing a customer inside.

For the last ten years, an older couple, Ellen and Walter, had lived in the loft upstairs and helped out in the store. But the month before, they'd moved back to L.A. Ellen had worked as store manager, Walter as carpenter, handyman and unofficial night watchman. In the last year, Walter had painted the loft and its bathroom, refinished the floors and built a new staircase. Ellen had designed geometric cutouts in the faces of the steps, and I'd installed blue lights behind them, so that at night they threw sharp patterns on the treads of the stairs. Just before they'd moved out, we discovered water stains on the ceiling beneath the claw-foot tub in the loft. Walter did his best to make repairs. In hindsight, I ought to have called a professional plumber. Perhaps if I had, the tub would not have fallen through the floor the very night you were flying from a car.

I mourned Ellen and Walter's leaving, and badly needed to replace them before your sisters were out of school for the summer. But I also found myself reveling in the solitude.

The front doorbell made its tinkling sound, and I looked up. A young woman was standing at the locked door. I checked my watch. Ten minutes to ten, nearly time to open, anyway. I stood up and flipped over the sign.

"Come in," I said. "I was just about to open."

"I love your store," she said.

"Thank you," I said.

"I'm Emme Greatrex," she said, extending her hand.

"Emma?"

"No," she said. "Just Emme. One syllable. Like the letter *M*. Might I have a look around?"

"Certainly," I said. "I'm Annie Black. Take your time. Let me know if you have any questions."

I sat down at my desk. It was my policy never to hover, but I glanced up now and then to observe her. She looked like a model out of a Free People or Anthropologie catalog. She wore a short skirt with an uneven hem, textured tights and a patch-work sweater that exposed her midriff. She had bangles on her wrists and combat boots on her feet, and she'd tied a scarf around her head that pulled her long blond hair back from her shapely face. She had large, round eyes, gray-green headed toward blue, the eyelids thickened by many colors of shadow.

She was tall, and her limbs moved loosely as she walked through the store. Her head bent slowly from side to side, as if to some private music. She stared at a lamp — one of my favorites — the paper shade an archival giclée print mounted on a base of Vermont slate. She tapped the globe of a blood-red sconce, as if fascinated by the sound her index finger made on the glass.

Then she stood, swaying, looking out the front window.

"Do you have any questions?" I said, and she turned toward me with a start, as if she'd forgotten I was there.

"No," she said. "Your things are lovely, but I'm afraid they're all a bit beyond my resources. I'm actually here about the loft?" She pointed to the LOFT FOR RENT sign in the window.

"Oh," I said.

I took her upstairs and showed her the apartment, then she sat across from me at my desk and we talked. She spoke softly, and I detected a faint accent.

"Where are you from?"

"England, originally," she said. "But I've been living in New York quite a while."

"Is your family still in England?"

"Well . . . my parents are no longer alive," she said.

That stopped me. Not just the fact, but the bruised way she said it.

"My last tenant paid a thousand a month," I said. "I'm prepared to keep it at that level. Even though I could probably ask a bit more, given what San Francisco rents are these days."

She looked at me steadily. "I'm afraid I can't afford quite that much."

33

"Oh," I said. "Well, then —"

"I wonder . . . Might there be a way I could pay you in the future? Once I've found work? I've only just driven out from the East Coast and as yet, I'm unemployed."

"Well," I said. "I don't know about that."

She held herself very still, waiting for me to say more. She was the right age — I guessed late twenties — and she was fashionable and beautiful. She would appeal to the young customers working for high-flying start-ups who were more and more the people in the Bay Area with money to spend. And, most important, she was ready to start right away.

"Maybe we could figure out some kind of work-rent exchange," I said finally.

She smiled. "That would be lovely."

We shook hands. She moved into the loft and started work in the store. She knocked on the door to our lives, and I invited her in, and it very nearly cost us yours.

THREE

The second week of March 2012. I sit at the kitchen table and make my pen move across the page. I resist imagining the present — the store flooded and shut, your father absent, you absent, too — in order to finger my way along the thread, backward to the beginning. But what is the beginning? It depends on who you ask. When I ask myself, my hands take me too far, back and back, down through the decades of marriage and the days in Paris and the months in London, until I am still living at home in Los Angeles, not yet twenty, and my own father is backing his truck down the driveway with an odd smile, insufficient amid the heavy bones of his face.

Where does the thread begin for you? Perhaps on the Fourth of July, when Emme stepped out of the store and into your life.

Where does it begin for your father? When did his seamless happiness begin to unravel?

The evening in late August when I made my confession? Three days later, when you were helicoptered to the trauma center? Or the afternoon in September, fourteen days after the accident, when he and Mitch met privately to discuss the results of the tissue tests? The preliminary kidney-donor screening had been reviewed. We knew your father's blood type was compatible. The next step was to assess tissue compatibility and perform the cross-match test. His blood had been drawn three days earlier for that purpose.

There were no protocols to violate. There were no precedents to follow or not follow. I thought the meeting was routine, best handled by Mitch and your father, since they were both doctors, even if your father had never really practiced. And because one did not question a doctor of Mitch's stature — chairman of the Department of Neurology at Stanford, a celebrated researcher, and one of GQ magazine's 2008 "Rock Stars of Science." We'd teased Mitch no end after he received the award and was pictured on the cover of the magazine in rock-star sunglasses and scrubs, even though he hadn't spent time in an operating room in years. Not until you landed in one, at least, and he stepped in to manage your care.

The trauma-center doctor had decided you were stable enough to emerge from the medically induced coma, and the plan was to take you off propofol the following morning, when the success of your dialysis and the need for a kidney transplant could be better assessed. So when Mitch and your father went off for their meeting, I was happy enough to visit your bedside alone. I sat and watched your face for a long time. I took your bloated hand in mine, and I took comfort in the promise that the following day, or at least within a few days after that, you would wake and be returned to us.

Later, I found Jonathan standing at the window in the waiting room. He was staring into the courtyard below, where a single sycamore tree had been planted. Its leaves had already fallen and its branches were bleached and bare, like bones long buried, dug up and scrubbed clean and displayed in the late-summer light.

I stood next to him at the window. I let my fingers brush his forearm, but he moved a step away from me. He didn't look at me when he spoke. He told me your body was sensitized to his blood. You had antibodies to some of his antigens. If he were the donor, your immune system would turn on his kidney and destroy it.

"I'm sorry," I said. "I know you wanted it to be you."

"It's all right," he said.

But it wasn't.

Driving back to the city from the hospital, at twilight, there was a thickening of color in the sky behind the hills, and I felt hopeful, in spite of everything. We'd known it was possible your father would not be a match. We'd known there was only a 50 percent chance of a match for each of us, and though I knew he was disappointed he would not be the one to make the sacrifice, I felt sure that my own tissue test would show a positive, and that my kidney and I would be up to the task, if required, and that your body would embrace your new organ with its usual grace and competence. You would come out of the coma the following day and we would all set out on the road to recovery.

"Are you all right?" I said to your father.

"I'm fine."

But he did not hold my hand across the center console. He did not take the scenic route we sometimes took, pulling off at the coast to watch the sun drop behind the horizon before we drove home.

That night, he slept on a camping mat, as

he had in August, when I returned from London.

"Why are you sleeping on that again?" I asked him.

"My back hurts," he said.

I handed him a pillow off the bed. "Take this, at least."

"I don't need that," he said. He bent down and began to blow up the attached inflatable compartment.

"Maybe you should let me do that," I said. "I've had more experience blowing things up."

I had wanted it to seem like an apology, for London, but it came across sounding bitter. He didn't even acknowledge I'd spoken. He did not kiss me good night, and I did not lower myself to the ground and ask him to. I lay on top of the sheet, the covers shoved aside, sweating. This was how I would live if your father never forgave me. This would be the trade I'd made. A moment's friction for a life in which I would never again be free of my own body. I would never again press against his coolness beneath the sheets. I would be encumbered by my own reckless heat, the way I had been the winter I met him.

The way, perhaps, you had been last summer, Robbie, when you first met Emme.

FOUR

It was eight months ago, last Fourth of July. Emme had been living and working in the store for just over a month. I'd extended her a last-minute invitation to join us for the day, and I'd promised her we'd pick her up on our way out of the city. We all piled into the Suburban and set off, and when we reached the store, I knocked on the glass door, then returned to the car to wait.

" 'The Salvaged Light,' " you read. "Did you repaint the sign?"

"Yes," I said. "The old one was getting faded."

"I used to call it 'the Savage Light,' " you said.

"Because you had a lisp."

"It wasn't the lisp. I really thought it was 'the Savage Light.' Because of that book we had, remember? About the savage."

"I remember that book," your father said. "We must have read it to you a thousand times. It was about a boy who writes a story about a monster, right? Then the monster comes to life."

"It wasn't really a monster," you said. "It was just a person who went wild. The boy starts writing the story when his father dies, to distract himself. When the savage comes to life, he can't tell where he ends and the savage begins."

"I always wondered what the writer was trying to say, metaphorically speaking," your father said.

"Something about the power of the stories we tell ourselves to fend off despair," I said. "Or am I being too literal?"

Polly piped up from the third row of seats. "I know that story. I remember it. We still have that book."

"No, we don't," Clara said.

"Yes, we do," Polly said.

"No, we don't. Mommy gave it away to the library with all the other books."

"I didn't give all the books away," I said. "Just the ones nobody ever reads."

Emme emerged from the store, cutting short the argument. She was wearing very short shorts and her combat boots, and she carried an enormous fringed bag over one shoulder. Her legs were thin and pale and her hair was so thick and blond and long it

41

was more like a Barbie's hair than a woman's. I had never seen it down before. I'd only seen it tucked beneath a hat or a scarf or pulled back in a headband or wound around her head in a braid, like a crown.

She stepped toward us in the fog. Did it shoot through the air between you right then — the speeding bullet of recognition or desire?

She climbed into the car next to you. She was holding a book, which she dropped into the side pocket of her bag so she could shake your hand.

"Robbie, this is Emme," I said. "Emme, this is Robbie."

"Nice to finally meet you, Robbie," she said.

You lifted the book out of the pocket of her bag and examined the cover. *"Zen Ko-ans?"*

"Yes," she said quietly.

"What's a Send-Going?" Polly asked from the back.

You laughed. "Zen ko-an," you said slowly. "It's a paradox, or a puzzle, used to teach enlightenment. For instance, 'What is the sound of one hand clapping?' "

"Why do you know this?" I said, turning to look at you.

"My department chair is interested in the

42

link between physics and enlightenment."

Jonathan glanced back. "He is?"

"Yep."

"Wow," your father said. "Interesting. So if a tree falls in the forest, does it make a sound?"

"Actually, when a tree falls, it creates shock waves. And when the shock waves reach an ear or an artificial mechanism like a microphone, they're transmitted into what we call sound," you said. "The shock waves themselves are not sound."

"But does it make a sound or not?" Clara asked.

"We don't really know," Emme said. "That's the mystery we're intended to sit with."

"Are you a Buddhist?" you said.

"Oh, no," Emme said. "I just saw the author speak at a bookstore in the Mission. He made it all seem so simple. He said we can achieve happiness not by remaking ourselves, but by subverting unhappiness. By throwing it overboard."

"I like that," Jonathan interjected enthusiastically. "Let's all throw unhappiness overboard."

"But you're already happy," I said to him, not altogether kindly. His optimism and good humor occasionally struck me as

43

bordering on delusional. "You don't need to throw it over, because you never invited it on board in the first place."

He looked at me and grinned. "Nothing wrong with happiness."

It was seven months later that he announced he was moving out. You had been gone from the house for a week. It was a bright February afternoon, and we were driving in the car. The sun was making metallic streaks on the windshield. The girls were at home with a sitter. We were returning from Sunday brunch at Mel's, a tenuous reenactment of what had often been our version of date night. It had been a relief to escape the relative quiet of the house since the holidays had ended and the leavings had begun. First my brother had returned to L.A. and my father to Maine, inviting us all to come visit him there soon. Then my mother left, and finally, Robbie, you did. Things were still strained between your father and me, but he had been the one to suggest the date, and I was encouraged that he was making an effort.

He squinted forward and lifted his hand to shield his eyes from the glare. Then, without a preamble of any kind, he announced that his author friend who lived in

Gold Hill, the one who'd invited us all over on the Fourth of July, was leaving in a few days for a year abroad. He'd offered to let your father move in as a house sitter.

"You're moving out?" I said.

"Yes."

"When?"

"As soon as I pack up."

He told me he planned to work in partnership with a team of researchers he'd met in the fall on a major new initiative at the Stanford University Medical Center — the development of content on health-related topics that could be packaged and sold for digital distribution. He was giving up the office space he'd leased in the city for fifteen years. He intended to work directly out of the house in Gold Hill. It made sense professionally and economically. Also, Stanford had made a sizable investment, which would pay all the hospital bills. And he could take a higher salary than he ever had before. We would no longer need to worry about money, at least not in the short term. We'd be fine without the salary I'd been paying myself since the store turned profitable a decade earlier. I wouldn't have to rush to reopen as soon as the damages from the flood were repaired. I could wait until I was ready.

We had reached the business district, almost deserted on a Sunday afternoon. The street was deep in the shadow of downtown. He pulled over and parked. He didn't look at me.

"You did all this without telling me?"

"Yes," he said.

"Why?"

"I guess I feel like we need some time apart."

I sat in the seat beside him, stunned. I should never have confessed. I should have wiped my one indiscretion — one indiscretion in more than twenty years — from my conscience, and our marriage would still be intact.

I started to cry. Then I groveled. I pleaded. I grew angry. But his mind was made up. He'd thought it all through. He figured the girls could stay with him alternating weekends and an evening or two a week until school got out. Then, in the summer, they could split their time between us.

He had been facing straight ahead, looking out the windshield, but now he turned to me, and I could see in the relentless blue of his eyes that he was not going to change his mind.

"Are we getting a divorce?"

"No, we're not getting a divorce," he said.

"Not yet, anyway. We're just . . . I don't know what we're doing."

"You don't know what *you're* doing," I said. "I'm not doing anything."

"You've done enough."

"It was one night, Jonathan. It was stupid. It was pointless."

He said nothing. Because the thing that had broken him was not the thing I was trying to explain away.

FIVE

Saturday, March 17. St. Patrick's Day. Seven weeks since you left this house, six since your father did, too.

On Thursday night, your father came to collect the girls for an overnight in Gold Hill. I had been crying earlier, and before he arrived, I looked at myself in the mirror — really looked — for the first time in months. I smoothed the wrinkle between my eyes. I put drops in to clear away the red. I put on lipstick and mascara. I ran a brush through my hair, wishing I'd taken the time to wash it. I studied my profile, then my back side, in a hand mirror — the curves I'd always tried to camouflage, which your father had claimed to love, and the hair he'd claimed to love as well. Welsh hair, from my mother's side, straight and long and still a dark brown, except underneath, where the gray threatened. The face was my mother's, too

— thick black arched eyebrows, the eyes beneath the same as yours, a fiercer, lighter green than people expected to find in our olive-skinned faces. A narrow nose flanked by what your father had once called "discriminating" cheekbones. Fullish lips and straight front teeth. Crooked bottom teeth I'd long ago learned to hide when I smiled.

I forced my face into a smile now, looking to see if whatever your father had first fallen for was still there, but my relationship to my overall appearance was as erratic as ever. I looked once, and glimpsed the old prettiness, but when I looked again, from another angle, it seemed to have been a trick of the light, and I could find only a series of small but certain flaws — in the skin, the shape, the hair — that were growing in strength and number as time marched on. I fell back into the tired script I'd been running all my life: If, when I looked, I was not perfect, how could I be beautiful? And if I was not beautiful, how could I be loved? I was not the only woman who ran that script. A worldwide industry promoted and supported its story. But since last summer, it had reached deeper for me. It had moved from the skin and the shape and the hair straight to the heart.

Polly appeared in the doorway as I was

staring at my face.

"What are you looking for?" she said.

I turned away from the mirror. How ridiculous to indulge in vanity with the question of your well-being hanging in the balance.

"Nothing," I said to Polly. "Nothing at all."

Jonathan did not ring the bell or knock. He opened the door with his key and came in. Polly pushed past me down the stairs. Clara emerged from her room and followed. I watched as your father embraced them.

"Hey," I said.

"Hey."

The girls went to collect their things, and your father stood for a minute with his hands in his pockets, surveying the room as I came down the stairs. He walked into the kitchen to get himself a glass of water.

"What's that whirring noise?" he said.

"It's the refrigerator."

"Why is it making that sound?"

"I don't know."

"How long has it been doing that?"

"I don't know. Awhile."

His tone was vaguely accusing, vaguely annoyed, which I took as a good sign — he was still territorial about this house. He dragged a chair over and lifted a panel at the top of the refrigerator and peered inside.

"Do you have any tools?"

"I guess I have whatever you didn't take."

He found an old toolbox in the garage and stood on the chair again and lifted off the panel. He stuck one tool in, then another.

"There," he said, putting the panel back and returning the tools to the toolbox. He was so appealing, standing there, so useful and solid and familiar, I wanted to fall into him and demand to be forgiven. But Polly and Clara came into the kitchen with their backpacks, and Polly wrapped her arms around your father's legs and he laid his hands on her head. I could tell he was taking sustenance from Polly's embrace just as I so often have, especially since your accident. Even before it, in August, when I dragged myself downstairs the morning after my return from London, and Polly looked at my face and opened her arms and squeezed me while I cried. Which is not to say that Polly is always kind. Or that Clara is, either. What six- and nine-year-old girls are always kind to their mother?

I forgot that it was St. Patrick's Day today, and when I picked the girls up from soccer practice, Polly reached up and pinched the flesh at the back of my arm.

"Ouch," I cried. "What was that about?"

"It's about you're not wearing green," she said bitterly. "And it's about you didn't tell me I was supposed to, and I got pinched."

"I'm sorry I didn't tell you, Polly, but you shouldn't pinch me like that. It hurt me."

"She's right, though," Clara said. "You should have told us."

I turned to look at Clara, suddenly angry. "You know what? I'm doing my best," I said sharply. She blinked up at me, and I continued. "Mommies can't always be perfect."

She took a step backward, away from me, and Polly burst into tears. I picked Polly up, and she laid her head on my shoulder. I reached toward Clara and held her against me, but I could feel the resistance in her. At nine, she had begun to see a truer picture of me than Polly could. She had begun to see what I saw — not beauty, but imperfections. I let her pull away from me.

"I'm sorry I pinched you, Mommy," Polly whispered, sounding very sorry indeed.

"I'm the one who's sorry," I said.

Mothers can't always be perfect, but they can be much better than I was last summer.

You returned home from your third year at Northwestern on June 9, our wedding anniversary, the day before the photo arrived. We'd planned a dual celebration in honor of our long marriage and the recent announcement that you'd been named a Northwestern STEM Scholar, making you eligible to spend your senior year studying at research institutions around the world that partnered with Northwestern. During the summer and fall, you'd be at Lawrence Berkeley working on an optical computing project. In January, you'd head to the National Institute of Information and Communications Technology in Japan, to work on space weather research, specifically solar wind. Then, for the grand finale, you hoped to find a project in the area that most interested you — light-source machines.

"Whatever those are," I'd said to your father when we received the letter from the dean outlining the plan and informing us that tuition, travel and living expenses were to be provided through a STEM scholarship.

The girls had spent the day making a cake, elaborately frosted on one side with a *22,* for the number of years we'd been married — close enough, your father said to me, with a wink — and on the other side with a long green painted stem (they had not understood *STEM* was an acronym) topped with a real daisy they'd picked from the backyard.

"Did you know that the name of that flower is translated as 'the day's eye' in Old English?" your father had said. "Because of the way it opens at dawn."

"You're full of fun facts, aren't you?" I said.

"Can we watch it?" Polly asked. "Can we get up really early and go in the backyard and see?"

"Sure," your father said. "Sure we can."

I gave him a look. "Dawn? Really?"

"Why not? It'll be fun."

You'd allotted us only two nights, because your classes at Berkeley were beginning in a few days and you wanted to settle into the room you'd rented in a shared house off-campus. Over dinner, you told us you'd been lucky enough to secure a three-month stay, beginning in April, at a research institute in Oxfordshire, England, with a light-source machine.

"What is a light-source machine?" Clara wanted to know.

"It's a synchrotron, technically," you explained. "It generates infrared and ultra-violet light invisible to the naked human eye. Researchers use it to see unimaginably small things no other apparatus, much less

54

the human eye, can see."

"It can generate light ten billion times brighter than the sun," your father added.

"Wow," Clara said.

"Why do you know that?" I asked your father.

"Because I'm full of fun facts," he said, smiling.

"Dad just knows about interesting stuff, Mom," you said.

"Oh, really?"

You caught yourself. "Not to say that you don't."

But of course that was exactly what you were saying, and I felt the old tug of discomfort. Your father was trained as a doctor; you were a STEM Scholar; I didn't even have a college degree. And the thing that concerned me — the lighting of homes — was trivial compared to the matters that preoccupied you and your father. You, science in its purest form. Your father, science as it applied to the health of the body. Never mind that my salary from the store contributed significantly to the family income. Never mind that it had helped support us, over the years, when the books your father edited and published — books on chronic disease, arthritis, diabetes, cancer — unexpectedly failed to sell, or cost too much to produce. Or when the book publishing business as a whole felt the reverberations of the changing economy.

"Looks like we're both going to be in the business of making light," you said, trying to appease me.

"But Mom's lights aren't brighter than the sun," Clara said.

"And why do people want all kinds of lights made of junk, anyway?" Polly asked.

"Well, because it's beautiful junk," I said defensively. "And people need a little beauty now and then."

"As long as it's not form over function," you said.

"What's wrong with a little form over function?"

"Give her a break," your father said. "Someone does need to put beauty in the world, and your mother does it very well." He stood up and fished a box from a drawer in the hutch and handed it to me. "Speaking of beauty."

"Jonathan," I said, taken aback. "We said no gifts."

"I know. But this is long overdue," he said. "Open it."

Polly pulled the box out of my hand. "Can I open it?"

"Sure," I said.

She opened the box. Inside was a diamond wedding ring. I picked it up and slipped it on and held it up to the light.

"You didn't need to do this," I said.

"You're crying," Clara said.

"It's all right if she cries a little," your father said.

"I'm crying because . . . it's beautiful."

It was the diamond from your father's grandmother's ring, he explained, and the three smaller stones in the setting were to represent each of you. He'd had it made to replace the cubic zirconium he'd bought me when we were first married, which in turn replaced the gumball-machine ring he'd slipped onto my finger when he proposed.

"I wasn't sure whether you'd like gold or white gold," your father said. "I figured you could have it reset if you wanted something different."

I stood up and kissed him.

"I don't want something different," I said, and I meant it. And not just about the ring, but about our twenty-one years of marriage. The people we'd made. The life we'd shaped together, exactly the life I wanted. I had no reason to suspect, standing there, that the very next day, I would begin to act not as if I wanted to give that life away, but as if I wanted something different to go along with it.

After dinner, we all played charades. Then you read the girls a bedtime story, and your father promised to wake them up early so they could try to watch the daisies open. You slept in your old room.

"I changed the sheets," I said, pulling the covers back.

"Gee, thanks, Mom. 'Cause I'm not used to sleeping on dirty sheets."

"I know, I know."

"I brought my laundry."

"That was collegiate of you."

"If you don't have time, it's no biggie."

"I have time."

I threw a load in right away. It gave me pleasure to wash all those dark T-shirts and dark sweatshirts and dark jeans that smelled of aftershave and outdoors. Some of it, I guessed, had not been washed since I'd laundered it at Christmas. Thinking of it now, I can't help remembering the clothes you were wearing when the car flipped. The clothes they cut off you, which I washed and kept, because I could not bear to throw them away.

By the time I woke up, the girls had been

58

watching TV since six, and you and your father had taken the dogs and your mountain bikes to Mount Tam. A wig of fog had overtaken the city in the night, and apparently the daisies had not known it was dawn, and remained closed. Your sisters were disappointed, and overtired from waking so early, and now they were arguing over what to watch on TV. I turned the television off and made pancakes, then set the girls up at the counter to make lemonade from lemons a neighbor had brought over the day before. Polly spilled half a bag of sugar on the floor, and I pressed my fingers over my eyelids and sighed.

"You're sighing," Polly cried out. "You said for us to tell you when you were sighing."

Clara nodded. "You said you were giving up sighing for Lent."

"That was just kind of a joke," I said. "And anyway, Lent's over, and I can sigh from time to time if I want to."

When the lemonade was made, I poured the girls each a cup and we went outside. The sun battled through the fog, and the girls sat on the swing on the front porch, and I sat on the top step with my coffee and pulled my knees up to my chin. It was an ordinary morning. An ordinary day in the life of an ordinary family. The last of its kind, for us. But I didn't know that then.

You and your father pulled up in your truck, your muddy bikes and the dogs in back. It was your father who'd insisted on two dogs, so they could keep each other company. The breed was his idea, too — German shepherds — the same as he'd grown up with. He got out of the truck and took off his cleats and sat down on the step next to me. The dogs waited, their tails wagging wildly, until your father called them. Then they jumped out of the truck and ran toward us. He snapped his fingers and pointed, and they dropped to the ground.

"If only you could control children as well as you can control dogs," I said.

"Who says I can't?"

"I say you can't."

He flung his arm over my shoulder.

"You're muddy and smelly," I said.

He pulled me toward him and kissed me hard on the mouth. "You love it," he said. "Admit it."

You stood in your shorts and cleats, pushing the girls on the swing. You seemed rugged and healthy in your biking gear, your calves caked with mud, your back and shoulders and legs strong like your father's, but stretched over a six-foot-three-inch frame. We were a family made up not of averages but of absolutes: you and Clara large-boned and tall; Polly so small and slight even Clara could still lift her up. Watching you together — your hair and eyes, your flesh and bone, your three bodies so frank and solid in the world — gave me immeasurable pleasure. It was pleasure derived not from parental pride, but from gratitude. We had been blessed by the existence on this earth of our three particular children, and we had been assigned a blessed task in keeping you all safe in the world.

Then Polly wanted more lemonade, and I said she'd had enough. She jumped off the swing in protest and began to cry. Your father picked her up and took her inside. You lifted Clara onto your shoulders and trotted into the backyard. I walked down the steps and retrieved the mail. I stood at the kitchen counter, flipping through the stack, dropping the junk mail in the garbage and making a pile of the bills. On the very bottom was an oversize white envelope. I slid my finger through the flap. I pulled out a smaller envelope and dropped the outer one in the trash. Inside the smaller envelope was a photograph — the White Cliffs, the chalk down, and a version of myself at roughly the age you are now, staring back. His name came into my head — *Patrick Ardghal* — and my breath caught in my chest. I fished the outer envelope from the trash, but the postmark was indecipherable.

Your father walked into the kitchen, and I slid the photograph under the stack of bills. I wanted time to think. I wanted a chance to confront the old longing that had so suddenly overtaken me. What was the nature of that longing? What was it I wanted, exactly? An explanation? An accounting? Perhaps. But also something wholly unbefitting a married woman of forty-one, mother to two young daughters and a nearly grown son: I wanted to see Patrick Ardghal again.

When I was alone, I took the photo and the bills upstairs to the hall closet. I placed the photo in the heavy, round gold-foil hatbox that once held my wedding veil, and where I keep the important artifacts. Nine months later, when I could not reach you to tell you this story and I began to let it bleed from my fingers instead, it was in the hatbox I was to hide this half-decipherable scrawl.

The longing to see Patrick Ardghal took the shape of obsession as the summer progressed, and my days became haunted with half-formed fantasies. Those fantasies shamed me, but I could not get rid of them. I spent many hours in the weeks after the photo arrived imagining him tracking me down, sending me the photograph, seeking me out. I wondered where he might be living. I searched the Internet, and checked my email many times each day, and wandered the rooms of the past. I ran headlong into memories, not just of Patrick but of Malcolm, too. I did not dwell on the memories of Malcolm — from our time together in London and Paris — because they were painful, and nonnegotiable. It was not Malcolm who appeared in my sleeping dreams last summer, but Patrick. One especially vivid dream was of Patrick stepping out of the fog and knocking on my front door and presenting me with a ring box, in which, instead of a ring, were a dozen old library cards — a symbol for love that could be borrowed, perhaps, but never kept. That dream, and others, came again and again, plaguing me all day after I woke up and flooding me with a useless, unsubstantiated longing — a colored emotional fluorescence with which the plain waking world could not compete.

At the same time, I was happy with your father. The heart is large, and there is more than one material in the bucket we call love.

I loved your father. I loved the new ring —
with its old stone and new stones — and I
wore it proudly. I loved the laden, harried,
unremarkable events that were our days. I
loved the whole barely observed construction that was our life. But I also loved the
way the idea of Patrick opened an ordinary
day to the feeling that something out of the
ordinary might happen to me at any moment. Perhaps I inherited that appetite from
my father. Perhaps it was not shame at all
that kidnapped my father that summer day
when I was nineteen and he backed his
truck down the driveway and set off for
Maine. Perhaps it was not regret, or remorse, my father felt as he looked for the
last time at that rock-and-timber house.
Perhaps it was the same cocktail of self-
indulgence and abandon and want — and
an unaccountable wish to be free, if only for
a little while — I discovered in myself last
summer.

It seems almost impossible that less than a
year has passed since that June day. I've
noticed I don't often sigh anymore, as I did
making lemonade with your sisters that
morning. There isn't much room for impatience when real worry has claimed the day.
And there isn't much need for most of what

64

you can find in the bucket of love at a time like this. Somebody said — some poet, I can't remember which one — that unrequited love is the best kind. But I can tell you with certainty, Robbie, that the other kind of love, the kind I received from your father for more than two decades, is far more necessary.

Six

I pull the thread, and it grows longer. I tug and tug, from this spring of 2012 to the fall of 1989, when I first went to London. Then I tug further, even, until the story makes a stop in a place that is more mine than yours, since I lived there before your beginnings.

I was nineteen, taking classes at a community college in the San Fernando Valley, majoring in French, of all things. I had been to the travel-studies office at the college and learned I could not afford tuition for a semester in Paris. I also learned I couldn't work in France unless I was a citizen, but I could apply for a work-exchange program in the United Kingdom, which would get me to Europe, at least. I submitted my application and waited to hear.

I was living with my mother and father and my brother, Ryan, ten years younger, in Pine Crest, which, in spite of its picturesque name, was a wasted place at the lip of Los

Angeles, slung above the valley's miasmic flats. It was one in a series of towns strung together in the foothills, bounded by the western edge of the San Gabriel Mountains and linked by an unbroken thoroughfare of biker bars and auto shops and liquor stores. The downtown was a single block without sidewalks, home to the post office and a Pic 'N' Save and our single dining establishment — a Mexican restaurant where I was working part-time as a waitress.

Winters were brief and wet. The rain fell in sheets and the creeks bulged and the wash overflowed and the canyon at the base of the mountains became a swift brown river. By April the rain was gone and it was as hot as it would be at the height of summer. Under the baking sun were three-story apartment buildings painted pastel colors, bounded by concrete and chain link, whole communities of children contained within. A handful of single-family dwellings had survived rezoning — flat-roofed ranchers and spec houses and the odd old cabin made of river rock and timber, set on a long, slim, sloping acre of wild poppies and weeds. Out back of such a house, our house, was a curve of driveway and a detached garage abutting an empty field, in winter neat and green as grass, turning in spring to

67

parched yellow weeds beneath an arc of blue sky.

The front porch had been halfheartedly enclosed by the previous owners to make two children's bedrooms, rooms whose interior walls were the cement and stone and wood of the outside of the house. The cement had crumbled away here and there and cobwebs grew. Ryan and I lay on my bed in the summers and watched the sun leak through the gaps, making feathery designs on the backs of our hands.

It was a town that had not yet been connected to the sewer. We had a cesspool that frequently overflowed, flooding the slab of concrete beside the back door. We could not afford to have the cesspool pumped, so for years we had been engaged in a conservation campaign that involved flushing rarely, washing both dishes and vegetables in a bucket in the sink and siphoning the shower water into the yard. We would each take our turn with the plug in the drain, the collective runoff trapped inside the walls of the small, square blue-tiled enclosure that was both shower and tub. Then my father latched the hose to a bib out front and dragged it up the front steps, over the threshold and into the entryway, across the living room carpet, through the back hall and into the shower. I turned on the water outside, and he yelled when the bubbles stopped. He was a great one for yelling. Bellowing, really, not with venom but with authority, a kind of verbal clap on the back for a job well done. These verbal claps grew louder as the day wore on, a phenomenon I did not associate with his drinking until long after he, and then I, had left home. One winter evening, my father whacked a hole in the siding that flanked the front door and ran the hose through, making it a fixed feature of our home, and a more or less permanent excuse for not entertaining.

My father was often without a regular job. During these spells, my mother worked double shifts as an emergency-room nurse to keep the family afloat, and my father involved Ryan and me in important projects. These projects always began with my father pacing the back patio, talking, while I took notes and made pencil sketches on a white pad, I having been deemed "artistic" by the art teacher at school. The pencil sketches led to formal plans and the purchase of supplies and a burst of activity that might last a week or a month or a season, until the current project was set aside in favor of the next. There was a device that would turn your television off when you clapped your hands. There were two exotic parrots and the construction of an aviary, the idea being that we would train the birds to do tricks and form a traveling bird show. There was a beekeeping period, and a leather-working period, and an organic vegetable garden, the products of which we intended to sell at farmers' markets around the valley. But we never did.

Sometimes we drove to a reservoir twenty miles north, off the highway. We sat in the roped-off sandy area and ate tuna sandwiches and swam in the dirty green water while my father drank beer on the beach. I did not understand how paltry a pleasure those days had been until I chased my father to Maine and saw the white clapboard cottages with their window boxes full of flowers, and the bright-green lawns, and the endless blue of Somes Sound.

The alliance of my father and brother and me seemed to trump normal adolescent activities. I was more often at home than out with my friends, and any entanglements I had with boys, I kept secret. My entanglements never went very far, anyway. I wasn't afraid of the sin of it, or of getting pregnant; I was afraid the main event — sex — would not be any good, and I would have to pretend it had been. Or I was afraid that when the moment arrived, I would change my mind, but I would move forward anyway, betraying myself. I was afraid the boy would turn out to be inferior to me, or at least inferior to my father's hopes for me. So I held on to my virginity even as I watched every single one of my friends get rid of theirs. The longer I waited, the more embarrassing a burden it became — one it seemed I might never shed.

My father brewed exotic beers in the basement — porters and pale ales and red ales — and sometimes cider or barley wine. In the evenings, he drank until he achieved oblivion. Not just his beer but whiskey, too. I remember once, or maybe it was many times, walking into the kitchen at night and finding him standing beneath the open door of the liquor cabinet with a bottle to his lips. While I lived with him, that image was stored inside me not in the place of memories but in the place of lucid dreams, and I was not sure I believed what I saw.

Taking the garbage out had always been my job. One Sunday when I was nineteen, I collected the bag from the kitchen and tossed it into the aluminum garbage can out back, then crushed the bag down with my hands so the lid would close. Something in the bag sliced through the flesh below my right thumb, and I howled. My father emerged from the house and barked at my brother to get a towel to stop the blood, then he set his beer down and walked toward me to inspect the wound. He was moving the way he moved when he was very drunk — his torso pitched forward, his legs unnaturally stiff, his steps heavy — as if he had suddenly gone blind or grown old.

He leaned over me. "Looks like this one needs a stitch or two," he said.

I could smell the alcohol on his whole body, as if he'd bathed in it. It was whiskey I smelled, not just beer. But I pretended not to notice. I pretended his words weren't rushing together, and he wasn't stumbling. I pretended so hard, I failed to protest. I got into the cab of the truck next to my father, and Ryan climbed in after me. My father drove us halfway across Los Angeles to the hospital. I couldn't drive myself, since my hand was gushing blood through the rags wrapped around it, leaking onto my lap. My mother couldn't drive me, since she was already at the hospital, beginning her second shift.

She was standing out in front of the emergency-room entrance when we drove into the parking lot, wearing her white nurse's dress and her white tights and her white shoes. Lit from behind by the hospital's lights, she looked like an immaculate ghost. My father pulled up in front of her and opened the driver's side door, but instead of putting the truck in park, he'd put it in reverse. At first I thought it was the car next to us moving. I watched it, fascinated, until I saw that it was us heading backward, and that my father was half in and half out of the cab of the truck as it lurched in reverse toward a parked car. He hit the brakes. He turned the ignition off and staggered around to open my door. I watched my mother watching him. I watched her turn from a ghost to a person made of flesh and blood and resolve. I saw the change first in her face, then in the clipped motion of her steps as she came toward us. In that moment, I saw her break free of the dogged loyalty — and love — she'd struggled under all those years.

It would not have occurred to me to wonder what it was in that garbage can that had sliced open my hand. But it occurred to my mother. She looked later that night and found a broken whiskey bottle wrapped in a paper bag.

There was an intervention. A soft-spoken gray-haired woman affiliated with the Betty

Ford Center was in charge of it. I had been taken to see her, beforehand, and she'd asked me to write my father a letter. At the intervention, she looked at me kindly and made me want to flee. There were other people in the room besides that woman and my mother and brother and me, but I don't remember who they were. I read the letter I'd written, under duress, enumerating the wrongs my father had done me when he was under the influence of alcohol, wrongs I didn't believe in, even though I knew them to be true. He had dropped a glass and broken it, now and then, and forgotten to clean it up. He had stood in the kitchen, in the dark, late at night, with a bottle to his lips. He had driven my brother and me to the county hospital when he was very, very drunk. I imagined my letter was the hardest blow. I looked up after I read it, and saw in my father's face a helpless bewilderment I was never able to forget.

I was not angry with him, though I see I ought to have been. I am not sure I believed he was an alcoholic. I clung to my allegiance to him, even when it was discovered, some time after he'd left home, that the bank account that held my life savings had a balance of zero. It was a custodial account, never switched out of my father's name.

There was a lien on the property in Maine he'd inherited from his mother. The IRS was entitled to property taxes that had not been paid, and the money to pay them was sucked directly from my account. Twenty-six hundred dollars was all it was, but it was all the money I had.

At the end of the intervention, he solemnly promised to enter rehab the next day. Instead, at dawn, he backed his truck down the driveway and set off for Maine and never returned.

"There's a woman there," my mother told me later. But I don't think I believed her, and when the summer ended, I announced that I was not going back to community college. Instead, I planned to take a Greyhound bus to Maine, collect the money I was owed and go to Europe. My mother and Ryan took me to the bus station. My mother cried as she slipped two one-hundred-dollar bills into my hand. Ryan stood awkwardly at her side. I had prepared a little speech in my head for him, but at the last minute it seemed there was nothing I could say that he would not learn on his own, one way or another.

SEVEN

In February of this year, the girls spent their first weekend with your father in Gold Hill. I drove them from the city and dropped them off on Friday afternoon. Jonathan didn't invite me in, exactly, but I came in anyway. I stood in the foyer. I looked out the picture windows at the view of open space, green hills turning to deeper green mountains against a pristine blue sky.

He stood in the doorway between the hallway and the kitchen. He had a dish towel over his shoulder.

"There's a trampoline next door," he said to Clara and Polly. "The neighbors said you can come over and use it anytime."

They ran outside to peer through the fence.

"I hope there's a net," I said.

He took the dish towel off his shoulder and tossed it on the kitchen counter. I was struck by the physicality of the gesture, struck, anew, by his raw athleticism. Every movement he made was masculine and energetic and graceful. I had loved that in the beginning. I could not decide whether I loved it now. I was putting all such assessments on hold until I knew whether or not we were going to remain married.

"Of course there's a net," he said. "Give me a little credit."

"I was only asking," I said. "Just because we're separated doesn't mean I'm obliged to stop being a parent."

He looked at me as if considering me for the very first time, but he said nothing.

"I'm sorry," I said. "I didn't mean to sound so brittle. Do you like it here?"

"I do."

"What do you like about it?"

"Everything."

"But what, specifically?"

"I like the view, and the space, and the neighborhood. I like that there's no traffic. I like the paths that connect the streets. I like the people. And I love the backyard."

"The dogs would love the backyard, too."

"I was going to ask you about that, actually. I was thinking they could come along when the girls visit."

"They're your dogs more than anybody

else's. You can have them when you want them."

"They're not my dogs. They're . . . they were . . . our dogs."

"Do you miss the city?"

He laughed. "I've wanted to get out of that city for years, Annie."

"You never said so."

"Sure I did. I hinted, anyway."

"Why did we stay so long, then?"

"Because you seemed happy there. With the store and everything. And I wanted you to be happy."

"At the expense of your own happiness?"

"Yes," he said resolutely. "But I didn't understand that. I didn't understand just how many decisions I made at the expense of my own happiness."

He picked up the dish towel and started wiping down the counters. I noticed his hand, and I felt my heart pound faster in my chest.

"You're not wearing your wedding ring."

"No, I took it off," he said, without looking at me. But I could see from the color creeping into the back of his neck that he was embarrassed.

I drove around the neighborhood after I'd said goodbye to the girls. I stopped at a realtor's open house. I wandered through the uninspiring living room, with its aluminum-framed windows and carpeted floor and cheap fluorescent lights. I picked up the flyer and studied the binder on the kitchen counter. I made a show of reviewing the inspections and the property lines and the floor plan. I ate a home-baked cookie and chatted with the selling agent. She told me she lived in the neighborhood. She gave me a bit of its history. A lower subdivision was built in the fifties, a planned community for university professors and staff. A second tract was added in the seventies. Tree-shaded paths connect one street to the next. A community center sits in the middle, with a pool, a tennis court, a soccer field and a bocce-ball court inside a grove of evergreens.

But of course you know all this. You were there, Robbie, two months before the accident. I don't know how much of Gold Hill you took in that day. In your memory, that Fourth of July must be marked only as the day you first met Emme. She made quite an impression, splayed out on a chaise, one elegant knee breaking through the barrier of her red cover-up to draw the sun.

"Do you live in the area?" the realtor asked me.

"No," I said. "I live in the city. My husband is house-sitting here. Temporarily."

"Oh," she said. "Is your husband Jonathan?"

"Yes."

"I guess I didn't realize he was married."

"He's married," I said. "I mean, we're married."

I looked at her left hand. There was no ring there, either.

A few other realtors wandered through, dropping their cards on the counter. Two or three neighbor women stopped in. The selling agent seemed to know them all. They wore khaki pants and loafers, like she did, or exercise pants and tennis shoes. It was the same uniform I'd seen women on the sidewalks wearing as they waited for the yellow school bus to deliver their children home. I studied their faces as they chatted with the real estate agent. I watched them smile, then laugh. I felt the old contempt for the monotony of suburbia, but I found that contempt was trumped, now, by envy.

Jonathan drove the girls back to the city two days later. He didn't come in. He walked them to the door and turned around and left.

Polly threw herself into my arms. Clara

hovered, wanting a hug but not wanting to appear as if she did. I noticed their painted nails right away. Clara's nails were a rather raucous purple, and Polly's were a bright pink. There were flowered decals on their thumbs. What person had had the patience to paint those twenty tiny nails? Not your father, certainly. Not any man. The nails were in direct contrast to Polly's hair, which clearly had not been brushed that day, or perhaps the day before, either.

"Make sure Daddy brushes Polly's hair when you stay with him," I said to Clara, later.

"I can brush it for her," Clara said, unwilling to pin anything on her father.

I caught myself, and retreated. "It's okay," I said. "It's not your job to talk to Daddy about it, or to brush Polly's hair."

Polly came and stood next to me.

"Your nails look pretty," I said to both of them.

They flashed their hands around proudly.

"Was there anyone else at the house with Daddy?" I asked, as offhandedly as I could.

"What do you mean?" Clara said.

"I mean, was there anyone over for dinner or anything like that?"

"Nope," Clara replied. "But there was a puppy. From next door."

"That must have been fun."

"He put his teeth on my finger, but it didn't hurt," Polly said.

"That's good," I said. Then I couldn't help myself. "Who painted your nails?"

"A lady," Polly said. "She didn't tell us her name. It took a long, long, long, long time."

"But it was worth it," Clara said importantly. "Because you never paint our nails."

"I have a secret," Polly said suddenly.

"Oh?" I said. "What's your secret?"

I was sure it was another woman, the woman who had painted their nails. The realtor, perhaps. Or a neighborhood widow or divorcée. I was certain, even though it seemed implausible. It was womanhood Jonathan was trying to get away from, after all — the treachery of hidden machinery, the probability of betrayal, the dangerous seduction of bodily parts.

Polly put her lips close to my ear. "If a bird's heart beats too fast, it could die."

"Really?"

"Yes," she whispered solemnly.

"Where did you hear that?"

"On PBS."

"I didn't know that," I said. "Thanks for telling me."

She ran off to her room, and the interview

was over. I wondered, later, if what was true for birds might also be true for humans. Or I wondered, at least, if the worry over a broken marriage, or a lost child, even a nearly grown one, could make your heart beat so fast it could break.

EIGHT

The journey to confront my father about the money took three days. The Greyhound got me as far as Bangor, then I caught a shuttle to the town of Northeast Harbor. I found a mail boat to take me across the sound to Little Cranberry Island and drop me at the dock in Islesford. There was a tiny museum where I stalled and looked around. On one wall was a photograph from 1923, the year the water froze from the Cranberry Isles to the mainland. The photo showed a man riding an old-fashioned motorcycle on the ice in front of the dock. The man was my own grandfather, but I didn't know that yet.

I walked the half-mile to the house. The drive was flanked by fir trees and undergrowth, opening to a wide lawn that surrounded a pretty green house with white trim, shingled flower boxes and a veranda. The sky was changing color, and the color of the ocean beyond the house was changing, too, deepening as night came on. Walking up the drive, I tried to fend off all that voluptuous beauty. I tried to rehearse what I was going to say. I could not really imagine pronouncing the word *money*. It would be like bringing up my father's leaving, or his drinking; it would be the intervention all over again.

I saw her before I saw him — the wide white face and the thin brown hair beneath the straw hat. I saw her overalls, and under them a white sleeveless shirt — a man's undershirt, presumably my father's. The straps of her bra were exposed, cutting into her sunburned shoulders, straining under the weight of her heavy breasts. She was tall and heavy all the way around, not exactly fat, but big-boned and generous. That was what most shocked me, that the woman for whom my father had forsaken his family and traded his future was not even thin. My mother told me later he had known Veronica Cox all his life. She had apparently always been in love with him. She had never gotten married. She had been waiting for him all this time.

She was holding something in her hand. A piece of wood, and in the other hand a little shovel, and she had on gardening gloves.

This was what they did, then, on a Thursday in September as evening came on and the sky filled with color and the harbor turned from blue to black and the lobster boats hauled the day's catch onto the dock: They gardened.

I stood behind a redwood tree and watched as Veronica Cox began to dig with the little shovel in a clearing beyond the house. My father appeared, carrying in his arms a black dog, its legs stiffened and its head hanging back on its neck. It took me a minute to realize the dog was dead.

Not gardening, then. A burial. I had happened upon them as they were burying Veronica Cox's dog.

My father laid the dog down and took over the digging. He lifted the dog's body into the hole and covered it with dirt. He placed one hand on the small of Veronica Cox's back and the other in her hair and held her to him. I could not tear my eyes away, though I was sickened watching them.

Finally, I stepped from behind the tree.

My father saw me. "I'll be damned," he said.

I stood still. He came toward me and opened his arms so wide there seemed no other place for me to fall but into them.

■ ■ ■ ■

We ate a dinner of beef stroganoff. There were tomatoes from the garden, and home-made egg noodles over which Veronica Cox poured the stew. My father set out three wineglasses. This surprised me. Not only a glass being set for me, but that they would drink in front of me. My father poured wine for Veronica and for himself, then held the bottle over my glass and looked at me. I nodded. I don't know why. Because it was easier than refusing, I suppose.

I drank the wine. I got quite drunk, in fact, for the first time.

For dessert, there was a tart made from cranberries that grew wild on the island. A bottle of port appeared, and there was more drinking. The wine made me bold — it dropped a curtain that left me on one side and my inhibitions and doubts on the other. At some point I asked for the money. He said he didn't have it and that he didn't know when he would. I stood up from the table and walked resolutely out of the house. In the dark, I stumbled down a grassy slope to the water. There was a boat tied up at a dock, a small aluminum dingy. I got in and rowed around. My father called to me from the shore but I wouldn't come in. He swam out to get me but when he reached the boat, I dived off the other side.

The cold water was shocking, but not shocking enough to immediately sober me up. I tried to swim away from him but he was faster and stronger. Eventually he caught my arm and hauled me in to shore. He handed me a towel and showed me to bed, and neither of us ever spoke a word about the incident again. What lesson did I take away? Possibly that one could get very drunk and act stupidly and not have to account for oneself.

In the morning, still a little drunk, I announced I'd be leaving that day for Europe. I had sixty dollars left, plus the two one-hundred-dollar bills my mother had given me. Not enough to buy a plane ticket to London, but somehow I believed I would get there anyway.

Veronica Cox cooked me a meal of eggs and sausages and set it before me. While I sat alone in the kitchen eating, I could hear her talking quietly with my father in the living room. She disappeared down the hall and returned with an envelope.

"It's the best we can do for now," she said. The "we" in that sentence pained and infuriated me, but I took the envelope. I didn't open it in front of them. I simply nodded and shoved it in my daypack and managed to say thank you.

They insisted on walking me to the dock. While we waited for the mail boat, we looked around the museum. I pretended I hadn't already been inside. I pretended I hadn't seen the photograph of the man on the motorcycle, the man my father explained was his own father, my grandfather, who had once owned much of Little Cranberry Island. It was an ancestral history that until then I'd known nothing about. I was saddened, and angered, that it had been kept from me. I imagine you will be saddened and angered that yours was kept from you, of course for different reasons.

The mail boat never came. A lobster boat pulled up to the dock. Veronica Cox knew the old man driving it and arranged for me to ride in it back to Northeast Harbor. As I stepped onto the boat, my father grabbed my hand and said he would get me the rest of the money somehow. He said he would wire it to London as soon as he possibly could.

Through a combination of buses and trains I made it to Boston. At the airport I slept on a bench and in the morning I paid for a flight to London with the cash from

Veronica Cox. I had only the two hundred-dollar bills left after that. Enough to see me through, I reasoned, until the rest of the money arrived.

NINE

I took a train from Heathrow to London and checked into a youth hostel at Earl's Court, where I slept in the girls' dorm. I went to the agency that had granted my work visa and flipped through index cards with job listings. I made phone calls and sent out letters. I worked on my typing speed on the typewriter at the agency. I ate bread and cheese on my bunk bed at the hostel, then went next door to the pub. Each night, I took enough money for only one pint, but there was always someone — some boy or man — willing to pay for more.

I tried to moderate myself according to how much others were drinking, but the more I drank myself, the more difficult it was to remember to keep track. After the first drink I wanted a second, and after the second, I wanted a third, and after the third, I wanted to remain. I wanted all of us to remain — the Australian backpackers from the hostel, the bartenders, the businessmen who came into the pub after work. I wanted the pub not to close and the night never to end. I wanted that whole society frozen in revelry, and I wanted my feelings frozen, too. My life and all the things that had happened or might happen to me seemed distilled and poignant, and the evenings themselves timeless and meaningful. I was no longer self-conscious or afraid. I could say anything, and often did. I do not think I worried, at first, about ending up with a drinking problem like my father, though I have no idea now why not.

I might have gone off with one of the Australian boys — back to the boys' bunk room or the dark corner of the basement of the hostel, with its well-worn brown couch and its velvet curtain, officially known as "the lounge." I might have done away with my virginity that very first fortnight in London. That was clearly the inspiration behind the hands on my knee, and on my neck, and all those free pints of beer. But I wanted an experience more promising than the one those boys were offering. I wanted money — I needed money — and if I could not get it the way it had been promised, in a wire from my father, which never did arrive in London, I would have to find it some other way. Not by trading my body, but by trading my skills. It seems to me now that what I wanted when I set off for Europe was not so much adventure as deliverance. What I wanted, more than anything, was an office job.

The work-study agency finally sent me on an interview. The man who opened the door was Malcolm Church.

"You may as well leave your sweater on," he said, after our first brief exchange. "I've got a meeting at the Isle of Dogs with colleagues from the London Docklands Development Corporation. You can come along and take the minutes if you like."

He took very fast steps on long legs, so that as we walked toward the tube I had to break into a trot to keep up with him. I began to worry about the money for the tube ride, but when we reached the station he bought me a six-month pass and stood in front of me and fitted the card into its red plastic holder. On the tube, and after we'd transferred to the Docklands Light Rail, he told me more about the historical redevelopment of the Docklands, and his affiliation with the London Docklands Development Corporation. He had worked for the firm that was granted the structural engineering contract for the initial Dock-lands Light Rail system. He himself had designed the station at Mudchute, just south of Canary Wharf. He was especially proud of Mudchute, which transported people to a wildlife habitat preserved during the redevelopment as an open-space park and city farm. Now he had struck out on his own and was preparing a bid to replace the small wayside station at Canary Wharf with a large one that could serve the needs of a thriving retail and commercial enterprise. The new station was to include six platforms serving three tracks and a large overall roof connected to the malls below the office towers.

It was crowded on the train and Malcolm was standing very close to me, both of us holding on to the overhead bar. He leaned in as he talked so I would hear him over the noise of the train. He explained that if he — if we — were awarded the contract, it would be the largest project he'd ever engineered, the final link connecting the Docklands to London, a triumph of twentieth-century re-development.

He had a quiet voice that trailed off at the end of his sentences. When he spoke, I had the odd sensation of a warm whirring at the back of my head, an almost hypnotic sense of friendship and safety and calm. Instead of using his authority to his advantage, he seemed to be trying to even things up between us.

The train stopped. Malcolm placed his arm under my elbow as the doors opened and we stepped onto the platform and walked up the stairs, onto a sidewalk cast in shadow by the tallest skyscraper in London. The meeting was on the top floor. Men were assembled around a table. Malcolm gave me a chair and introduced me.

"This is Annie Black," he said. "She's come from California to keep us organized."

I took careful notes on a yellow legal pad Malcolm produced from his briefcase. I recorded the technical terms as best I could. Lunch afterward was in a pub. All the men ordered pints, and I ordered one, then another, no longer caring that women in England customarily ordered only a half. I had been full of doubt that morning, dressing for the interview. I had stared at myself in the mirror and seen not clear skin and long legs and long hair, but my eyebrows, too thick and dark, and my overlapping bottom teeth, and the earring holes in my ears, one lower than the other. But after the second pint in the pub in Canary Wharf that day, the curtain dropped again, and the men began to talk to me, and I felt attractive. I felt it was a wonderful country I had landed in, where I could pass a workday afternoon in the company of men who were paying me to drink for free.

When we returned to the office that first day it was nearly six o'clock.

"There's a computer for you," Malcolm said.

I sat down at what would become my desk. Malcolm handed me an office key and said that unfortunately he'd have to be heading home. He said he would pay me in cash every Friday, so I wouldn't have to worry about taxes, and he would pay me double for overtime. He cautioned me against staying too late. He didn't want to tire me out on my first day.

"You don't have to pay me for tonight."

"Of course I'll pay you," he said. "Don't be silly. It's not my money anyway."

"Whose money is it?"

"It's the investor's money. The investor being chiefly my father-in-law. If we can get a bit more out of him, we can move into proper office space in Canary Wharf."

He seemed to be sharing a confidence, so I did, too. I told him how I was waiting for a wire from my father, and how, in the meantime, I'd persuaded the hostel to let me stay on credit.

He said nothing for a moment. Then he set his briefcase back on the desk and popped it open. "Let me give you something for this week," he said. "An advance."

"You don't need to do that."

"It's no problem," he said. He removed a handful of bills and held them out to me. "Please."

His hand was trembling and his voice seemed suddenly tender. The change alarmed me so much I nearly refused the money. But I didn't. I took it. And I didn't refuse him the other time that really mattered, either.

I stayed in the office a long while that first night, studying the picture of Malcolm's wife and daughter on his desk, reading documents about the Docklands redevelopment Malcolm had left for me, and fiddling with my computer. By the time I locked up it was midnight, and when I reached the tube station it was closed. The streets were empty. There were gates pulled across the windows of the shops and even the pubs were shut. There were no taxis and no buses and I had left my street map at the hostel in Earl's Court. I stood on the sidewalk at the entrance to the tube station, pushing the metal chain back and forth across its entrance with my foot.

I set out walking. I reached the Thames at Westminster. The river was black and quiet. Big Ben and the Houses of Parliament were lit yellow in the night sky. I had no hat and no gloves and no coat, and I could sense the cold, along with the possibility of fear at being alone in a foreign city late at night. But it was as if I stood inside protective glass, and those feelings could not really reach me. Some new power had risen in me. All my tight cavities were opening and warning voices were fading. I had only myself to worry about, and if I wanted, I could simply choose not to worry at all.

Finally there was a red double-decker bus creeping through the roundabout at Whitehall. I got on, then got off again after a while because I was not sure the bus was headed in the right direction. Somehow, I found my way back to the hostel. The very next day I took the money Malcolm had given me and bought myself the winter coat.

TEN

Late March. Frost on the window this morning, and outside, a cold, cloudless sky. I turned the heater off last week but now I've turned it back on again. I feel you not as an absence today, but as a presence. It's your hurt that's here, though we don't know exactly what the hurt is about. It's a large, cold hand I can't scoot around because I can't see it, but I know it's present, because I helped put it here myself.

I will try to paint for you London as I remember it at nineteen, then twenty, all the while knowing my picture will be imperfect. Not only because memory itself is imperfect. Not only because I was young. Not only because I was a stranger in a foreign city, seeing it then and remembering it now in my own dialect, through the veil of my own customs. But also because the London I paint is colored by the pencil I hold, and the pencil I hold wants a picture with an ending we can all bear.

Malcolm arrived at the office each morning at nine o'clock sharp. He had two suits, which he alternated, and a gray raincoat that draped like a tarp over his enormous frame. Each evening at seven he prepared for his departure, lifting his briefcase from the floor beside his desk, popping it open, replacing his notebook and pen and snapping the case quietly closed. It was an old-fashioned briefcase with a hard shell, the kind that could withstand the trauma of being ejected from the back of a motorcycle taking a roundabout at an unsafe speed — and had, he told me. He injected this story and others, abruptly, into random conversations, as if trying to make me understand that what I saw of him was not all there was, that he existed beyond the walls of the office we shared. It was in this same way that he first told me about his wife.

It was a Friday, and we had, at his suggestion, left work at five for a drink in the pub around the corner. We sat in a booth and he ordered us pints and asked me pointed questions about myself — my course of study in college, my aspirations, my childhood. I told him about the failed intervention, the money, Veronica Cox. I told him I had been majoring in French, and that once

I'd saved enough money I hoped to travel on the Continent, beginning in France. He told me his wife's family kept a Paris penthouse — the top floor of a small hotel — and that I must come along sometime for a holiday.

I told him my mother was a nurse and that my father was currently unemployed. He told me that when he was young his parents had wanted him to go into medicine or law. He'd wanted to be a scientist. Somehow he'd ended up in civil engineering, with a specialty in structural engineering. He and his wife had lived in central London when they were first married, then moved to Richmond after their daughter was born. They had a cottage out back they let out to boarders sometimes, or friends in need of a place to sleep. Right now it was inhabited by the son of a family friend, John Ardghal, who'd given Malcolm his first job out of university. The son's name was Patrick.

Louise spent quite a bit of time in the garden, he told me, and was involved in the Royal Horticultural Society in London. That was what she'd gotten involved in when their daughter had gone off to school. She was also interested in collecting art, especially photography. Patrick, their boarder, liked to take pictures.

"Patrick's not a bad bloke," Malcolm said. "Only his father ran into financial trouble, and I'm afraid that sent Patrick off course. He's been out of university I'd guess eight years now, but he's still dallying with the photography. He needs a bit of keeping on track."

Then, in the same halting tone he'd been using all evening, he told me that Patrick and Louise shared other interests, too, not just photography.

He raised his eyebrows. "If you can guess what I mean," he said.

I set my beer down on the table.

"But it's all on the up-and-up. It was never hidden from me. In fact," he said, "I engineered it, in a way."

"You mean they're having an affair?"

He laughed a funny little laugh. "If you want to call it that."

I must have looked shocked, because he took pains to explain that it had been his own idea, intended to bring Louise up out of what he called "a midlife malaise." This malaise had been brought on by turning forty and being alone in the house after Daisy went off to boarding school, where she was not adjusting as well as they'd hoped. The worry over Daisy had gotten to Louise, or Daisy's absence had, or some combination of that and turning forty and confronting the future in a new way. Malcolm thought what she needed was a distraction, an outside interest, and he'd suggested the Horticultural Society, but that hadn't helped. Then Patrick moved in, and Malcolm observed a mutual attraction, and engineered an encounter, or at least encouraged it, after their annual summer party. He'd even thought to go upstairs and get a condom and bring it out to the cottage, knowing that under the circumstances Louise wouldn't think of it herself.

I leaned close, not wanting to miss any inflection or detail. I was not shocked or disgusted by his confidence. I was intrigued, and impressed.

"We were young when we met, you see," he said. "When we married. Neither of us had a chance to come into our own, romantically speaking. More than anything, it's a decision not to be threatened. In a way, it's been invigorating."

There was a tentative, almost helpless quality in him that affected me. There were also the low lights, the thick mugs of beer and the rowdy abandon of a London pub on a Friday afternoon. A wave of feeling rose in me. I wanted to comfort him. I wanted to offer him something. I wanted to reach out and lay my hand over his. I did reach out and lay my hand over his, and I smiled.

He leaned in toward me, without warning, and delivered a kiss that landed not on my lips but on the crease under my nose. He laughed self-consciously. He folded his other hand over mine and began to stroke my knuckles with his thumb. I looked at his hand and, perhaps under the influence of the beer, I studied it with some absorption. His thumb was extraordinarily large, something extra he'd been given, a special piece of bone and flesh moving back and forth across my skin. I wanted to remove my hand. I wanted to undo, unequivocally, what I had done. But I did not want to put an end to the action before it had begun. I was ever conscious of my virginity, a burden that seemed more weighty and ridiculous the longer I carried it with me, and Malcolm was a man in a suit, married, twice my age, wholly unsuitable on several counts and therefore able to offer me precisely the sort of romantic entanglement I'd envisioned when I set off for Europe — one that could be indulged in, then abandoned without further complication. I took what seemed to me the middle ground. I liberated my hand slowly, then reached for my pint and downed what remained of my beer.

"But you're married," I said.

It was an entirely fabricated moral sentiment, but I put it forward that night, and
over and over again as the autumn ebbed
and winter took hold, because it was conve-
nient to claim the high ground while I
decided what I wanted. In this way I set
down a pattern — advance followed by
halfhearted retreat — that pursued us all
day in the office as he talked into the Dicta-
phone and I typed, as we assembled the bid,
the mammoth document, the tables and
drawings and photographs, then as we
revised and reassembled and resubmitted.
We retired more and more often to the pub
in the afternoons, always drinking the same
bitter beer and always sitting in the same
corner booth. Malcolm left the pub duti-
fully each evening at seven, encouraging me
to leave when he did and walking me to the
tube, or sometimes giving me a ride home
on the back of his motorcycle. I'd wrap my
arms around his waist, the sky pressing
down overhead, any words attempted between us lost to the wind. It was at the end
of these rides, when he'd ridden onto the
sidewalk in front of Victoria House, that I
often nearly invited him to my room.

What stopped me? I was not afraid of getting hurt. I was not worried about offending his wife, though I pretended I was. I was afraid something would change. I liked my job very much. I liked having my own key and my own desk and my own computer, and I didn't want to risk losing that, or the camaraderie we had settled into, our bantering and our flirtation, our friendship. His devoted efforts to win me, not only by complimenting me often, and anticipating my needs, but by doling out more and more responsibility for the bid, and by giving me raise after raise and even a new title, "office manager," which he had printed on thick white business cards. If I gave in to him, if we consummated our flirtation, our days together in the office would be changed. And if we went to bed together, I might not live up to the expectations that had been building in him all this time. I would be a disappointment, or worse, he would be, and I would have to pretend he was not.

"Let me walk you up," he'd say.

"That's all right."

"Are you certain?"

"You're married, Malcolm."

"So is my wife."

But he did not push me. He was a gentleman, and I loathed and admired him for it. He must have had no idea how easily I would have given in, if only he'd taken me in hand. Once, standing outside Victoria House in the cold, he told me that in a perfect world he would begin again with me. I would be the woman with whom he made a family. I knew for certain, at that moment, that I had been right to refuse him.

And yet, as the weeks wore on, I imagined it unjust that at seven every night he left me to collect his wife. I imagined I was lonely in my blue room at Victoria House, and maybe I was lonely, but I also remember a singular happiness and relief returning there in the evenings as long as I had not had too much to drink. When I was drunk, I sometimes became indignant thinking of Malcolm abandoning me to make his way to the Horticultural Society to collect Louise and drive her home. Was Malcolm's devotion the result of obligation or duty? Did he perceive Louise as a noose around his neck, or did he love her? Did he refuse to keep her waiting because he was afraid of her, or because he did not want to make her unhappy? I suspect it was the latter — he wanted her to be happy — and what is that, if not love?

I wonder now, too, whether he wasn't a little relieved to leave me at the end of the day. Perhaps Louise was relieved, too, when she found herself in her own bed, with Malcolm, instead of in the cottage with Patrick. Their arrangement was intoxicating, but it must have been burdensome, and wearing, too.

ELEVEN

This morning I woke to a silent house. I checked the girls' rooms, first Polly's, then Clara's, and found them empty. Had they been taken from me in the night? Who would take them? Jonathan? Why would he take them when he has them half the time?

I called out their names. Silence. I called again, growing frantic, opening and closing the front door, then the back. I had misplaced you, and now I was losing them, too.

Then I heard them scream "April Fools!" and they threw the living room curtain from over their heads and emerged, squealing and beaming. They'd been hiding over the heating vent, impressively silent, sheltering themselves from the frigid spring morning.

Later, Clara said, very seriously, "Can I tell you something?"

"Yes," I said, "tell me something."

"There are a lot of answers to one question."

"Which question?"

"Well, like, what's black and white and red all over?"

"What is black and white and red all over?"

"Well, a newspaper. That's the easy answer."

"And what are the hard answers?"

"A penguin in a blender," Clara said.

"Ooh. Ouch."

"A zebra with a sunburn," she continued.

"My goodness. What else?"

"That's all," she said, and she reached out and hugged me around the waist. She's begun to hug me differently than she used to. She doesn't turn her face to the side but keeps it straight ahead, so that her nose is pushed directly into my belly.

I leaned down and whispered: "Did you miss me when you were at Daddy's?"

"Not really," she said.

I kissed her on the forehead. "Good," I managed to say. And I almost meant it. I'm happy she's independent. I'm happy Polly is, too. You weren't when you were their age. Sleepovers, school trips, me going away to work in the store: You used to throw your arms around my neck and hang on until I detached you limb by limb.

■ ■ ■ ■

On the fifteenth day of your stay in the hospital last September, you were taken off propofol. The trauma-center doctor expected you to emerge from the coma within a matter of hours, or a few days at the very most. It was a week shy of your twenty-first birthday, and I was already imagining my mother and father bringing the girls to the hospital to see you on the big day. I was anticipating the joy on your face, and theirs, when they presented you with a birthday cake you would not be able to eat, but that you would know had been baked in your honor.

I refused to leave the hospital while we were waiting for you to emerge from the coma, and a room was found, a closet, really, into which a hospital bed was rolled for your father and me. We slept in the bed together the first night, the only night I can remember that autumn that our limbs were entangled the way they had been the rest of our married life.

At the end of your second day tapering off propofol, Mitch came to check on you and ushered me out of your room by the elbow. "Go get something to eat," he said.

"We can't have you fading."

So I walked to the cafeteria, but the smell of food made my stomach turn. I returned to the waiting room outside Trauma. I hadn't minded the space before. The sea-foam-green carpet. The gold pendant lights over the receptionist's desk. The chairs patterned in silver and teal. But during those days we waited for you to regain consciousness, the heavy quiet of that waiting room made me feel like I was going mad.

On the third day, the trauma-center doctor's brisk reassurances began to lose some of their briskness, and I felt panic rise in my gut.

We paged Mitch. He grilled the trauma-center doctor, whom he himself had hand-picked. He moved around your bed, studying your chart, checking your vital signs, touching your body — your head and eyelids and ears and chest and neck and belly and knees and feet and toes. He moved like an athlete, or a dancer — the steps he took so practiced as to take on a stylized grace — but his hands were an artist's hands, imprinted with a vision of a healthy human body, and gifted with the power to bring that vision to life.

When Mitch finally spoke, it was to your father, not the trauma doctor. "I would recommend putting him back in a coma."

"Why?" your father asked.

"I've never seen that done before," the trauma doctor interjected.

"Well, now you have," Mitch replied.

Mitch took us aside. He explained to us that he suspected the doctor had been too ambitious in bringing you back. He was of the opinion you had experienced a kind of cognitive overload, and your body, as a defense, had clung to its unconscious state. His view was that sedating you again would actually allow you to recover consciousness more quickly than if you remained on the path you were on, which he was afraid was going to cause seizures, or even a stroke.

A memory came to me of Mitch sitting in my store, years ago, after his wife left him, fat tears falling down his face. How could a man with such powerful intuition in the matter of human health have so badly miscalculated in the matter of human love? Could a man like that be trusted now to be infallible?

I could not stand my own doubt, and I could not stand the certainty in Mitch's face or the uncertainty in your father's. So I turned away and let them decide.

If a mother is only as happy as her least

happy child, that day began a series of the most unhappy days of my life.

TWELVE

In London, I began to stay on in the pub after Malcolm left for home each night.

"You'd better go," I'd say to him, at seven.

"I hate to leave you."

"I'm fine."

His voice would become throaty and tender. "Are you certain you won't allow me to give you a lift?"

"I'll stay for one more beer."

"Let me give you money for a taxi home."

"I can take the tube."

Then as soon as he was gone, I was bereft. I told myself there was no sense staying on drinking alone and waiting for something to happen. I told myself, each time, I would finish just the one pint. But when I finished, it was difficult to leave the comfort of the pub, the guarantee that the hours of the evening would pass without any conscious effort on my part to fill them. I'd order the pint, and drink it, and the by-now-familiar

115

curtain would drop, cutting me off from worry and fear and pain. The matter of why I was so far from home. The situation with Malcolm. The question of college. All that was swept behind the curtain, and the present moment became what mattered. I grew confident in my own intelligence, and wit, and beauty, and I often simply stood up and took a stool at the bar and talked to whoever was next to me, and the night went on from there.

Sometimes, the curtain failed to drop, and the drinking backfired, sharpening my awareness of being alone instead of softening it, and making me hungry for human contact — for just one man, or a woman, even, to sit down beside me. But that hunger crippled me, and on those evenings I did not have the courage to speak to anybody at all.

One night, still feeling the effects of a hangover from the night before, I vowed to myself I would not drink after Malcolm left. My father was an alcoholic, after all. I, more than most people, needed to watch myself. I told myself I would let the unfinished pint of beer sit on the table in front of me, and if I could do that, I would have won, and there would be no need for further vigilance. I made a little game of it. I watched the minutes passing. I made it four minutes without taking a drink, then five, six, seven. I gained strength with each full rotation of the minute hand on my watch. Ten minutes passed, then fifteen. The foam began to flatten. The pub filled up. I began to feel silly taking up a whole booth alone, so I moved with the untouched beer to a stool at the bar. The foam in my glass was thinning but the bubbles were still rising, propelled by some mysterious private force, like waves beating the shore.

The man sitting on the next stool spoke to me. He began to tell me about a problem he was having with his tooth, which was crumbling, causing him pain when he drank something too cold or too hot. He went so far as to hook his finger in his mouth and pull his lip back to show me the damage.

"Do you need a filling?" I said. "Or a root canal?"

"Dunno," he said. "Haven't been to a dentist."

"Why not?"

"Dunno," he said, laughing wildly.

I turned away. I did not want to become involved with him, and I was intent on not drinking my beer, which required all my concentration. I waited in silence until I had been sitting not drinking for exactly an hour, and I told myself now I could go. Now I would take the tube home and walk the blocks from the station to Victoria House alone. But what sort of reward was that for having won?

I took a deep drink from my glass and turned again to the man next to me. A few of his friends arrived, and they all took an interest in me. There were three or four of them and they made sure there was always a beer in front of me. Eventually I found they could make me laugh, and a breezy camaraderie rose among us. When the pub closed, we went on to a "club," which seemed to be only a name for a pub licensed to stay open when the rest shut at eleven.

Hours later, when the club closed, we all stood outside in a taxi queue, the idea being that I would come along with them to wherever it was they were headed, a flat where we could continue to drink. But when we reached the top of the queue, I found myself alone with the man with the crumbling tooth. He was holding my hand as he climbed into the cab, trying to pull me in after him.

I resisted. If I got into that taxi with him I would be entering a new life, a cheapened one, where gums swelled, where teeth rotted, where bones and muscles and skin grew thin, where books and houses and cars and furniture and all the objects of order in the world were allowed to corrode and decay.

"I'm not sure I will come," I said, pulling my hand out of his. "I'm tired."

"Come on now, love. We'll put you straight to bed," he said. He got out of the taxi and tried to take my hand again. But I'd crossed my arms over my chest.

"Come on now, love," he said again. "Taxi's waiting. Taxi won't wait forever." He was slurring his words and his face had grown hard. "Get in now."

"No," I said. "I won't, after all."

We stood eye to eye. He was a small man, which I hadn't noticed before, small and fierce.

"You frigid cunt," he said venomously.

I was stunned. I'm not sure I'd ever heard the word spoken out loud.

He tried to get his arms around my waist, but I slipped out of his grasp and jumped in and locked the door before he could come in after me. The taxi sped away, and my head began to spin. I vowed, in the morning, that from then on I would keep my drinking in check. But I found I couldn't, or wouldn't. I carried on drinking excessively as long as I could — right up to the moment I decided to become a mother.

It was not so difficult, then, to stop. The stakes changed, and you grew inside me, and the muscles of restraint I hadn't known were there became strong.

THIRTEEN

Decay. Corrosion. Neglect. Things we found readily enough last fall at the Salvaged Light, which I'd mostly abandoned after the night of your accident, when the claw-foot tub in the loft fell through the floor and smashed the lights below. Repairs could not begin until negotiations with the insurance company were complete. And I really did not have the energy to address the problem, anyway, given my preoccupation with you.

We also found neglect at the Mermaid Inn, where your father and I alternated nights, each of us taking a shift to be close to you, then a shift at home, to be with Clara and Polly. But we didn't find neglect in the places we might have expected to — inside the hospital, with its expensively framed art and butter-colored paint, or in our own house, which was kept clean and orderly by my mother last fall, and animated by my father, who'd effectively moved in, too. The evenings I was home from a shift attending to you, my mother and father attended to me. I imagine they did the same for your father the nights he was home, at least when he let them. They took care of me as perhaps they wished they had when I was a child. I'd come home long after dinner and they'd sit me down at the table. My mother would put a grilled cheese sandwich and a bowl of tomato soup before me. My father would cut me a piece of some concoction he'd invented and baked with the girls — caramel chocolate pie or peanut-butter-and-banana cake or his famous bread pudding. My mother whisked around, cleaning and straightening and doing laundry. My father played with the girls, and played the piano, and sometimes sat with me on the front porch while your sisters worked on perfecting their cartwheels on the lawn. He never took a drink that fall, as far as I know. He settled in. He made it clear he would stay as long as we needed him. He'd stay out the year, if we'd have him.

It was as if two decades had not passed, and there had been no estrangement. I was unable to keep myself at a distance from him. I needed to confide in someone, and as soon as he was there, I knew he was that person. So I talked, and he listened. Sometimes, when I spoke about your condition, and the accident, and the summer that preceded it, I laid my head on his shoulder and wept. I ended up telling him everything, and it was as if the burdens of the story were absorbed into him, and lifted from me, at least while we sat together that way.

My mother and father were often in the kitchen together, deliberating over the question of dinner. My father did the grocery shopping, always bringing back something extra, Life Savers or licorice or, most often, a double package of Oreo cookies he opened in the store and shared with the girls as soon as he returned home, even if it was right before dinner. He was not so different sober from how he'd been drunk, which is to say the best of him survived both conditions. He told me the addiction to drink had simply lifted a year earlier, the day he'd found out he had hepatitis and a barely functioning liver, and that if he continued to drink, he was going to die. Just like that, he knew he wanted to live, and that want canceled out the wanting of alcohol he'd been trying to fight his entire adult life.

On weekends, when the girls were home from school, my father involved them in elaborate projects like those from my childhood. When your father was home, he helped them. They built model rockets and shot them off at Crissy Field. They installed a zip line in the backyard. They sketched plans for a tree house and purchased supplies, then the rain came and the project was set aside. When my father left in January, he promised to finish it next time he came to visit. The wood is still stacked against the fence. I keep forgetting to put a tarp over it to protect it from the weather.

After a night at the Mermaid Inn and a long day at the hospital, it was a relief to come home, but in a little while, I wanted to be back at your bedside, speaking with Mitch or another doctor, or wandering the halls of the hospital or sitting in the waiting room reading. I fought off panic by immersing myself in research. I reread *The Art of Kidney Transplant,* the second book your father acquired when he started a publishing house focused on specialized medical topics. He had changed careers after his mother, your Grandmother Catherine, died of heart disease; he had become disillusioned with the practice of modern medicine. He believed he could make more of an impact publishing health books that were accessible to the general population than trying to treat that population one by one.

I had read your father's books over the years, but other than that, I had left the unseemly insides of things mostly to him. He was the one who had cleaned the dogs' ears and pulled ticks and foxtails from their skin. He was the one who had poked at your belly when as an infant you had colic. He was the one to apply antiseptic and Band-Aids to your cuts and scrapes and to wrap your wrists and ankles when they were sprained. He nursed you and the girls while I nursed my squeamishness — until last fall, when the insides of you became a landscape it was necessary to investigate and master.

The first book Jonathan ever published was Mitch's book on Huntington's disease. The book sold well enough to enable your father to move from practicing medicine to publishing full-time. Mitch had been one of Jonathan's instructors at Chapel Hill. He moved to the West Coast to accept an appointment at the University of California, San Francisco, not long after you were born. A friendship developed. Mitch took a shine to you right away, and as you grew, he mentored you in your study of science.

When we'd known him just a little while, he got married quite suddenly to a twenty-six-year-old medical student named Jessica. We invited them to dinner, and I bought a glossy cooking magazine. I made pork kebabs and corn custard, and for dessert, a lemon tart. At dinner, I remember, Jessica nibbled at the pineapple and peppers on her kebabs, but the bits of pork I'd marinated overnight were left in a forlorn little pile at the side of her plate.

I have to admit to disliking her right away. I suppose I thought she was exactly wrong for Mitch — too fussy and thin and shallow and made-up, and possibly exhausted by the strain of being not quite as intelligent as she pretended to be, and not quite as pretty, either.

After dinner, in the kitchen, Mitch told me she was a vegetarian. "I should have warned you beforehand," he said. "I'm sorry."

I held her plate in my hand over the garbage can, fighting the urge to rescue the meat by shoveling it into my own mouth.

Most people have two kidneys, one on each side of the spinal column in the back, just below the rib cage. We never knew you had only the one. I dreamt of rescuing it — that fist-size, bean-shaped mass of cells that filtered waste and balanced minerals and maintained your blood pressure and kept your bones and blood healthy — but since I couldn't, I prepared to give you one of mine in case yours did not recover.

Three years after that dinner, Jessica left Mitch for another man. There was a year of despair, during which Mitch was more often at our house than in the apartment he'd rented in Pacific Heights. At the end of that year, he moved out of the city to become the head of neurology at Stanford and a noted researcher at the Stanford Synchrotron Radiation Lightsource facility, where you spent the summer after high school in an internship Mitch arranged.

He never remarried. He came to dinner when his work allowed. He always arrived with an excellent bottle of wine and told me I looked ravishing. He was a fixture in our house at holidays. He always insisted on doing the dishes. For years, he put money into 529 accounts for you and Clara and Polly that we didn't find out about until you were on your way to Northwestern. He said to me once that your father and I were the people who'd held him up after the divorce, and that he'd always be in our debt. But it turned out it was not with us his loyalties finally lay.

The days at the Mermaid Inn merge together in memory, but I do vividly recall waking the first morning after your accident

127

beneath the scratchy white sheets. I remember staring at the stains on the ceiling and listening to the roar of traffic on El Camino Real, a sound that seemed to lay the fact of your accident on my chest like a stone.

I got up and dressed quietly, letting your father sleep. I walked in the already-warm morning to the Starbucks. There was a woman standing at the counter barking out one of those ridiculously precise and long-winded orders, a nonfat decaf triple-shot mocha, extra hot, no whip, or some such thing. While her "coffee" was being prepared, she went outside to check on her dog. By the time I'd ordered my coffee, she was back. She took a sip of her drink and made a face. It didn't taste at all like it normally did, she told the barista. It tasted all chocolate and no coffee, and was the barista certain it was decaf, because usually they do such-and-such to the decaf, and usually it doesn't look like this, and, by the way, could she have some water for her dog?

The barista apologized to me for the long wait, and handed the woman a cup of water. She stuck her finger in it, and made another face. "It's really not like me to be fussy," she said, "but this is awfully warm. Do you think you could get me some cold water for my dog?"

It occurred to me that not so long ago, my concerns had been like hers — trivial enough. But I had been set straight about what could go wrong in a life, and you were lying in a hospital bed with a compromised kidney, and I couldn't waste another minute. So I pushed my way through the glass door, leaving the coffee I'd paid for behind.

FOURTEEN

The day after the night I met the man with the crumbling tooth, I was sick with the worst hangover of my new drinking life. I forced myself to sit at my desk, typing the final revision of the costings for the bid, sneaking away again and again to the bathroom to be ill. The hangover never ebbed, even as the day did, even as the windows darkened and Malcolm looked over at me, pacing and glancing at his watch. Then I heard quick, light steps on the stairs and the door banged open and a woman stood in the doorway.

It was the woman from the photograph on Malcolm's desk — his wife, Louise. She struck me as less like a woman than a doll, carved in miniature. She had smooth, high cheekbones and small, perfect ears that dangled with diamonds. She had china-white skin and blue-gray eyes and short, shiny blond hair. She wore a blue velvet sequined dress that clung to her tiny waist and flared out at her ankles. On her feet were black patent-leather heels as high as any I had ever seen.

I felt like a giant as I stepped toward her to offer a greeting. But she seemed not to have registered me standing there.

"The engine's smoking, Malcolm," she said in a wild, accusatory voice. "I told you last week there was something wrong with the car. You never believe me when I tell you these things. You hardly listen when I speak to you."

She turned back toward the stairs. Malcolm raised his eyebrows at me.

"Louise," he said. "My wife."

He followed her down the stairs.

I sat in my metal chair, the wind blown out of me. It was so undignified and unnecessary, the way married people behaved. The indiscriminate airing of grievances, the incessant flinging of blame and complaint. Of course, I had no idea back then what a marriage required. How the resentments and oversights and misunderstandings could pile up, sometimes moving ordinary kindness beyond reach. Love piled up, too, if you were lucky, but it seemed to be locked away in a separate compartment, sometimes unreachable when it was needed most.

In ten minutes, Malcolm was back.

"Is the car all right?" I said.

"It was only a little engine oil," he said, then he cleared his throat. "In any case, Louise wondered if you'd like to come along for a drink. Bit of a party we're having over at the Photographers' Gallery, where Patrick works."

His voice had halted a little before leaping over the name *Patrick*.

"What's the occasion?" I asked.

"Our twentieth anniversary, actually."

I could not tell whether he wanted me to come or not. But he was already collecting my coat and holding it open for me. "Louise doesn't like the idea of you here alone at the weekend. And don't be put off by her, just now. It's not that she doesn't want to get to know you. It's only the way she is about the car. Any sort of engine trouble puts her into a state."

I could have refused. I had been refusing Malcolm for weeks. The invitation had not come from him, though, and I found myself unwilling to turn Louise down. There was something else, too. I had begun to feel, as the afternoon wore on, that an alternative to sleeping off my hangover would be to drink it off. I could not very well go to the pub on my own, after the night before, and

I was not so far gone as to drink alone in my room. A party, on the other hand, was ordained. A party might be a reasonable justification for putting off, for another day, the vow I had made that morning never to drink again.

Malcolm slipped my coat over my shoulders and I followed him to their car. Louise sat in the front seat.

"I'm so happy to finally meet you," she said, turning and squeezing my hand, her small fingers feeling very cold over the hot tips of mine.

It was not just a few friends, as I'd imagined. It was a fancy cocktail party, and I was hideously underdressed. That was the first hardship. The second was that I was not immediately offered a drink. The third was Patrick — the first sight of him at the bar, the shock of him under my ribs. His dark suit and open collar. His lean body and long legs and long, thin hands. His narrow green eyes and dark, curly hair and marbled skin. His full pink lips. The way those lips moved suddenly into a smile when he saw us, and the way his body leapt into motion. How he rubbed his hands together when he reached us, as if now that we'd arrived, the fun could finally begin.

He was not handsome — his face was too pale and his ears were too large and he was too thin — yet by the time he reached us, the lens through which I'd perceived the world of men had been altered. Malcolm, ten years Patrick's senior, seemed no longer mature and distinguished, but staid and used up. Malcolm's attentiveness was no longer comforting, but overbearing. His voice was too tender, his manner too hesitant, his face too square.

Patrick said something to Louise about the food, which was being passed on trays by servers. Then he said something about the new installation on the far wall, photographs by a little-known but promising photographer — he grinned — Patrick himself. If he'd been not only charming but incontestably good-looking, perhaps he would have been better behaved. He might have been accustomed to his gifts, like old money is accustomed to wealth, and been modest and generous and less careless with others. He might not have been so set on extracting every ounce of pleasure for himself before the game was up.

The gallery proper was upstairs. The party was being held in the café that made up the ground floor, transformed that evening with round tables and candles that softened the

134

sparse white walls. I did not much like the look of Malcolm and Louise's friends, especially the women. Their features and bodies seemed dragged down by effort and gravity. Louise, on the other hand, looked beautiful, and I was deeply envious of her dress and her shoes.

Malcolm brought me a drink and told me I looked lovely. I did not, at all, believe him. My face felt crumpled and I had a terrible headache and I hated my cheap skirt and shoes. But I kept drinking, and after two glasses of champagne, I began to feel better. Malcolm and his friends seemed not so bad, and perhaps my outfit was all right, and I liked sitting on the bar stool, keeping an eye on Patrick.

Then Patrick himself sat down beside me. He faced away from the bar, toward the room, so that in order to speak to him I had to shift around on my stool until my legs were stretched out beside his.

"You must be bored silly," he said. He did not ask me my name or offer his, and I assumed — correctly, it turned out — that he had been informed of my identity and he assumed I had been informed of his.

"I'm all right," I said. "The champagne helps."

"And how are you finding your stay here?"

"I'm loving it."

"Good," he said. "But you mustn't spend all your time in London. You must see Ireland, too."

"You're Irish?"

"I am," he said. "I come from Howth, in North County Dublin. I came here for university, initially. Then work. Malcolm has been good enough to give me a place to sleep."

I replied without thinking, and without checking myself. "And you've been good enough to sleep with his wife."

What had possessed me to speak so boldly? The champagne, which had seemed to reconstitute the drunkenness of the night before, and his knee touching my thigh, and an instinct I had about Patrick, that I would need to act boldly to win him. I would need to be not so much myself as the person I felt inside me who had so far not been unleashed.

He grinned. "You've been apprised of that situation, have you?"

"I have."

"Malcolm told you?"

"He did."

"You two are on intimate terms, then, are you?"

"Not exactly."

He looked at me intently. "Well, it's ancient history, that is. I suppose it was a mistake."

"Really? I don't believe you."

"That it's over or that it was a mistake?"

"Both."

He laughed. "It's true — I don't really believe in mistakes. There's only what you do, and what you don't do, isn't there? It was a mistake to the extent anything like that is a mistake. The before and after of it looking differently from each other. In any event, you can believe or not believe whatever you like."

"Thank you for your permission."

"You are very welcome, so you are. An odd pair, our Mr. and Mrs. Church. You'd have to feel a bit sorry for them, wouldn't you? For Louise, at least. Beneath all her fierceness she's a timid bird."

I said nothing. I was trying to work things out in my mind, to understand whether Patrick's sentiment was sincere or condescending, and, more important, whether he was available to me or not. He was watching me closely, and for a moment it seemed he might lean in and kiss me. I felt that would be the right thing, for us to fall upon each other immediately.

"Stand up a minute," he said.

"Why?"

"Stand up and let me look at you."

Did I hesitate? I don't know. Probably I didn't. I simply stood and presented myself to Patrick.

"You are attractive, aren't you?" he said, as I sat down again. He spoke as if my appearance were a difficult but unavoidable burden. I imagine it was a line he used with women, a line he'd perfected over the years. But I didn't suspect that then, and it made an impression.

He showed me his photographs hanging on the gallery walls. They were black-and-white images with blurred backgrounds, each with a single swipe of color painted by hand. He told me the series made use of an effect called solarization, which was the process of reexposing photographic paper in the darkroom. Areas that had been exposed the least in the original print were affected the most during reexposure. Silver outlines emerged, and light and dark were reversed.

"I've seen a photograph like this," I said. "At the office. On Malcolm's desk."

He smiled. "I took that years ago, when I was an art student."

He described each image for me, speaking with authority, pointing out how the foreground was transposed against the background, and how solarization, along with the swipe of color, called the subject's integrity into question, creating what he called dissonance. I didn't really understand what he meant, and I'm not sure he did, either. If I met him for the first time now, I'd challenge him. I'd think him pretentious. But I didn't do either then.

Late in the night, he sat down at the piano. I don't remember what song he played, but I remember Louise watching him, how bright her eyes were and how flushed her cheeks as she smiled. She looked across the room at me, still smiling, and I felt as if I had seen into her soul. I did not know what I was seeing then, but I imagine I do now. Not dashed hopes so much as helpless want. Want like a small dirty creature, waiting all the years of her marriage for a sign. Patrick was not the sign; she herself was, her own blue dress, her tiny waist, her small, round breasts. And her want was not for dogged faithfulness — and not even for love — but for unfamiliar flesh, for bone against her own bone.

The end of the evening at the gallery was like my dream of the library cards last summer. I could borrow Patrick for a little while, but I would not be the one to keep him. He was waylaid by Louise, and I by Malcolm, who'd made an elegant toast to Louise early in the evening, then proceeded to get so drunk he shed his usual restraint. Each time he approached me, he was more demonstrative. He took my hand. He whispered in my ear. He once slipped his arm around my waist and tried to embrace me. I was embarrassed. I was afraid Louise would see us, and I would be blamed.

When the evening ended, I found myself outside with Louise and Malcolm under a city sky lit by a bright round moon. Patrick appeared in their car. Louise insisted on dropping me at Victoria on the way home. Patrick drove, since Malcolm was too drunk. Louise sat up front with Patrick and I sat in back with Malcolm. He had to be laid down, so that his head was nearly in my lap and one of his arms was draped over my legs. I was terrified Louise would look back and see us in this position. Or worse, Patrick would. But neither of them did. They were alone together, and I was alone with Malcolm, and I was pierced with indignation and jealousy.

When we reached Victoria, it was Patrick who walked me up the front steps of the boardinghouse. He held the door open for me, and I thought that was going to be the end of it. But he said quietly, "Come to the gallery, won't you? Come tomorrow afternoon."

FIFTEEN

Say it, I tell myself.

Say it, even if it's not the only name that matters.

Emme.

One syllable.

Like the letter *M*.

She worked out well enough, last summer, as a tenant and assistant. She was smart, and she listened well, and she was efficient. Every morning I gave her a list, and by evening she had it all done. She didn't ask many questions. She figured things out on her own. She didn't seem to have many plans, besides yoga classes, and I felt a little sorry for her. I began to ask her to babysit now and then, in the evenings. She seemed happy to do it. She came to the house on time. It was always clean when your father and I returned from dinner or a movie, and Clara and Polly were always asleep in their beds. They had a pet name for her, Emme-and-Emme, and they liked her accent and her long hair and her exotic clothes. They liked that she taught them to play card games — gin, gin rummy, even hearts. Her moods were unpredictable, though. Mornings, she could be quiet and subdued, then by late afternoon, she was often radiant and expansive. Sometimes she retreated again by evening, and as the summer progressed, I began to feel a nameless discomfort when I headed home and left her alone.

The retail space next to the Salvaged Light had been vacant for half a year, then the FOR LEASE sign disappeared, and one morning last July, Emme pointed out that a new sign had finally gone up, THE GREEN UNDERTHING: LINGERIE WITH A CONSCIENCE. The day after that, she told me she'd just introduced herself to the owner, Michael Moss, whom she described as "a lovely man."

"What is 'lingerie with a conscience,' exactly?" I asked her.

"Environmentally correct lingerie," she said. "Chemises. Camisoles. Teddies. Bras. Panties. All in hemp, silk and bamboo. Never cotton."

"Why not cotton?"

"According to Michael, cotton lacks a

143

conscience. Cotton production requires massive pesticide use. Developing countries account for less than thirty percent of global pesticide consumption, yet the bulk of pesticide poisonings occur in the developing world."

"It sounds a little like a marketing gimmick."

"Not to me," Emme said.

Was there something off about her? Her eyes seemed glassy, and her manner too bright. Had she been getting high with Michael Moss next door?

I walked over a day later to introduce myself. He was very good-looking. He also had a ring on his finger. To me, he seemed like just the sort of man who would be attracted to Emme. But what did I mean by that? Every man was that sort of man.

A week later, I stopped at the store on my day off and found him leaning back in a chair with his feet up on the dining room table, beneath the chandelier display. Emme was wearing a skirt and cowboy boots, and she was sitting on the table with her knees pulled up, offering him what I imagined was quite a display of her own.

Then, on Tuesday morning, I saw him leaving the store just as I was arriving. To me it was unseemly — the two of them together. I wanted to tell her to stay away from him, and him to stay away from her. But who was I to say so? It was none of my business with whom either of them spent their nights.

When I left home this morning, there were gray clouds in a pale-blue sky and a feeling of impending rain. I drove out of the city to Gold Hill to collect the girls. I was early, so I parked in the little shopping center and got a cup of coffee at the neighborhood café. I had brought along a couple of magazines and a book in a tote bag I'd grabbed from the hall closet. The tote bag was one you'd decorated for us some long-ago anniversary. It had a child's drawing of an oddly intricate human heart ironed on it and words written across the top: *Mom and Dad: I love you. From Robbie.*

Mom and Dad. Words you've strung together, without thinking, all your life.

On the other hand, I didn't string those words together about my own parents for the more than twenty years after my father left. Then, last fall, the phrase returned to the lexicon of my life.

"My mom and dad are here helping out," I'd say to people, feeling like a child telling a hopeful fib. But it wasn't a fib. They were indeed here, together, and they took care of things while Jonathan and I shuttled between the hospital and the Mermaid Inn. My father walked the dogs. My mother took the girls shopping for school clothes. My father took it upon himself to pack up your apartment in Berkeley. He assessed the damage of the flood at the Salvaged Light and hung a sign on the door announcing that the store was closed for remodeling. Then he appointed himself investigator of your accident.

We knew that sometime that night, after Emme came to dinner and made a scene, you climbed into the passenger seat of her car. We knew she was the driver at the time of the accident. We knew she had a valid New York State driver's license. We knew she was interviewed by the police, and that she rode to a hospital in Santa Cruz in an ambulance, and that she passed the sobriety test. We knew she was released with barely a scratch — and after that, she disappeared.

My father made some calls and scoured the web. He found a few dated photos of her online as a hand model but none of those leads pointed us anywhere useful. The modeling agency she worked for in New York provided an address in Manhattan, different from the address on her driver's license, but she hadn't resided in either location for years. The emails we sent to the address the agency provided us bounced back. She seemed to have willfully dismantled herself, then vanished.

We didn't press you to tell us what happened that night. It was clear, when you emerged from the coma, that you had no memory of it, so we simply chose not to speak of it. In the end, I was the one who told my father to give up the search; I didn't see a good reason for trying anymore to find her.

Sixteen

I had no idea what time I ought to arrive at the Photographers' Gallery the day after Louise and Malcolm's party. I didn't know what time Patrick's shift started or ended. I didn't even know if his invitation still stood. But at two o'clock, I took the tube to Covent Garden and walked until I found the gallery. I had another reason for being in Covent Garden that afternoon, an alibi of sorts, which was that I was hat shopping. Malcolm had arranged a chartered train to take the two of us and a group from the London Docklands Development Corporation to the horse races at Newbury — a boondoggle intended to favorably dispose the committee toward our bid — and I had gotten it in my mind that I would need a hat.

The café at the gallery was very different in daylight. It was a single, stark, narrow room with white walls and gray concrete floors and photographs sparsely displayed on the walls. There were long wooden communal tables with benches down the middle of the room, and a counter at the far end that had served as the bar the night before.

There was no sign of Patrick, so I ordered a cup of tea and pretended to read the newspaper. The gallery was full of students and artists wearing dark, grungy clothing. It's exactly the sort of place I would avoid now — the trendy crowd, the self-conscious modernity of the space, the harsh white walls and hard benches and humorless fluorescent lights.

Patrick arrived, finally. He walked down the stairs and saw me.

"You came," he said, smiling and embracing me and giving me the idea, right then, that everything was settled. "What shall we do?"

"I need a hat," I said. "For the races. Malcolm's chartered a train to take us to Newbury on Wednesday."

"It must be Ladies' Day, then, if you're in need of a hat?"

"I don't know. Malcolm said I would need a hat."

Malcolm had not said I would need a hat; I had thought of that on my own. I had imagined all the ladies would be wearing hats at the races, and the matter had been troubling me for a week. I did not have a hat, and moreover, I did not have anything appropriate to wear with a hat if I bought one. I had only my plain work skirts and blouses and my cheap, low black leather heels.

"A hat it is, then," he said, and we set out. It was raining. Patrick's camera was slung over his shoulder and he held an umbrella over us as we made our way to Covent Garden Market. The market was originally built for fruit and vegetable wholesalers, he said, converted to retail in the seventies. He said he knew a shop there; he knew the shopkeeper.

"Now is it only a hat you need or an ensemble?"

"I don't know," I said, as he looked me up and down.

"We'll see, shall we? We'll see what we can find. My mother always dressed spectacularly for the races," he said. Then after a pause, "She's dead now."

"I'm sorry."

"It's all right. It was ten years ago, when I was at university. But when she was alive she was quite fashionable. Famous in our little corner of Ireland for her dinner parties."

I imagined the scene — an elaborate dining room, an antique table set with china and glittering crystal, a female version of Patrick holding court in an elegant dress. It was that image that would have given Patrick his idea of what a woman should wear and say and be.

He pushed open the door of a shop.

"Henriette!" he said to the woman inside.

"Hello, Patrick," she said brightly. He took her hand and kissed her on the cheek.

The shop was small but airy, with fans turning in the ceiling even though it was spitting rain. There were a few sweaters folded on dark wooden tables. Blouses on metal rods against the walls. Furlined gloves in glass cases. Hats on hat stands. Scarves — wool and cashmere and silk — tied over round wooden hangers. There appeared to be no prices on the tags of the garments.

Patrick began to pick out articles of clothing — dresses, jackets, skirts, blouses — holding them up not for me but for Henriette.

"What do you think, Hen?" he'd say, and Henriette would nod and murmur and smile.

He held one or two things up against me, his hand touching my shoulder, then my hip. He seemed not to be aware of this touching, but I was. I was also aware of a particular feeling of foolishness. On the one hand, of course, I wanted to be beautifully dressed. On the other hand, I felt the time and energy the enterprise demanded was the worst kind of waste. I had an urge to demonstrate to him, and perhaps to myself, that I was a person of substance. But here I was letting him speak about what I ought to wear as if I weren't there, and hold garments against me, and touch me, and talk about my body as if it were only a collection of parts.

"Accentuate the legs," he said. "Camouflage the hips. That was always my mother's policy."

"There aren't any price tags," I said quietly.

"Aren't there?"

"Not that I can see."

"Not to worry," he said.

Henriette held up a dress. "We just got this in. Would you like to try it on?"

It was a black knit dress with a fitted bodice, a white fur collar and a purple suede belt. It had a full, short skirt, puffed up by a kind of netted slip.

Patrick took the dress from her and held it up to me. "This would be excellent on you," he said, "with your legs."

He held the dressing room curtain open and I took the dress from him. While I worked at the zipper, Patrick's hands appeared beneath the curtain — long white hands with long clean nails that I watched remove one of my shoes. A moment passed, then Patrick's hands were again under the curtain, sliding in a pair of knee-high black boots and a black felt hat with a wide brim and a white sash.

I zipped the dress. I pulled on the boots. I arranged the hat on my head and posed experimentally, assessing myself in the mirror.

It was then that Patrick pulled the curtain aside. I straightened and turned away. But he — and Henriette — had already seen me all dressed up, smiling at myself.

Patrick crossed his arms and raised his eyebrows. Henriette nodded. They were not smiling, but serious and approving.

"Lovely," Henriette said.

"I should photograph you in that," Patrick said.

"It's a little over the top, isn't it?" I said.

"Don't be ridiculous," he replied, with an edge of impatience. "It's only a matter of confidence."

I pulled the curtain closed and took the clothing off. I put the dress carefully back on its hanger and handed it to Henriette, along with the boots and the hat. Patrick walked outside to smoke a cigarette. Henriette began to write up the order.

I fingered a few things on the racks, hoping Patrick would return. Or hoping he would not, and that I would come to my senses and ask Henriette how much all this was going to cost. I'd had some idea that Patrick had intended to pay for whatever I chose, or that he would make some deal with Henriette, since they seemed to know each other so well, a discount, or a layaway. Vaguely I'd thought he'd had a plan when he'd told me not to worry.

I watched him outside, taking long drags on his cigarette and leaning against the store window. He was staring up at the vast ceiling of the market, at all that metal and glass, exhaling slowly, leisurely. He seemed to have forgotten about Henriette and me altogether.

Henriette finished writing up the order. I approached the counter and took my wallet out of my knapsack. I removed the credit card my mother had given me for emergencies, knowing there was no guarantee it would actually work, since my mother was more often than not over her credit limit.

Henriette slid the merchandise slip toward

me and smiled, her hair smooth against her scalp, making her sharp features even more pronounced. I studied the receipt. How was it possible these bits of leather and felt and silk could add up to such an enormous sum? It was more than I made in a month, including overtime. It was more than I'd spend in a year on clothing, and the bill would be sent directly to my mother.

I snapped the credit card up off the counter. "I'm sorry," I said. "It's too much. But thank you, anyway."

I walked out the door, right past Patrick.

"What's the rush?" he called, as he came after me. "I thought we'd go for a drink, and maybe a meal later."

"I can get a free meal at the boarding-house. Already paid for. No sense wasting it."

"What's wrong?" he said, seeming suddenly truly concerned. "You didn't like the clothes?"

"I liked them. I just couldn't afford them."

"What a pity," he said. "I won't be able to photograph you in them."

"If you can only take my picture when I'm dressed up in thousands of dollars' worth of clothing then I don't want my picture taken."

"Whoa, now," he said. "Let's not get our

155

knickers in a twist."

I was walking as fast as I could, fueled by my humiliation in the store and my indignation at Patrick's abandonment. But he was keeping up with me easily. It had stopped raining, and as night threatened, the sky was smeared with color. Patrick lifted his camera out of its case and started taking pictures of me.

"You're very pretty when you're angry," he said.

I turned my face away from his camera.

"If you won't have a drink with me, let's take a walk, at least."

So we walked. I was not comfortable walking beside him, but he was clearly at ease. He hummed. He pointed out the sites. Trafalgar Square. A church whose name I've forgotten. The Embankment and the Thames. It was dusk. Lavenders and pinks had drained from the sky and collected in the fat clouds, casting their mirror image on the surface of the river. There was a fiery line at the horizon, and the trees were shivering with water from the afternoon rain. I snatched a look at him now and then. He had a narrow face and a broad nose and big ears and curly hair that was almost black. He had a way of walking — his arms swinging energetically, his camera slung over his shoulder — that made me feel we were headed toward fun.

I was to learn that he had a tendency to lose track of time, to get on the trail of something, someplace he wanted to photograph, a derelict corner of London, or a particular Irish pub he wanted to find, or an Indian restaurant. An idea like this might at first seem whimsical, but over the course of the chase it could take on a dark necessity, and he would become impatient, or even angry, if he could not find what he was looking for, or if, in finding it, he could not have it. In Paris, at Christmas, when we came upon Mary McShane at Montmartre, I imagined he felt that way about her. Never mind the obstacles that might present themselves. Never mind me, standing mute beside him. Never mind Louise. Never mind Malcolm sitting down to rest.

We turned away from the river and came to a pub. We sat down to drink. Time and inhibition fell away. He told me he'd noticed me as soon as I'd arrived at the party the night before. He told me he could almost see the heat coming off me, the sparks. He put his hand on my knee, and we drank until the pub closed.

I don't remember the journey to Victoria House. I do remember he held my hand as we climbed the stairs to my blue room. We lay down on the bed. I told him I was not on the pill. He pulled a condom from his wallet. The long-awaited event — the loss of my virginity — finally transpired. What did I think of it that first time? I was swept up — if not physiologically, then at least romantically. I was if not adventurous, at least pliable, and as far as I could tell he was not disappointed.

I woke at two in the morning to the sound of rain hitting the window. Patrick was asleep, turned away from me, half covered by the sheet. His clothing was tossed upon the floor — jeans, shirt, blazer, belt, boots — stylish clothes that made an impression even discarded about my utilitarian room. His back was pale and smooth and I wanted to touch it, but I resisted. Already I sensed that to claim him, to take something of him without asking, would be to drive him away.

When I woke again at seven, he was gone. He'd left a note stuck to the inside of the door to my room. There was no salutation or signature, only a few lines from a song:

Love's young dream, alas, is over
Yet my strains of love shall hover.

What did he mean by that note? What did

he mean by any of his notes, with their bits of poems and songs? Were they actually warnings? Or was he just playing at being a romantic and winning women?

There are thirteen notes in all. I kept them in a sealed envelope in the hatbox for two decades. I finally read them again last summer after I received the photograph. I studied them for clues, but they didn't tell me anything I didn't already know.

Seventeen

Tomorrow is Easter. The girls are with your father for a whole ten days. They'll be in Gold Hill through Easter afternoon, then they'll fly to Wisconsin to spend their spring break visiting distant Gunnlaugsson cousins. It is still winter there, and your father has promised your sisters ice skating on the lake, and hot chocolate, and sledding. He has promised me that we will all meet here for Easter Mass tomorrow morning, then brunch, before the three of them catch their flight to Wisconsin. I find myself holding my breath, waiting to see them for a few hours tomorrow. And I find myself dreading the week alone. Yesterday, Good Friday, I was already at loose ends without them.

I stopped in at the store and surveyed the water damage. My mother and father had cleaned up the debris as best they could while we waited for the insurance situation to be resolved. But they had not been able to move the tub, or fix the gaping hole in the ceiling, or replace the lights that had been smashed. I did not really care. I had more pressing matters on my mind. As I was locking up, Michael Moss, from the environmentally correct lingerie shop next door, detained me, asking about you, as well as my plans for the store.

I told him that I didn't have any plans, yet. He said he'd be interested in taking over my lease, if I decided to close my doors.

"What would you do with the space?" I asked him.

"I'd expand."

"More room for bamboo panties?"

He smiled. "Actually, we're adding a line of clothing."

"Oh," I said. "Well, I'll let you know."

I took a long walk across the city after that, all the way to Russian Hill. I ate an early dinner alone at a restaurant. I went so far as to skip the chicken and order salmon on my salad. Who was I trying to fool? It was the Good Friday offering of an unbeliever, but I can't really afford the luxury of faithlessness anymore. That's something I've learned: When luck turns, and the chips are down, and you've lost something you can't live without, faith claws its way back. It may be the brand of faith Clara will have this

161

year about Santa Claus — not Polly's absolute certainty but a nine-year-old's hanging-on-with-your-fingertips kind of faith. Maybe faith isn't even the right word. Maybe a better word is hope.

On my way home, I stopped in at Grace Cathedral to light a candle for you. Yes, we're going to church on Sunday — another offering — but I won't light a candle in front of the girls, since they don't know you need prayers, or hope, or whatever it is. They think you're where you were headed when they last told you goodbye.

There was a memorial service in the church, so I sat silently in back and bowed my head. I didn't pray, but I thought hard, I hoped hard, that the life that was being celebrated had been well lived. During the scripture reading, I had the feeling I always have when God and death become entwined — that God is stepping in to steal the thunder of a human affair, a glorious union of flesh and blood, the miracle of two bodies making a new life out of love, a strictly human life that, like all lives, can end only in death.

Human love. Human death. What's that got to do with God?

Outside, I carried on walking. I walked until I could see the sun setting over the

162

bay. The bridge was a gray ghost in the distance. The sky was shifting with golden light, and the wind was full on my face.

I closed my eyes. I felt the memory of the mourners in the cathedral stirring inside me, a hundred human voices raised in song. I stood that way for I don't know how long, hearing that song and thinking of you and hoping. I hoped with every mothering cell in my body. I hoped with every scrap of power and will, every particle of knowing you, the years and years of you, the joy and hurt, the work and pride, the worry and love. I hoped until it hurt. I hoped so hard I felt it finally turn to prayer.

EIGHTEEN

In London, I turned twenty. I didn't tell anyone it was my birthday. I was afraid if I told Malcolm, he'd make a fuss, and if I told Patrick, he wouldn't. The day of the races arrived, and that morning, I couldn't find the right platform at the train station. I was afraid I'd miss the train, and ended up running, and sweating, and I did not like my clothes, and I did not have a hat. When I finally reached the platform, the engine was humming, and everybody was already on board except Malcolm, who was waiting for me. He took my hand and led me into the first-class cabin. A large crowd from the LDDC was already on board, mostly men, laughing and drinking even though it was only nine in the morning. There was a built-in table of sorts between mine and Malcolm's seats, a protective barrier onto which a waiter placed two glasses of champagne and a basket of miniature croissants and breakfast rolls. I drank the champagne and allowed myself to forget Patrick and to take pleasure in Malcolm's attention. Was it a great capacity for love I had then, or only great neediness and greed?

It turned out not to be Ladies' Day at all. There were very few women in the stands when we reached the track. There had been no need to worry about a hat.

If the drinking on the train had predisposed me toward Malcolm, the drinking that followed seemed to release me from my obligations toward him. I remember entering the elegant dining room of the pavilion, taking not the seat next to Malcolm but the one across from him. I remember standing up to place a bet and being waylaid by a young architect contracting for the LDDC, and forgetting, for a long time, to return to my seat in the stands next to Malcolm.

I passed out on the way back. When the train stopped, I found that I had been sleeping with my head on Malcolm's shoulder and my hand in his on the table between us. I sat upright and tried to collect myself, moving my hand away and running my tongue over my teeth and blinking the sleep from my eyes. There were a number of men from our party heading from the train to a pub, and I wanted to join them.

"I think it's time I took you home," Malcolm said.

"I thought we could go for a drink," I replied.

"I think we've had enough for now."

"It'd be fun to go to a pub, wouldn't it?"

"It would, it would," he said. "But I thought we might have some time alone together."

"Don't you have to get home?"

"No, not tonight."

"Why not?"

"I told Louise this morning I'd likely spend the night in London."

"With whom?"

"I didn't say with whom."

"But where are you spending the night?"

"I was hoping to spend it with you."

Had I led him on to such an extent that the request was reasonable? I didn't know. But I know that what I felt as we stood on the train platform was that here was a problem — Malcolm beside me with a pleading look on his face — and there was no way to solve the problem except to acquiesce. It was not a romantic impulse, but a practical one, that led me to agree.

We took a cab to Victoria. We walked into the boardinghouse, up three flights of stairs to my room. We lay down on the bed, and he began to kiss me. His lips were trembling. Instead of making me resist, the trembling worked to his advantage. I wanted the awkwardness between us over with as soon as possible, so to hurry things along, I removed my own clothes. He lay staring at me, and I saw that now his whole body was trembling. He leaned over and kissed me. The kiss was so tentative, it repulsed me. I rolled toward him anyway, my determination growing with each failed advance.

"I don't know that —" he said, when my body was crushed against his, but he didn't finish.

"You don't know what?"

"I may be too excited, just now," he said, so quietly I barely heard him.

"Too excited for what?"

"To, well, to perform."

I rolled abruptly away from him. It was just as I'd feared. Worse than I'd feared. It was a disastrous embarrassment that would ruin everything between us. I felt that all the blood in me was rushing to my face in shame, and I knew it was my fault, even as he apologized again and again.

"It's all right," I said, grabbing my clothes and putting them back on. "I've changed my mind, anyway. I think it's best you go, now."

"Please," he said. "Let me stay. We can just spend the night together. We don't have to try again. I could just hold you."

I could not stand his desperation. It made him seem weak and unattractive. It severed any remaining obligations.

"No," I said. "I want you to go, now."

I felt a rush of longing for Patrick — his nonchalance, his selfishness, his unfailing ability to perform — and I knew it was a night he was working at the gallery. If I hurried, I might still catch him.

"All right," Malcolm said. "I'll go. We'll have other chances."

He hugged me goodbye. I had to force myself to keep from squirming out of his embrace. I knelt on my bed after he'd gone, watching out the window to make sure he exited the building and was out of sight before I put my coat back on. Patrick was just locking up as I arrived at the gallery. He seemed happy enough to see me. He caught me up in his arms. We went somewhere and ate curry, then returned to my room and made love, though it was a stretch to call it that. I was making love, I think; he was taking what I made. Sometime in the night he wrote me a note, a goodbye note, as always. In the dark, he stuck it to my left breast and kissed me and took his leave.

NINETEEN

Easter Monday. Your father and your sisters
have flown off to Wisconsin, and I am alone
in the city for the week with the dogs. I
stepped outside this morning, determined
to distract myself by taking pleasure from
the day. I stretched out on a chaise longue
with my coffee. The dogs lay beside me. The
yard was still and hot under a cloudless sky,
and there was that summertime silence we
sometimes get early in the spring. A column
of gnats hovered above the grass. From
where I reclined, it looked like rain afraid to
land.

I thought of Emme stretched out at the
pool on the Fourth of July. I remembered
her walking beside you, her red bikini hanging on the stark bones of her hips. I remembered that she smiled — a smile I know now
was for you. Sometimes I try not to think of
you. Or at least I try not to worry. But I am
superstitious; it might be when I fail to

worry that you will slip away for good. Not that basking miserably in the sunshine, thinking and worrying, was going to turn up any more leads, or loosen any threads, or reveal any untaken paths.

The hatbox was waiting for me inside, on the kitchen table, its contents laid out like museum artifacts. The yellowing photographs. The ancient notes on scraps of paper. The official documents with their damning, printed type. And my own words on these pages, ready for me to take up where I'd left off.

Wednesdays and Saturdays. Those were the days I was allowed to see Patrick, or at least those were the days Patrick indicated he was available to see me. I spent the time away from him replaying the time together, thinking of him constantly, wondering if he was thinking of me and waiting to see him again. I tried to keep my obsession in check, but I had no one to share it with, no friend to force it out of my head into the open air, where it might have lost some of its power. Malcolm was the only other person I really knew in London, and he was the one person who could never know that I'd fallen for Patrick.

I don't know what Patrick did with the

rest of his week. I was desperate to ask whether he saw other women, and whether Louise still crept out to the cottage at night to sleep with him. But I knew I could not ask Patrick. Nor could I ask Malcolm. A door had closed on that conversation and I was afraid if I pried it open, I would give myself away.

Wednesday evenings, I went to the gallery straight from work. Malcolm never asked why I rushed off one day a week like that, and neither did I volunteer an excuse. I simply packed up my things and said good-bye, secretly pleased that now I, too, had someone else in my life. Saturdays I forced myself to pass the day alone and arrive at the gallery no earlier than four o'clock, half an hour before Patrick's shift ended. I always ordered tea and read the paper while I waited. Sometimes he was there. Sometimes he wasn't. Sometimes he hadn't shown up for work at all. Sometimes I was told he'd left early. Alone? I wanted to ask, but I didn't dare. When he was there, he greeted me with enthusiasm. He bounced toward me and sometimes he lifted me up and spun me around.

"Annie Black!" he'd say. "You're just in time."

Then he'd describe whatever it was he had

in mind for us, a journey or a meal or a show. One Saturday afternoon, we walked from the gallery all the way to Victoria Station. We stared up at the departures board, the white letters flickering on their black signs, announcing all the places a person could choose to go. There was no reason, Patrick announced, that we couldn't just board a train and see where we ended up.

Canterbury. That was where we ended up.

We walked from the train station, passing under the ancient stone arch that was the original gate to the city. It rained. The ground was mossy and the air was damp. There was a forlorn little cemetery with stone coffins and headstones leaning sideways and a stone structure, a keep, it was called, where valuables were kept safe from invaders. We stood beneath a rusted green crucifix outside Christ-church Cathedral. A brown river ran between brown brick buildings. There was a Norman castle made of piled-up rubble and cement, and Canterbury Castle itself, with its massive walls of flint and limestone. Across the brick street was a courtyard outside a tiny house where laundry hung in the rain.

Patrick said we ought to spend the night, and we found a bed-and-breakfast on a side street. He paid. We ate dinner in the dining

173

room. He paid for that, too. I already knew he was a person who could focus intensely on a single object. He could direct his sensibilities, and his camera, and the whole force of his personality, toward uncovering its special qualities. But until that night, that object had never really been me. After dinner, we climbed the stairs to our room. There was music coming from somewhere, and we danced. He was tender. He put his lips on my neck, and my breasts, and later, the flesh at the back of my knees. He told me he could taste the sparks on my skin. He could see my heat outlining my body like an unholy halo. When he fell asleep, I pressed my front into his back. I lay awake as long as I could, trying to hold on to time. But it passed, and morning came. Patrick grew remote, as he always did, and I tried to beat down the hope that more nights like the last would come my way.

Hope doesn't like to be beaten down, though, does it? Hope is what gets us through. Hope, and the prayer it wants to become.

TWENTY

Tuesday, the second week of April. The girls are still away. The store is shut. If it were not for the dogs, who need their walk, I'm not sure I would force myself out of bed at all. I give them a full hour, up and down the hills, then I sit again at the table and begin. I try to force my pencil to stay in England, in 1989, where it belongs. But it wants to leap forward from that London winter to a memory of Christmas, here in the city, last year.

The holiday season did not really begin for your father and me until we collected you from the rehabilitation center on December 20. There was a bright winter sun in the sky, and the wind was flushing leaves from the trees as we left home. Then, when we were returning, the daylight was ebbing and the wind was dying down and you were in the backseat looking very nearly like your old self. We pulled up to the house and found that my father and brother had strung our holiday lights. I could see the Christmas tree through the front window, and I could see my mother inside, stepping from the kitchen and pulling off her apron.

Your father parked the car in the driveway, but he didn't open the door. Instead, he turned up the volume on the radio. Natalie Merchant was playing the piano and singing an acoustic version of a 10,000 Maniacs song, "These Are Days," that your father and I used to listen to when you were a baby.

These are days you'll remember,
Never before and never since, I promise,
Will the whole world be warm as this,
And as you feel it,
You'll know it's true
That you are blessed and lucky.

I remembered your father and me stretched out on our living room rug, listening to that song, you an infant between us. You used to fall asleep on the floor like that sometimes, and we were afraid to move you, so we simply watched you as you slept. We dozed off occasionally ourselves, the three of us passing half the night that way together.

I looked over at your father beside me in the car. He was staring straight ahead, and he was crying. He wasn't trying to stop the tears or hide them or wipe them away. He was just letting them run down his cheeks. I'd never seen him cry like that. I'd never seen him claim his own feeling with that kind of abandon. I reached over and squeezed his hand. I felt lost in my feeling, too — that we were indeed blessed and lucky now that you were finally coming home — but I know now that his emotions were much more complicated than mine.

From the backseat, you couldn't tell your father was crying. I wonder if you have ever seen your father cry. I don't think you were listening to the radio, either. You didn't notice what song was playing. You didn't know what it meant to us. You were in your own world, in back, staring at the house and its lights.

"Everything looks different," you said. "It's weird. It's like I don't know my own house."

"Maybe it's the lights, Robbie," I said. "It's the same house. Nothing has changed."

"Some things have changed," your father said, but so quietly, I don't think you heard him over the music.

■ ■ ■ ■

The ebbing day. The house ablaze with light. Your father's tears. The images of that homecoming evening are merged, in my memory, with those of our Christmas Eve celebration, four nights later. Clara and Polly in their finery, dragging the dogs under the mistletoe and smacking their furry heads with kisses. My brother, Ryan, sprawled on the couch with a guitar in his lap. Your father shoving wood into an already blazing fire. My own mother and father standing together in the kitchen spooning the stuffing from the turkey. My mother pausing entirely by accident under the mistletoe, and my unexpected happiness as I watched my father lay a deep kiss on her unsuspecting lips. Then Mitch arriving at the front door with an outrageously expensive bottle of champagne, and a moment later, the star of the show — you, Robbie — materializing in a bow tie at the top of the stairs. In that moment I felt again that we were blessed and lucky. I hoped that this time I could make it last.

December had arrived in London. I remember that it snowed, but the snow melted as soon as it hit the ground. In the office, I pretended Malcolm had never come to my room that night after the races. He never brought it up, and nothing changed between us, at least not that we acknowledged.

I wrote my mother a letter. I told her I was not coming home until spring, at the earliest. I did not detail my holiday plans, since I hadn't made any. I was holding out hope Patrick would invite me to Ireland. In the meantime, Malcolm invited me to France.

I can't quite reconstruct the circumstances under which he first introduced the idea that I come with him and his family to Paris for Christmas. I only know that as December marched forward, it became the principal item of discussion between us. He did not approve of my spending the holidays alone in London. He thought I would enjoy Paris. I had studied French, after all, hadn't I? It was no imposition, since there was plenty of room. Louise was enthusiastic about the idea. The penthouse had been in Louise's family for generations, so it didn't cost them anything, and Louise thought it would be nice for Daisy to have a companion.

"Is that why you want me to come?" I said. "To babysit Daisy?"

"Of course not. I want you to come because I want to be with you. And I don't want you to be alone."

I didn't tell him, of course, that I hoped to be with Patrick. My plans for the holidays had not come up in conversation with Patrick. The future rarely did. Not even the immediate future. Not a day or an hour and sometimes not even a moment in advance did I have any idea what Patrick had in mind for me, or whether he had me in mind at all. This uncertainty lay like a sore under the surface of my skin, erupting again and again, then subsiding, but never healing.

Sometimes I told Malcolm I would think about coming to Paris. Sometimes I told him no, outright. But he would not give up, and every day he had a new prop. A photograph of the penthouse. A description of the holiday decorations on the Champs-Élysées. A review of the restaurant he'd booked for the twenty-third of December.

I ventured to the gallery on the Wednesday two weeks before Christmas. Patrick wasn't there. On Saturday, he wasn't there again. The following week was the same, until finally, beside myself, I inquired with the owner and was told that Patrick's work schedule had changed. I could not call Patrick, because the only phone he had was in the cottage, and he shared the line with Malcolm and Louise. He couldn't call me, because the only place I could be reached was at work, and Malcolm would be there. He did not once come to Victoria to find me.

Two days before Malcolm and Louise were to leave for Paris, Malcolm pulled up a chair next to my desk and sat down. He leaned toward me and put his elbows on his knees and folded his hands.

"It's not too late to change your mind and come to Paris," he said.

I didn't say anything.

"If you don't come, who will sort out my French?"

"I'm sure your wife can sort out your French."

"She could, but she won't."

"Why won't she?"

"She'll be too timid. She won't want to speak French in front of Patrick."

"Patrick?"

"Louise has invited him to come along and he's agreed. We received news that Daisy won't be arriving until Christmas Eve. She's been invited by a school friend to ski at Saint-Moritz and she seems quite set on going. So Louise said she'd like to invite Patrick, and there was no reason I should object, and now there is absolutely no reason you should not allow yourself to come."

He looked triumphant. He had played his final card, and he was about to win, but not for the reasons he thought.

"Louise is all right with this, Annie," he said quietly.

"She's all right with what?"

"Us. The two of us. I mean if you will ever . . . if we were ever to try again to be together."

"You asked her?" I could not believe he would do such a thing.

"Yes," he said. "I did."

"When?" I asked, wondering if it was before or after that first failed attempt in my room at Victoria, which I'd worked so hard to pretend had never happened.

"I cleared it with her when you first arrived," he said.

TWENTY-ONE

We left for Paris three days before Christmas, at seven-thirty sharp. I waited on the sidewalk in front of the boardinghouse with my duffel bag. The sky pressed down flat and cold, and the street was emptied of life. The car pulled up to the curb. Malcolm put my bag in the trunk and opened the front passenger door. I had imagined that for appearances' sake we would pretend this was an everyday sojourn, a married couple and their younger friends traveling from London to Paris — and I thought I would sit in back with Patrick. But it appeared Louise was to have Patrick to herself, and I was to be stuck with Malcolm. I had to remind myself that officially Patrick and I had met only once — at the gallery the night of the anniversary party. I turned halfway around to the backseat to say good morning.

"We meet again," Patrick said, smiling.

Louise was directly behind me and I

turned and extended my hand and she gave it a halfhearted squeeze. Malcolm handed me a map. He'd drawn a black line to indicate the route we would take from Victoria out of the city to Dover, where we would catch the ferry, then another dark line from Calais to Paris. The darkness and thickness of the lines had blocked out some of the names of the roads, so I couldn't tell where we were, or what direction we were heading, or even which way to hold the map. Impulsively, I passed the map back to Patrick.

"You don't mind navigating, do you?" I said.

"Not at all," he said.

It was foggy and cold, and now and then Malcolm had to turn the wipers on to clear the mist from the windows. From the back, Louise kept telling Malcolm to slow down at the roundabouts and reminding him when he'd left his blinker on. How many times had this commentary run between them? A hundred, a thousand times? I was suddenly weary of them. I had barely slept at all, wondering about Patrick, wondering why he'd agreed to come, and why he'd slipped out of my life, and what Malcolm was expecting of me, and whether I had packed the right clothes. Louise would be stylish, and I would not be. Patrick would take note of the disparity. Patrick had said something to me once, when we'd been window-shopping and I'd pointed out something I liked in a shop. He'd said that at some point in my life, I would arrive upon a more definitive sense of style. The statement had deeply offended me, but it had also worried me every day since.

I fell into a half-sleep. I sensed the three of them in my dreams, their breaths and separate thoughts. Also Patrick's humming — incessant and beautiful and unselfconscious. In my dream a thin, silver thread extended from me to Patrick, tying us thinly by the wrists. I woke with Malcolm's fingers on my arm. We had reached Dover.

"Those are the White Cliffs," Malcolm said. "And Dover Castle's just beyond. We'll have time to walk along the ridge before we board the ferry."

I peered out the car window but I could not see the castle in the fog.

"It's awfully damp out," Louise said. "This wretched fog. We'll barely be able to make anything out."

Malcolm ignored her and opened the car door.

"Really, dear. I don't know that we all want to trudge out in this weather."

"It's barely spitting," he said.

"But this wretched fog."

Malcolm sat for a moment with his door open. "Let's at least pose for a photo," he said shortly.

"You three go on," Louise said. She stayed where she was, her tiny hands folded in her lap, her thin lips made even thinner by determination.

Patrick brought his camera. We walked against the wind to the cliffs. Malcolm made me stand alone for a photograph. I tied my scarf tightly around my neck and hugged my coat close, until Patrick ordered me to let the coat blow open and the scarf fly free.

Then Patrick went to the car and I tied the scarf around my neck again and buttoned my coat against the wind. Patrick returned with the tripod, and Louise.

"Our lady has agreed to a photo after all," he said.

He set up the tripod and placed us — Louise, then Malcolm, then me — leaving a space beside Louise for himself. He set the timer, then slid into place, slipping his arm around Louise's waist. Malcolm, in turn, put his arm around mine, but I must have pulled away, because in the photo there is a gap between us, evidence of my unsuccessful protest. And that is the immortal moment, preserved for more than two decades, then transported into our mailbox last June.

You'll want to know how it found its way to us, and why. You'll want answers to the same questions that plagued me last summer, until I went to London and behaved foolishly, and the car expelled you into a ravine, and the whole matter became irrelevant.

What did I notice, some twenty years after the fact, when I first held the photo in my hands? The silver-halo effect, yes, and the swipe of red, but also, to be perfectly frank, my clothes — the ill-fitting coat, the clunky boots, the scarf tied much too tightly around my neck. My face was not so bad. My features were the right size and shape. My skin was clear. My hair was long and dark and thick. I was young, after all.

Patrick returned the tripod to the car. Louise decided she could brave the weather, after all, and we took a look around. The White Cliffs were not really white; they were the color of dirty sand. The fog was dense. The ground was frozen in places, muddy in others. A single tower of Dover Castle was visible in the distance, poking through the low-lying fog. Malcolm explained it was chalk downland we were standing on, a rare material that contained more species of plant life than an equal size of tropical rain forest. That was because it was inhospitable. It was difficult for plants to take root in it, so many tried, and the result was diversity. Where the down met the sea, Malcolm said, the chalk was exposed to the wind and weather to form the White Cliffs.

I stood on the frosty ground at the edge of the cliff. It was very steep and there was no railing. I could have jumped. Or pushed someone.

I was furious with Patrick for not standing beside me in the photograph. And for failing to touch me the whole morning. And for absenting himself from my life after our trip to Canterbury, and appearing, now, completely at ease with the distance imposed between us. And for acting as if I were nothing to him — perhaps I *was* nothing to him — and forcing me to pretend he was nothing to me.

On the other hand, he had been solicitous of Louise. He had opened the car door for her. He had persuaded her to stand for a photograph. He had referred to her as "our lady," and posed beside her.

But of course I did not push him off the cliff. I believed I could not be happy without him.

Below us was a sharp drop onto another plateau, then the ferry terminal and the sea. Malcolm said that on a clear day, you could see the Continent from here.

"Not today," Louise said bitterly.

Announcements for the ferries embarking and disembarking were being made in various languages — French, English, German. Our ferry was named, and we piled back into the car and drove onto the ferry. We climbed the stairs after leaving the car and sat inside at a table by the window. The wind had picked up and the ferry had begun a gentle rocking. Louise said she hoped the motion wouldn't make us all sick. Malcolm brought us weak coffee in foam cups. Louise said she'd changed her mind — would Malcolm go and get her tea instead?

"Tea with lemon, dear," she said, "not milk."

The air was warm and stale. The windows were covered in a film of salt that obscured the ocean and the sky. Malcolm returned with Louise's tea. Patrick was uncharacteristically quiet. I was, too, probably, and a mood settled over the table, a vigilance, a determination not to say the wrong thing, which left nothing much to say at all. It was a relief, a distraction, when Louise began to feel sick from the motion of the boat.

"Have you got the Kwells?" she asked Malcolm.

"They're in the car, my dear," he replied.

She stared at him silently, her mouth a frozen oval of discontent.

"I said it three times, Malcolm. 'Remember the Kwells,' I said. You know how I am at sea."

Malcolm tried to speak but she cut him off.

"Three times, Malcolm. How often must I say something? Or am I to do everything myself? All the packing. All the arrangements. Absolutely everything."

"It's no problem. I'll fetch them now," Malcolm said, standing up even as he was speaking and beginning to make his way toward the stairs that led to the cars below. The three of us sat silently in his absence, then Patrick began to hum, and Louise smiled at him weakly, and I looked away.

In a few minutes Malcolm was back at the table, frowning. Apparently, during a rough crossing the lower deck was locked in case the cars shifted. Passengers were not allowed below as a precaution. Louise did not speak, but it was as if the motion of her face were standing in for language, bleating out its awful, ugly, primitive complaints. She clutched the edge of the table and her

190

fingertips flared pink beneath her beige polished nails. Her upper lip pulled back on one side, revealing tiny, crooked yellow teeth that seemed out of place in her otherwise flawless face. She shook her blond head back and forth and rolled her eyes — elaborately, savagely — and blew a furious shiver of air out of her mouth.

It was beyond distaste. It was beyond disappointment. It was even beyond rage. What locked on to her face was dismissal; it was contempt. It was terrible to watch, but I was drawn to it as to a car wreck by the side of the road. I found it both horrifying and invigorating. Something would have to happen now. They would not be able to survive such a display. We would be witness, Patrick and I, to the precise moment of their marriage blowing apart. But Malcolm only sat, reduced and mute, his hands folded in his lap, staring out the filmy windows toward the sea.

What did Malcolm and Patrick see in her? How had they allowed themselves to fall in with her? Aside from her petite frame, and her sense of style, I felt myself to be in every way superior to her. I believed myself incapable of such a display, incapable of the ugliness underlying it. And I did not even really notice it, months or years into my own

191

marriage to your father, when I began to strike that pose myself, now and then — the sighing, the childish rolling of eyes, the exaggerated discontent — particularly, and this is the secret every woman tries fruitlessly to keep from every man, at that time of the month.

What happens to a marriage? A persistent failure of kindness, triggered at first, at least in my case, by the inequities of raising children, the sacrifices that take a woman by surprise and that she expects to be matched by her mate but that biology ensures cannot be. Anything could set me off. Any innocuous habit or slight or oversight. The way your father left the lights of the house blazing, day and night. The way he could become so distracted at work that sometimes when I called, he'd put me on hold and forget me, only remembering again when I'd hung up and called back. The way he wore his pain so privately, whistling around the house after we'd had a spat, pretending nonchalance, protecting you and your sisters from discord, hiding behind his good nature, inadvertently calling out my ill nature in the process, persisting in being optimistic, and cheerful, and affectionate, when there was clearly no call for any of that.

These were the tallies I kept, the grudges I nursed. Would I have indulged myself that way if I'd fully understood the situation?

I would have behaved better, I hope. I hope I would have been kinder.

Patrick was the first to recover from Louise's display. He raised his eyebrows at me and gave me a wink. He took out a handkerchief and wet the corners of it in a drinking fountain and gave it to Louise to put over her eyes. The color had drained from her face but she managed to smile, again, at Patrick. She placed her elbows on the table and held the cloth over her eyes with both hands. It did not seem fair that ill temper and a weak constitution should bring her the gift of Patrick's attention, and I was envious that she should be the one to hold something that belonged to him.

"I'll see what they've got behind the counter for motion sickness," Malcolm said.

"Is there anything I can do?" I asked, when he'd gone.

"Yes," Louise replied, without removing the cloth from her eyes. "Go and see what's keeping Malcolm, would you?"

He had been gone only a moment, but I did not object. I stood up, leaving Patrick and Louise alone at the table. I found

Malcolm milling around the cafeteria with his hands in his pockets. He was a good man. That was what struck me when I saw him. He was a good man doing his best, and I had a fleeting wish to carry him away and deliver him into a safer, better life. I touched his arm. He turned with a start and stepped toward me so that he was standing very close. I very nearly let my body fall into his body, but I reminded myself, in time, that it was not Malcolm but Patrick I wanted, and I took a step backward.

"Give me the car keys," I said. "Maybe I'll have better luck. Where are the pills?"

"The Kwells? They're in the boot in my suitcase," he said, handing me the keys. "But you won't be allowed down there."

I turned from him without answering and found the door to the staircase that led to the lower levels. I took the narrow concrete stairs two at a time. The door to the third level, where we'd parked, was locked. I ran back upstairs and found an attendant, a thick man in a blue uniform. I put my hand on his arm and gave him a pleading look. "Can you help me?"

He nodded with an official air and I followed him back down the stairs, where he opened the door. It was not quiet — there was clinking, as of metal on metal, and there was the roar of the ship's engines — but the effect was of quiet, and I stood still for a moment, happy to be alone.

I couldn't remember the color of the car. Was it gray or beige or possibly gold? And I had not paid any attention to the make. I had been too distracted by Patrick, and by the seating arrangements during the car ride from London. I walked up and down the aisles, feeling aimless and ridiculous. Then I saw the map folded up on the dash, and Patrick's wool sweater in the backseat. I opened the trunk and found the Kwells in Malcolm's suitcase, the label indicating one tablet every six hours for motion sickness.

Patrick and Malcolm were alone at the table when I returned.

"Here," I said, handing Malcolm the pills.

"Thank you," he said. "Louise has gone off to the loo. She's a bit under the weather, I'm afraid."

"Those will help, hopefully."

"She might be in there quite a while," Patrick said. "Can you make a special delivery, do you think?"

Malcolm handed back the pills and I made my way to the ladies' room. I could see her shoes under the stall door — tiny brown tasseled leather loafers — and the cuffs of her brown slacks. Those shoes, those slacks — were they stylish? I didn't know. I hoped they were not. I could hear her throwing up, not violently but reluctantly, as if resisting the vicissitudes of her own body.

"Louise?" I said. The word seemed absurd on my lips, as if she were a teacher or a surgeon or a nun and I was using her given name. But what else could I call her? I could not very well call her Mrs. Church.

"Oh, dear," she said. "Is that Annie?"

"Yes, I've got the Kwells for you."

"He sent you in here, did he?"

"I don't mind."

"I'm sorry about all this."

"It's all right."

"This can't be much fun for you."

"It's no problem at all."

Then I heard her throw up again. I felt as if I were seeing into her soul, as I had the night of the party at the gallery. But this time it was her other self I saw, not the dark fairy of want but a middle-aged woman, like the woman I am now, plain, chastened, mortal.

The toilet flushed.

"Just leave the pills on the sink," she said shortly.

"All right," I said, understanding that her moment of vulnerability had passed. This would be something we would pretend had not happened. We had not been in the bathroom together. I had not heard her throwing up. I had not seen her feet in their loafers under the stall door. She was not sleeping with Patrick. Her husband was not trying to sleep with me.

When I returned from the bathroom, Malcolm was alone at the table, and I sat across from him.

"How is she?" he said.

"She got sick but I think she's all right now," I said. "I left the pills for her."

"Thank you." He put his hand over mine on the table. "I'm sorry about all this."

"It's all right. I don't mind."

"I'll take her to the infirmary when she comes out."

We sat in an awkward silence. "It's lovely to have a moment alone with you," he said. "I wonder if you know —"

But he didn't finish. I was shaking my head, shrugging off the love he kept trying to pin on me. I knew it wasn't the right kind of love, because it required nothing of me. I did not need to worry about keeping it alive or putting it out since it was kept alive quite independently of anything I might or might not do. He would not be someone who demanded anything of me. He would hold on to whatever pieces I offered him, however flawed they might be. It did not bind me to him — somehow, it freed me.

Louise appeared, moving unsteadily toward the table. I slipped my hand from beneath Malcolm's. He stood abruptly and moved toward her, walking cautiously across the gently rocking ferry floor.

He was enormous. She was diminutive. He was sturdy. She was delicate. He was cheerful. She was not. They were each the farthest point on opposite ends of the curve of human creation. It was as if with the slightest genetic mutation they would evolve into separate species altogether. Unable to mate. Unable, even, to peacefully co-exist. How had it been possible for them to create a child? But they had. The evidence, the photograph, was on Malcolm's desk at the office. That child was skiing in Saint-Moritz. That child was to join us in two days' time.

Malcolm bent his knees so he could put his arm around Louise's waist. He supported her as she leaned into him and rested her head against the bulk of his arm. He turned her toward the stairs to the infirmary. For the first time I imagined them alone together in a bed. I had so often imagined Louise in Patrick's bed. I had conjured the cottage, the bedspread, his glasses on the nightstand. The window above them, letting in the cold night air. His lips behind her knees. But she had a bed in her own house, too, a bed she shared with Malcolm, in which they slept and in which everything else that occurred between them occurred. Why had I not thought of it before? In that bed, did he see that her skin was not as taut as it once was? Did he notice the gathering of lines around her eyes and her mouth and the slight pucker of skin leading toward her jaw? Or did he experience her through a veil of familiarity and love, as your father experienced me until I stripped the veil away?

He loved her. I could see that. And until that moment, I had not thought it possible.

He suddenly grazed her cheek with his lips, then touched the back of her neck so tenderly it startled me. I felt not jealousy so much as shame for not understanding the bond between them. The bond that was stalwart in the face of complacency and cruelty and wandering desire. The habit of each other that was the bedrock upon which they'd sunk the foundation of their mutual existence — and upon which they were standing, still.

I walked outside to the upper deck for some air. The ocean was rough and gray and it had begun to drizzle. The wind was strong and the clouds were becoming defined, taking on colors, dark grays and purples, gathering themselves for a storm. I wanted it — rain and lightning and thunder — I wanted anything that would upset the dullness that had overtaken the day, the preoccupation with manners, ailments, medications, complaints.

Patrick saw me. He brought me a beer and one for himself. It was warm, bitter beer in a can, but I was grateful for it.

"I'm glad you came," he said.

"I don't know if I'm glad or not," I said. "It's bizarre, isn't it, all of us here together?"

"Ah, come on, it's not so bad."

"It is for me."

"It was good of you to get Louise sorted out."

"It wasn't good of me. I was just fed up."

"Poor Louise. She tends to make a bit of a fuss, doesn't she? But she's not exactly what she appears to be."

"You would know," I said.

"Now, now."

We finished our beers and he took the empty cans and threw them away. When he returned the wind had shifted. It whipped my hair around my face, not in an orderly, possibly attractive way, but in a frenzy, into my eyes and mouth and up over my head.

Patrick's curly hair was blowing, too, off the white expanse of his forehead. His eyebrows were thick and dark and wild. His lips were thick, too, and his eyes were very green. He did not hold on to the railing but kept his hands in the pockets of his coat, unbothered by the significant rocking of the ferry. He was used to boats. In better times, his family had owned a yacht. This was something he'd told me many times as we'd walked beside the Thames in the evenings.

"If we were on a sailboat," he said now, "we could head out the Channel and around the tip of England into the Irish Sea. We could be in Howth by Christmas Eve."

"You'll be missed this Christmas, won't you?" I said.

"Oh, I wouldn't miss Christmas. I'm flying to Dublin Christmas Eve."

This was news to me. Awful news. I would be alone in Paris with Louise and Malcolm and their daughter.

"You'd love Christmas Eve at Hill House," he said. "Dad would take a shine to you. He likes pretty girls. Can you cook at all? He likes pretty girls to help him in the kitchen. He stomps around, since Mum died, can't find the baking pan, can't find the baster. It's amusing. And of course there's always plenty to drink."

"I can't cook much."

"Ah, well, not to worry."

Did he really mean that I should come? It was what I thought I wanted. To be claimed by him. To be taken into his family and his life. And yet the idea terrified me. I would have to work so hard to please him. I would be worried all the time about my clothes, as I was now.

Patrick began to speak of a pub in Howth he and his sisters visited every Christmas Eve, after dinner. The pub was called the Bloody Stream, so named because a vicious battle against the Danes in the twelfth century was said to have turned the stream beneath it red with blood. As he spoke, he grabbed the two ends of my pink scarf and pulled me toward him. I thought he was going to tell me he would book me a flight from Paris to Dublin. That he would not abandon me to Malcolm and Louise. I thought he was going to kiss me. He did kiss me, long and hard, then he let go of one end of the pink scarf and pulled it free and flung it over the railing of the boat.

I never knew, afterward, whether he'd meant to do it from the start. Whether he'd intended, all along, to be the one to cast it off and cancel out my efforts at reinvention.

Or whether it had been a whim. I only know that one instant it was around my neck and in the next it was gone. I watched it fall. It did not get caught in a gust of wind. It did not whip itself upward over the bow of the ferry and hang suspended in a sliver of sunlight, brilliant against the gray clouds. It simply mashed itself against the side of the boat, a pink smudge, a stubborn remnant of the progress I'd hoped to make. A little wave came up and sucked it under and it disappeared.

TWENTY-TWO

It rained hard during the drive from Calais into Paris. Patrick and I sat in back. Louise sat in front because of her motion sickness.

"Malcolm!" she said over and over as he drifted toward the center lane. She always hated taking the car to the Continent, she explained to Patrick and me, what with the confusion over the steering wheels, especially in the terrible rain.

I took my shoes off during the journey and tucked my feet under me. Patrick removed his own shoes and extended his leg across the seat and nudged one of my feet free and tickled the sole with his toe. I didn't smile. I didn't even look at him. I was afraid Malcolm would see me and we would be exposed. Exposure would be the worst possible thing, or would it? What would happen if it was revealed to Malcolm that all this time I'd been resisting his advances, I'd secretly been sleeping with the man who had seduced his wife?

We did not go directly to the penthouse, but parked the car in an underground garage, then walked to the base of the Champs-Élysées. The idea was to eat a late lunch, enjoy the holiday decorations as we walked up the grand avenue, then visit the Arc de Triomphe. Afterward, we'd take the métro to the Musée de l'Orangerie before collecting the car again to drive to the penthouse in time to clean up before dinner.

The holiday décor on the Champs-Élysées was meant to have involved the affixing of electric lights to the trees lining the avenue, then wrapping them in colored gauze. Louise had read about it in the travel section of the paper. But when we reached the avenue, holding our coats closed against the driving wind and rain, the trees were bare. Apparently it had been an exceptionally long, warm autumn in which the trees had not lost all their leaves. The gauze had lumped and bulged and, with the onset of unusually heavy rains the week before, the decorations had been deemed unsuitable and removed.

We received this information from an American tourist. Louise, in her disappointment, suggested we sit down to lunch right away. Her feet hurt, she said, and she was cold. Impatience shot through me, and for a minute, I wished I hadn't come. This was not how I'd dreamt of experiencing Paris. This was not the picture that had formed in me during the endless French classes in high school and community college. I watched the American walk away. He did not have an umbrella. He was young and bareheaded and unconcerned. I wished I could walk away with him — a countryman, a free spirit — but if I did that, I would miss my chance with Patrick.

"This one will do, won't it?" Malcolm said, stopping at the window of a restaurant with red-and-white-checked tablecloths.

"Oh, I don't know. It looks awfully touristy, doesn't it?" Louise replied.

"It is the Champs," Malcolm said. "We're not going to find anything especially authentic."

"You wanted to come to the Champs," Louise replied.

"I'm just saying, as far as restaurants go, we may have to compromise."

We walked on. We were halfway to the top of the avenue by the time a suitable compromise had been reached, and we gratefully stepped out of the rain into a little bistro and hung up our wet coats.

"The wine list isn't anything special, is

it?" Louise said when she picked up the menu, and for a moment I was afraid we would not be able to eat after all, or worse, that wine would not be ordered. But Malcolm grunted and said it was fine and ordered a bottle of Beaujolais.

"Why don't you order something we can share to start?" Malcolm said to Louise. He looked at me, then at Patrick. "Louise is quite fluent in French. She did her A levels and studied French literature at university."

"Oh, I don't know," Louise said. "I don't think I'll bother. All the waiters speak English on the Champs, anyway."

"Go on, my dear — you should give it a try."

"I don't want to, Malcolm. Stop making a fuss."

It was clearly an exchange they'd been anticipating and in some way gearing up for.

"C'mon, Lou," Malcolm said. "You shouldn't be shy, you know?"

"I said no, Malcolm."

Patrick changed the subject. He had picked up the *Herald Tribune* and began to read the weather forecast.

"There's some kind of system building offshore," he said. "Winds increasing through the afternoon and evening. Hard, steady rain predicted for the rest of today and tomorrow."

"It's so unusual for Paris," Louise said. "I've never known it to rain like this without letting up."

"Never know," Malcolm said. "Might clear up."

"If the paper says it's going to rain," Louise replied impatiently, "then it's not likely to just clear up, dear, is it?"

Malcolm said nothing. The waiter came and we ordered in English.

As we ate and drank, Malcolm laid out the itinerary for the weekend. Dinner would be nothing fancy tonight, since we were eating such a late lunch; we'd dine at the restaurant below the penthouse.

"Not very adventurous, I'm afraid, but it's really very good," Louise said. "We can bring our own wine. And I should think we'll all be exhausted by then, anyway."

The next day we were to take a tour of the Seine on a riverboat. In the afternoon we could do a little last-minute holiday shopping at Trocadéro, and if I liked, Malcolm would take me up the Eiffel Tower.

"After all, Annie being here gives us an excuse to be tourists, doesn't it?" he said with determined enthusiasm.

After that, we would head to Montmartre

and climb the hill to Sacré-Coeur. Dinner reservations tomorrow night were at La Tour d'Argent.

"La Tour d'Argent," Patrick said, impressed. "It must have taken some doing to get in this time of year."

Louise smiled, triumphant. "We made the reservation months ago," she said. "As soon as we knew we'd have the penthouse for Christmas. Of course we thought it would be Daisy coming along. We thought she might bring a friend for the holidays. We didn't know she'd abandon us for Saint-Moritz."

"She'll be here for Christmas, any event," Malcolm said. "We'll collect her Christmas Eve morning. You'll miss her, Patrick, if we can't persuade you to stay on. There's plenty of room, you know. Daisy's quite comfortable sleeping on the daybed in the morning room."

"I'm afraid I'd never be forgiven if I'm not home to cook the turkey," Patrick said heartily.

"Very happy you'll both be able to enjoy La Tour d'Argent, at any rate," Malcolm said.

"We'll be ordering from a list of nearly fifteen thousand wines," Louise said.

"Speaking of wine," Malcolm said. "Shall

we order a third bottle?"

"Oh, let's don't," Louise said. "It'll only spoil us for dinner."

We were obliged, after coffee, to leave the warm restaurant and enter the wet street again. It took us another half hour to reach the top of the avenue, then we walked through the tunnel to the Arc de Triomphe. We stood under the arch, out of the rain, and surveyed a plaque affixed to the stone, the transcript of a famous radio speech given by Charles de Gaulle.

"Why not read it out loud, my dear?" Malcolm said to Louise.

"Oh, I don't want to, Malcolm. Not now."

"I'll read it," I said, the wine having made me careless.

"Cette guerre n'est pas limitée au territoire malheureux de notre pays —" I read, and so on. I read sentence after sentence with only a vague idea of the meaning of the words.

Patrick looked at me. "You read French?" he said.

"She studied French at school," Malcolm informed him.

Patrick grinned at me, amused that Malcolm knew something about me that he did not. There were many things Malcolm knew about me that Patrick didn't. This was not because I had not tried to tell Patrick who I

210

was, but because he did not often listen when I talked, so I ended up telling him things more than once, after a while not bothering to tell him much at all.

"You have an excellent accent," Patrick said.

"Yes, you do," Louise said, looking not at me but directly at Malcolm.

Watching Louise's face, I was all at once ashamed. This was the formula that ruled the weekend's moral calculations — shame when I might have felt pride, greed when I ought to have been sensible, euphoria when I ought to have felt remorse, indifference when I ought to have been deeply concerned.

We took the métro and endured, again, the gusts of wind and the relentless rain as we made our way from the underground through the Tuileries Gardens toward the Musée de l'Orangerie. We walked on wide, orderly, paved paths between square lawns, and in spite of the day, I was moved. I was moved by the grand scale of it, and by the trees set in straight lines, uniformly bare of leaves, their branches ravaged by wind and rain, the whole scene blown and wet with trauma.

At l'Orangerie, we entered the vast room that housed Monet's Water Lilies. The walls and the ceiling were curved and white, slick as an ice cave, the only ornaments the enormous canvases sweeping the walls. I tried to take in the paintings, but I found them overwhelming, and I failed to be moved.

Louise wandered off to stand before a canvas, and Patrick joined her. Both of them appeared swept up. They walked slowly around the room, turning toward each other from time to time and murmuring. I wondered what they were saying. I wondered what it was the art was supposed to be telling me. I had been interested in art, growing up. I had at least been interested in drawing. But the sketches I made when I was young were driven by an opposite impulse. I had not been interpreting, or creating. I had been attempting only to replicate what I saw. I had been operating within clear limits. Lighting was not so different. Lighting had a function that limited its form, and that gave it a meaning and purpose abstract painting seemed to me to lack.

Malcolm appeared beside me. He took me by the elbow and sat us both down on a white bench in the middle of the room.

"I'm very much hoping you'll like the penthouse," he said.

"I'm sure I will."

"I'm very much looking forward to tonight."

"You mean dinner?"

"Dinner," he said decisively, "and the night together afterward."

Dread shot through me. Would I have to subject myself to a repeat of that mortification so soon after we'd arrived?

I didn't pose the question, and he said nothing more. He only sat beside me, his body an enormous burden in the white-walled room.

The penthouse took up the top floor of an old building on a side street set back from La Place du Châtelet. It had belonged to Louise's great-grandfather, then been passed down in trust, ultimately to be shared by Louise's mother and aunts and bachelor uncle. It was made available one week a year for each of their children, and Louise had been determined this would be the year she would secure the Christmas week; she'd wanted that for Daisy. Then Daisy had insisted on traipsing off to ski.

The building was completed in the middle of the nineteenth century, Malcolm said. During World War II it had been the headquarters for a Quaker mission, a safe house for wounded French civilians.

"La Place du Châtelet is the oldest square in Paris," Louise added. "It's the true center of the city. From the square, you can walk across the Pont au Change to the Île de la Cité and the Rive Gauche and the Quartier Latin. The Louvre is just a few blocks away, and Les Halles are not far beyond that."

She pronounced all the proper nouns in this speech with a perfect accent, but there was something halting in her approach, a brief pause before she leapt forward, as if she had to take a moment to persuade herself that her command of the language was sufficient to proceed, and that it was worth the trouble it cost her. It seemed to me this was the way she moved generally, in the world. She was so small and delicate, it did not seem it would take much to propel her along the street, but she walked as if she were bracing herself, pitching her body forward and keeping her arms tight at her sides. When she did swing her arms, it appeared to require both effort and resolve.

"Why don't you drop us here, dear, then park the car?" she said to Malcolm when we had pulled up in front of the building. "I'm beginning to feel a headache coming on."

"Right," Malcolm said. "I'll just pop in

and find *'le porter'* to take care of the bags."

Malcolm's French was abysmal, and his insistence on using it clearly pained Louise, but he didn't seem to care. He was not cultured or stylish and he did not pretend to be. It was the thing about him I liked most and that had put me at ease all the months we worked together so closely. He was forthright and unpretentious. He was who he appeared to be.

The lobby of the hotel had dark, shining wood floors and heavy furniture and there were objects set tastefully on each surface — brass candlesticks and polished lamps, photographs of points of interest in silver frames, carved iron horses and antique telephones. There was a globe in one corner and a reproduction of an early map of modern Paris, circa 1860, above the fireplace, with the location of the hotel marked with a gold star. The Seine ran through the center of the painting, broken up by bridges and contained by stone walls that would be overrun by water in a matter of two days' time.

The wine had worn off entirely, leaving me ill at ease. Malcolm's murmured sentiment at the museum, and the corollary question of the sleeping arrangements, began to trouble me immensely. I longed to have my own room. I longed for Patrick to come to me in the night when Louise and Malcolm were asleep, bringing with him the singular focus from our night in Canterbury. I could not allow Malcolm's intentions to interfere with that possibility.

We took the ancient elevator up to the fifth floor and emerged directly into a bright, airy, comfortable room with windows all around. The kitchen was in one corner, and a nook they called the morning room was in another. The walls were painted a sunny yellow. The kitchen was filled with chunky wood hutches and baskets and vases. In the center of the room was a living space with many sofas and chairs in cheerful mismatched upholstery. There were tasseled pillows stacked one upon the other on the faded Oriental rug, making themselves into a kind of stool. It was a French country room, well worn and authentic, with an element of the flea market in it. I did not know whether this effect had been achieved intentionally or whether it had accumulated organically over the years. I did not know, either, whether I should like the room or not. But I did like it, especially the lights.

There were pendant lights made from recycled jam jars. There was a chandelier with a shade covered in ostrich feathers.

There was an old birdcage in one corner in the shape of a woman's body, painted robin's-egg blue and converted into a lamp. Years later, when I first opened the Salvaged Light, I happened upon three birdcages in that same unusual shape at a flea market and picked them up for fifty dollars. I wired them and painted them by hand, and they sold in the store for four hundred dollars each.

When I asked Louise about the birdcage, she said, "Isn't it awful? Really, I have to apologize for the state of this place. It used to be so elegant. But over time, with so many people inflicting their taste upon it —"

"I like it," I said, cutting her off.

She looked at me curiously, wearing the same expression she'd worn when I'd read from the plaque at the Arc de Triomphe. It was as if she were reconsidering her estimation of me. As if until that day, she had perceived me as an attractive but mostly empty vessel. And, really, who could blame her? It's exactly the way I felt, Robbie, about the girlfriends you brought home over the years. All that smooth flesh and shiny hair. The high, bright cheeks. The push-up bras. The interests and intentions: a passion for journalism; a plan to join the Peace Corps;

a love of writing, or painting, or drama; a major in business administration, perhaps with a minor in psychology. Beauty and ambition, the twin currencies with which those girls hoped to purchase a place for themselves in the world.

Emme was different, of course. Emme's beauty was uncontested, but her faith in herself was tenuous, and her ambitions, to me, at least, were opaque. She wanted to be happy, I imagine, like any of us.

Louise announced she had a headache and was going to lie down. Would Malcolm mind bringing her things to the room? They disappeared down a hallway. I was not shown to a room, myself. The showing of guests to their rooms was presumably Louise's job, but Louise was ill. Patrick took a bottle of wine from a rack in the kitchen and opened it. Malcolm returned and the three of us stood in the kitchen drinking. The storm had intensified.

"Sounds dodgy out there," Patrick said. "I wonder about our river cruise tomorrow."

"Never know," Malcolm said. "Might clear up in the morning."

Patrick and Malcolm became involved in a conversation about World War II, inspired by the visit to the Arc de Triomphe. They were going on about de Gaulle and the Irish

Republican Army. I was surprised by Patrick's command of history and the sharpness of his opinions, though I have no idea, now, what those opinions might have been. I was also impressed by how respectful he was of Malcolm, almost to the point of deference.

Malcolm went to check on Louise. When he returned he said she was still resting and that we might as well go downstairs and have a drink in the bar while we waited for her to join us for dinner. I wanted to change my clothes, but I did not want to force the question of where I was to sleep, so I remained as I was. My neck felt bare without a scarf.

In the restaurant, there were white tablecloths and bud vases, each with a single white rose, but we sat down at a plain table in the bar to wait for Louise. Wine came, and hors d'oeuvres. The lights flickered, then went out and came back on again, then went out for good. There was a collective catching of breath, followed by a flurry of activity among the waiters. Candles were set down at our table, along with another bottle of wine. The waiter told us the electricity was out across half the city and it was not known when service would be restored.

Patrick's knee brushed mine beneath the table. His hand fell, once, against my forearm. Then his hand began to move up and down my thigh. Malcolm listened attentively to everything I said, and encouraged me to speak to the waiter in French, which I found easier to do as the evening wore on.

Malcolm wondered aloud about Louise, but he did not get up to find her. He slid his arm around the back of my chair. I found I did not mind Malcolm's arm, and I did not mind Patrick's hand on my thigh beneath the table. I did not mind the flush I could feel in my cheeks and the way the evening was changing, the way time was stretching out and slowing down and finally moving toward irrelevance.

Then the lights came back on, and there was a collective exhalation of breath, and after a few minutes Louise appeared a little distance from the table.

"I was alone in the dark," she said to Malcolm. "You never came. I've been waiting all this time. The storm was making terrible sounds." She crossed her arms as if she were very cold. Malcolm stood up.

"I'm sorry, my dear. I didn't . . . I thought you were sleeping. Let me get you a chair."

"I don't want a chair," she said. "I need something for my head. I've got a migraine."

Malcolm looked stricken. He tried to give Patrick money for the food and wine, but Patrick refused it, and Malcolm and Louise turned and left together.

Patrick kissed me once, then a second time, across the table. Quite suddenly, Malcolm was back.

"How is she?" Patrick asked.

"She's in a bit of a state, I'm afraid."

"That's a shame," Patrick said. "Anything I can do?"

Malcolm looked at Patrick. He stood beside the table and ran his hands through his hair and stroked nervously at his chin. "I wonder whether . . . I wonder if you wouldn't mind sitting with her awhile."

"I don't mind at all," Patrick said. He stood up and, with a small, chivalrous bow, turned to go. He left without a smile, but he placed something in my chest, a hollow thing that left no room for the hope and happiness that had been condensing there.

I did not have the will to allow the emptiness to remain, I suppose. And here was Malcolm, sitting down now in Patrick's chair, ready to fill it.

"You're so lovely," he said. "I'm sorry to have abandoned you. Louise is never herself when these headaches come on."

"It's all right," I said. I felt an impulse to

tell him everything, if only to stop him from apologizing when I knew myself to be the one who was treacherous. But how could I tell him I was in love with Patrick, knowing he had persuaded himself he was in love with me? He leaned toward me and lifted a strand of hair off my face. He touched the lobe of my ear, as if it were delicate and mysterious.

He said, "Shall we go upstairs?"

I remember wanting to object, but not finding the words, or the will, because I was drunk. I remember leaning on him as we left the restaurant, but I don't remember what came after that. I don't remember taking the elevator. I don't remember entering the apartment. I don't remember getting into bed. But all that must have happened, because when I woke up the next morning, I was under the covers, alone.

TWENTY-THREE

The bedroom in the penthouse was filled with gray morning light. I lay very still, not wanting anyone to know I was awake. I was fully dressed. My boots were placed neatly next to the bed with my socks hung over them. I would never have done that, hung one sock over each boot. Patrick would not have done that, either. Malcolm must have done it. Malcolm must have removed my boots, but not my clothes.

I could hear the storm still raging outside. I could also hear, breaking through the weather, muffled sounds through the wall behind the bed. Patrick's low laugh. Louise's higher one. Murmured conversation. I held my breath and listened, trying to decipher words, meaning, intent. Waiting for the mattress to squeak. For the headboard to slam against the wall.

There was a knock on my door.

"Come in," I said. Malcolm opened the

door and sat on the edge of the bed. Then he lay down on top of it, next to me, in his pajamas, which had the effect of pinning me beneath the sheets.

"Look. Here's the thing," he said, with an urgency that was unlike him. "Louise thinks I've misrepresented this. She thinks I made it out to be only a distraction. An interlude to shake us out of our malaise. A strictly physical attraction. And maybe I did. Maybe I misled her. But my feelings for you snuck up on me. Of course she knows I would never abandon her. But that might not be the only possibility. I've been turning it over and over in my mind. I've been thinking all sorts of mad thoughts. Ways to keep you in Europe. I'm terrified you'll leave. That's it, at bottom. I cannot allow you to leave."

He seemed to be speaking to himself as much as to me.

"In any event, she's agreed to go through with the weekend, then it's over as far as she's concerned. She doesn't want Patrick living in the cottage. She doesn't want you working for me anymore, either. She says she and I are done with this; we've had our bit of fun, but enough is enough."

He grew more animated. "Never mind that while she's been . . . well, she's been having her fun and I've been waiting . . . all this time I've been waiting for you, and trying, that once, anyway, and she's been . . . but never mind. Patrick's not as chivalrous as he appears, apparently. He blows a bit hot and cold. She's never been one to allow herself to be taken advantage of."

"Is he taking advantage of her?"

"I suppose she thinks he is. But it's not just Patrick. She's fed up with the whole situation. She's fed up with me, really. But how could I have known I would fall in love? It was you speaking French, funnily enough. You reading that plaque yesterday at the Arc de Triomphe. My fault, I suppose. She's quite fluent, you know, but she's timid. She's afraid her accent won't measure up. So when you were so confident, funny little thing like that, you reading a bit of French, that's when she saw it, I think. She saw the truth."

I did not ask him what the truth was, but he told me anyway.

"The truth is I can think of nothing but you. I can see nothing inside my mind but your face. It makes me happy, you see. To think of you."

He was not looking at me but up at the ceiling. He was lying very still, and I was lying still, too, because he had trapped me beneath the sheets and I could not move.

"On the other hand," he said, "I do think, I've thought for some time, that Louise's unhappiness, her lack of fortitude, has worn off on Daisy. She's allowed Daisy to think of herself as a young person requiring special considerations. In a way we've both allowed Daisy to think that."

"I would imagine that's natural," I said, "when you're raising an only child."

"But I never wanted to raise an only child, you see," he said. "I wanted a large family. Louise didn't. Or she thought she did, initially, but after Daisy was born, she changed her mind. She misunderstood life's possibilities. And I did, too, but now I don't. Now I know what I want, and what I want, in my heart of hearts, is to start a family with you."

He looked at me significantly. I heard Patrick through the wall, rising, walking about the room, opening the shutter and saying something to Louise, something that made her laugh.

"Louise isn't jealous, exactly. She's furious. She thinks I'm ridiculous. She doesn't understand what's between us."

I didn't ask what *he* thought was between us. That was clear enough. I could have put an end to the whole thing right then. I could have been frank, and delivered him out of his predicament. But I didn't, and I might not have been able to persuade him that I didn't love him, just as I could not persuade myself that Patrick did not love me.

Malcolm stood up and walked to the window. It had been open a crack, and the shutter had blown wide. He closed the window. Then he closed the shutter and stood looking down at me beneath the sheets.

He was so large, standing there; I wanted his largeness to make him invulnerable, but it didn't. His bulk, the weight of his bones, the strength of his fingers — all this gave him no protection. It made me think of my father at the intervention. The bewilderment on his face. The great stillness and sadness of his body.

"I'm so sorry," I said, and I was. "I'm sorry about the whole thing."

"Don't be sorry," he said. "It's a gift. A great gift to feel this way."

I reached my hand toward him. I meant nothing by it, but of course he took meaning from it. He pressed his lips to my hand. He bent over me and kissed my forehead, and then my lips. His lips on mine felt too light, too tender, too tentative, and the kiss brought back the abject failure between us the night after the races. I tried to turn my face away from him, but he surprised me. He took my chin in his hand and kissed me harder. He pulled away and looked me in the eye, then he kissed me again — quite persuasively — and I was moved, in the nether regions, in spite of myself.

He got in under the covers in his pajamas. I did not look at him. I did not touch him. I did not do anything at all. He put his hand beneath my sweater. Louise let out a sharp laugh in the room next door. I heard a door open and close. Malcolm began to kiss me more intensely. Then there were footsteps, and the sound of the elevator opening and closing, then only the sound of the storm.

There was a flash of lightning. A roll of thunder. The hammering rain. The sheets, I remember, were white satin. His hands moved over my body. He undressed me, then undressed himself. He rolled over on top of me, and I could feel him; I could feel there would be no failure this time. I told him I was not on the pill. He said it would be all right. He said I did not have to worry. What, exactly, did he mean by that, and what did I take him to mean? Or was I simply, by that point, beyond bringing myself to care?

I became a great internal shrug. All my organs gave way to the path of least resistance. I felt myself dislocating, but the dislocation did not have the expected result. Instead of removing me, it made me more present, more available, more pliable, more attuned. He entered me, feeling more certain inside me than Patrick had, and at some point, the universe tilted, and an unaccountable shift occurred. Something like abandonment overtook me. It was like the curtain that dropped when I was drinking, but even more absolute in its obliteration of worry and pain, its obliteration of everything. I gave myself over to the whims of my own body. I ceased to be who I had been, and I was swept up, out of shame and into pleasure, up and over the precipice for the very first time. Malcolm had achieved, on the first try, what Patrick never had. Or else I achieved it myself, by simply not caring, and by letting desire rule the day.

Is desire the right word? It was more like hunger, rumbling in a specific location inside my body, a location that couldn't be silenced until it was sated.

"I love you," he said afterward. "I love you more than you can possibly imagine."

He was still touching me, but too delicately, now that it was over. He ran the tips of his fingers along my arm — so lightly it was as if he were afraid he would leave a

229

scar — and it was all I could do not to swat his hand away. He was breathing very heavily, and I had an urge to put my own hand over his mouth to make the sound stop.

Shame was reinstated. What was it that shamed me? It was my tacit consent. It was the success of the thing, followed by the return of my distaste. I had received something I had not asked for. I had taken it on a whim. And because I'd taken it, I was at liberty to throw it away. I had not cared, and so I had come. I had been set down on the earth, and so I was loved.

TWENTY-FOUR

Wednesday morning. Hump Day. Appropriate enough.

I walk the dogs. Then I stand in the driveway, surveying the street. Easter has come and gone, but spring appears to be in retreat. The sky is a bland white. There is no sign of the sun. It's going to be one of those middling days that could grow warm or stay quite cold, making it hard to decide what to wear.

I take the dogs inside. The weather doesn't matter unless I plan to venture out again, and there is really no need. The girls are still in Wisconsin with your father. The store is closed. You are nowhere I can find you. And there is plenty to do, here, inside the past.

Malcolm and I found Patrick and Louise downstairs at the café, eating breakfast. I had showered, but I still felt they might see or smell or sense the residue of sex, and I kept my coat tightened around me. We could not take a cruise on the Seine, it was decided, because of the storm. We sat in the café and drank coffee and ate croissants. Louise dipped a sugar cube in her espresso and sucked it between her lips. I was terrified to sit next to her. I felt myself to be toxic and dangerous, but also disposable. And yet she gave no outward signs of rudeness or discontent. If anything, she was more polite than she had been the day before.

Her headache was gone. She was enjoying herself in spite of the weather. She always loved to be in Paris, she announced, especially at Christmas. She was so looking forward to dinner at La Tour d'Argent. She suggested we skip the Louvre, which could be overwhelming, in favor of the Musée d'Orsay.

We took a taxi in the steady rain. There were more Monets. There were Renoirs and Van Goghs. There was more standing and looking and, on my part, failing to be moved. I stood at a window and watched the rain fall and the river rise and the bare trees sway violently in the wind, and I longed to be outside experiencing the day.

"Next stop, Trocadéro," Louise said. "I

must find one or two more things for Daisy for Christmas."

While Louise shopped, Patrick and Malcolm and I walked across the Seine to the Eiffel Tower. We bought tickets and stood in line, but Malcolm said he was feeling a little dizzy and would wait below while we rode up. At the top, Patrick and I could see almost nothing because of the rain. We rode back down again and collected Malcolm and returned to Trocadéro. Patrick joined Louise in a shop. Malcolm and I waited outside. When Patrick emerged, he handed me a small shopping bag. Inside was a parcel wrapped in tissue paper. I pulled off the tissues and lifted out a wool scarf, pale gray with a faint green geometric pattern.

"A scarf of moonlight and whispers," Patrick said.

"Moonlight and whispers?"

"It's from a poem," he replied, opening his umbrella dramatically into the wind. "Can't remember the rest, I'm afraid."

"It's beautiful," I said. "Thank you."

Louise eyed Patrick curiously. "How sweet," she said.

"She lost her scarf on the ferry," Patrick replied.

I wrapped the scarf around my shoulders. Patrick reached over and rearranged it.

"More like this," he said.

"Very nice," Malcolm said. He rubbed the back of his neck. "Bit of a stiff neck. Must have slept at a bad angle on the pillow."

Where had he slept, and with whom? It was the first time I'd wondered. And what did he think of Patrick, whom I was supposed to have met only once before, giving me a gift? There is no way to know. No way, now, to reconstruct the probabilities of Malcolm's brain, or his heart.

Louise gave Malcolm her shopping bags to carry. "Look at that, now," Malcolm said. "There's a bit of sun fighting out."

"We'd better get over to Montmartre before the rain starts up again," Louise said. "We can take a taxi and walk to the top."

"Or we could take a taxi the other way around," Malcolm said. "The back way. Right to the church. Save the walk up the steps."

"That's a good idea," Louise said.

"I'd like to walk up the steps," I said. "If nobody minds."

I had read about the journey in the guidebook — the more than three hundred steps to the top, and the graffiti on some of the buildings that flanked the stairs. It was something I thought Patrick might want to photograph.

We found a taxi. We walked up the steps. Patrick took pictures. I stayed beside him, wearing my scarf of moonlight and whispers. Malcolm and Louise lagged. Halfway up I turned back to see that Malcolm was no longer climbing the stairs but standing beside Louise, leaning his hip against the railing. Patrick and I descended again, to join them. Malcolm's face was pale as he put his hands to the back of his head. "I'll just sit down here a minute," he said. "It's my head."

It was not like Malcolm to make a fuss. Not like him to feel unwell.

Louise sat down next to him. She took his hands in hers.

"I'll stay with him," Louise said to Patrick and me. "You two go on. We'll be up in a minute."

I did not hesitate. I did not worry about how Malcolm was feeling. Patrick and I climbed the stairs together. He linked his arm in mine. At the top of the stairs he leaned over and took my chin in his hand and kissed me deeply. We reached the church, gray and immense against the massing clouds. We walked around inside. We looked at the stained glass. He kissed me again.

Outside, a clearing of blue was visible

between the clouds. The day was fading, and a thin geometry of colored light lay over the city. In front of the church, a girl was tapping a tambourine against her hip and singing.

Patrick took a picture of her, then we moved closer.

"My God," he said suddenly, "it's Mary McShane. Her brother was with me at school."

He walked right over to her. There was a blue velvet hat at her feet, filled with coins and bills into which Patrick dropped a ten-franc note. When she finished her song, they embraced. A young man sat on the ground beside her. A guitar lay dormant in his lap, and in his hands was an emaciated gray rat. He let the rat run along the back of his neck, over his shoulder and along his arm.

Louise was suddenly beside me. "That rat turns my stomach," she said.

"Is Malcolm all right?" I asked her.

"He's just there, by the church, resting. He's got a terrible headache," she said. "Which isn't like him. We're going to have to go back to the penthouse. We'll take a cab. We could all probably use a little lie-down before dinner anyway."

"Patrick's bumped into someone he knows from home," I said.

He was standing with the girl, Mary Mc-
Shane, talking and laughing. He saw Louise
and walked toward us and the girl began to
sing another song.

"We're going to need to head back now,"
Louise said. "Malcolm's not well."

"I'll catch up to you, why don't I?" Patrick
said offhandedly. "I'll be back in time to
change for dinner."

"I might need your help, though," Louise
said, "with Malcolm."

Something rose in Patrick's face. I saw it,
and recognized it — an arc of resistance
stretching toward an outright refusal. He
would not allow himself to be reined in by
her any more than by me. I'll admit that it
pleased me to see him refuse her. He might
have come along out of deference to Malcolm, who had stood to join us now, but he
did not, he would not, once Louise had
pressed him to.

"I'll be all right," Malcolm said. "Let him
stay and talk to his friend."

"Suit yourself," Louise said to Patrick.

"I may as well stay for a bit, too," I said,
"since the weather's finally cooperating."

Louise sighed. "Fine," she said. She ordered Malcolm to stay where he was, and
Patrick to flag them a cab while she went to
use the bathroom in the church.

Malcolm and I were left alone. He sat down on a step. I sat down next to him. He looked at me. His eyes were watering and his face was drained of color. Did I worry that he was sick? I don't think I did.

"I want you to know," he said, "that this morning was one of the highlights of my life."

I felt my face color. What did I say in return? I don't know. I don't remember. Maybe nothing at all.

"You should stay and have fun," he said. "No sense my spoiling the afternoon for everyone. You'll be all right getting back?"

"I'll be fine," I said. And I was, but he was not.

TWENTY-FIVE

The sun dipped behind a cloud after Malcolm and Louise had gone, and it began to rain again, hard and fast. Mary McShane picked up her hat and the boy put his guitar in its case. Patrick finally introduced me to Mary. She had blue eyes and a small nose and her hair was dyed black and cut short, like a man's. She had earrings all up and down her ears and she was wearing a peasant skirt she kept clamping down against the wind.

It was decided we should all get out of the rain and go for a drink in Mary's flat. She and Patrick walked ahead, talking about people they knew, and the boy and his rat and I walked behind. It was still raining hard and we walked fast, holding our coats over our heads and winding our way through the narrow cobbled streets of Montmartre, past small galleries and shops and bars and cafés that smelled of garlic and rotting vegetables.

We climbed three narrow flights of stairs to an apartment. Mary and the boy lived there with a third roommate, Mary's boyfriend, who was asleep in the back room. It was necessary, Mary warned, to keep our voices down. Her boyfriend had trouble sleeping at night, so mostly he slept during the day while she worked the church.

Bright cotton scarves were hung over the windows. There were books stacked a foot high against the walls. There was a mattress in one corner, and a cardboard box in another, where the rat slept. There was cracked plaster peeling from the walls, revealing dark paint beneath, and spots on the ceiling like giant coffee stains.

Mary offered us red wine in water glasses. There were only two chairs. Mary sat in one with her guitar in her lap, so I sat in the other. The boy sprawled out on the mattress with the rat. Patrick stood at first, moving aimlessly about the room, then he perched himself on the arm of Mary's chair. He asked her questions about herself, about her sisters and her family. Her brother, Ian, had gotten away after their mother died. He'd gone to the States, she said. But she'd been stuck. The eldest girl, with four younger sisters needing caring for. She hadn't been able to stand it. The sadness and the grief and the God-awful mess. She'd told her father she'd found a post with a French family, as a nanny.

She laughed. "Imagine anybody in their right mind leaving little ones with the likes of me!"

"Give us a go," Patrick said, and she handed him the guitar. He played a few chords. I finished my wine and Mary refilled my glass.

Patrick put the guitar down and stood up again and walked around the room, picking up books. He began to read from *A Portrait of the Artist as a Young Man*.

"Such rubbish," Mary said, interrupting him. "For a while I loved that book. When I was naïve."

"Rubbish? Really?" Patrick said. "There's the McShane bravado at last. I've been waiting for it to reappear."

"You're one to speak about bravado," she said.

"You've got to admit Joyce was a genius," Patrick said. "You've got to at the very least give me that."

"I will certainly not give you that," she said.

I had not read Joyce. I had not read anything of importance. I had not finished college, and I had been wasting my time working in an office when I ought to have been pursuing art. Patrick had told me that often enough, but I had not believed him. I was happy working for Malcolm. I felt useful and important. But in this squalid flat in Montmartre, I was too purposeful. I was party to the bourgeois corporatism, as Patrick had once called it, that threatened the modern world. I was involved in an enterprise that had turned the historic Isle of Dogs into a capitalist circus.

The debate on Joyce was continuing, but I was not really listening. I was studying the girl — Mary — taking mental notes.

"You pretentious fuck," she said suddenly. She pronounced the word *fuck* so it rhymed with *hook,* and she said it with real fury. She leapt from her chair and snatched the book away from Patrick.

He laughed. "And is your boyfriend a Joyce critic as well?"

"No, he's a musician. But he's got a wee problem with the smack."

Patrick raised his eyebrows.

Her boyfriend was a songwriter, she told us, only he'd gotten hooked on heroin, and the heroin had affected his songwriting. But now they were tangled up together, and he couldn't give up the drugs, because he was

242

afraid if he did, he wouldn't be able to write music. But he couldn't start writing music again while he was using, because if he was successful he'd never give up the drugs.

I wanted to dislike her. I wanted the whole tableau to be a carefully constructed façade. I wanted her to be a fake. But I don't think she was. She filled my glass again and took my hand and squeezed it. "You're so beautiful," she said. Then to Patrick: "She's so beautiful. Wherever did you find her?"

"Here and there," Patrick said. "She doesn't really belong to me." And then to me, he said: "You don't really belong to me, do you, Annie B.?" Then to Mary: "Her loyalties are somewhat in dispute."

Did he know what had happened in the penthouse that morning after he and Louise had gone to breakfast? He couldn't know. But he seemed to.

The door to the back hall opened suddenly and the boyfriend appeared in the doorway. His head was shaved and his face was gaunt. His skin was so white it was almost blue. Deep circles seemed to be carved under his eyes, like vowels. His shirt was unbuttoned and his chest was thin and hairless. Around his neck was a silver chain with a cross.

He jutted his chin into the room and narrowed his eyes. "What's all this?" he said to Mary.

"We met them at the church," she said. "This is Patrick Ardghal. He was at school with Ian, back home. It started to rain and we all got wet. They came in to get dry."

She stood up and moved toward the boyfriend, slipping her arm under his shirt. He did not accept or reject her embrace; he merely stood squinting into the room.

Patrick was looking at Mary, as if trying to give her a sign. I now felt as he must have felt, too: She needed saving; she needed to be swept away from this place.

"How did you make out today?" the boyfriend said.

Mary handed him the hat. He took the money and shoved it in his pocket.

"And who are you?" he said to me.

"I'm Annie. Annie Black. We're here visiting from London."

"But you're not English, are you? You're American."

I nodded and looked at Patrick. "We'd better go," I said to him pointedly. "They'll be waiting."

Patrick looked the man up and down with an air of challenge. "You go ahead," he said to me. "Send my apologies, won't you? I can't suffer through that restaurant tonight,

I'm afraid."

"But they made the reservations."

"They'll survive."

"But —"

"It'll be fine," he said.

"Suit yourself," I said, not realizing until after I said it that I sounded just like Louise.

With some difficulty, I flagged down a taxi. It took two hours and cost me a small fortune to get back to the penthouse. There were traffic jams all across the city because of the storm, and the taxi driver had to keep backtracking and taking alternate routes. It was nearly eight by the time I arrived at the penthouse, and the power was out. The concierge gave me a flashlight and walked me up the stairs and opened the door for me with the master key. I wielded the flashlight and peered around the kitchen and the living room and down the hall, but nobody was there. I sat down to think. They must have already gone to the restaurant. I could find out where it was located and take another taxi to meet them. But I would have to explain myself. I would have to apologize for my rudeness, and for Patrick's. I would have to suffer through dinner alone with Malcolm and Louise, and I knew I couldn't do it.

I changed out of my wet clothes. I walked downstairs with my flashlight to the restaurant from the night before, which was open and lit with candles. They were not serving food, but they were still serving drinks. I sat and drank alone until the bar closed at midnight, then I returned to the penthouse. It was still empty, and it was very dark, and the storm was raging outside the window. I lay on the bed in the room I'd woken up in and tried to think, but the room was spinning. I hadn't eaten since lunch, and except for the taxi ride, I'd been drinking since we'd stepped into Mary's flat many hours before. I tried to find my nightgown in my bag. The difficulty of this task, the way my hands did not respond as I anticipated they might, the way I stumbled against the wall, informed me that I was even drunker than I'd imagined. I lay back down on the bed, still in my clothes, on top of the covers, willing the room to stay still. Dread overcame me.

After a little while I heard the door to the penthouse open. I listened for Malcolm's heavy steps, and Louise's lighter steps, in the hall. But it was Patrick. He entered my room and flicked the light switch, but of course there was no power. I peered at my watch. It was two in the morning. A great crack sounded outside.

"What was that?" I managed to say, enunciating carefully so he would not know how drunk I was.

"A tree, probably. This storm is shattering the city. I barely got back," he said. "There were trees fallen in the road. They're not back yet, are they? The métro is shut down and it'd be nearly impossible to get a taxi. I wonder if they're stuck."

He stripped off his jacket and the rest of his clothes. He dropped them on a chair. He made me get up so he could pull the covers back, then he climbed into bed and pulled me in after him.

"Now, then," he said, which was the thing he always said to begin.

There was to be none of the feeling from Canterbury. I could sense that, and yet I did not at first try to resist. I found I was happy to be in his arms. But something in me became shocked at myself for being so pliable, for already having forgiven him for abandoning me the night before and spending the night in Louise's room, and for ignoring me in Mary's flat, and leaving me to make my way across Paris alone. Then I remembered what I had done with Malcolm that morning. If there were amends to be made, it could be argued they needed to be made by me as well. I could feel Patrick's erection against my thigh and his hands moving along my body. I had moved against Malcolm that morning, not so differently from this, feeling not love but detached animal desire. Patrick might be feeling the very same thing, ignited not by me but by Mary McShane.

"Not tonight," I said, removing his hands from my body and rolling away from him.

If he'd protested at all, if he'd tried a little harder, I would have given in without a fight. But he fell right to sleep. I listened to him breathe deeply, then begin to snore. The sounds of the storm filled the room. Great crashing and groans. Wood bending and moaning in the wind. The rain hammering the windows. I could reach over and touch him and wake him. I could see if it might be possible, with Patrick, to achieve what I had achieved that morning with Malcolm. But I didn't do it. I remained turned away from him and went to sleep.

In the morning, he was not there. There was a note — an excerpt from an Oscar Wilde poem — written on a sheet torn from a pad and folded in half and perched like a tent on top of my backpack:

How sad it seems.
Sweet, there is nothing left to say
But this, that love is never lost . . .

I'm off home.

P.

The storm had ended and the penthouse was silent. I walked down the hall and put my ear to the door of the second bedroom. I opened it a crack. The room was empty. Louise and Malcolm were not there. Daisy was not there, either. I was alone.

I opened the drapes in the main room. The city was calm beneath a mild white sky. The only visible evidence of the storm was the tree we'd heard fall, cracked in two, hanging over itself like a failed sculpture, and the red awning of the hotel flung onto the sidewalk. There were no cars moving in the street. There was a building in front of me blocking the larger view of the city — the hundreds of felled trees, the scaffoldings crashed to the ground, the smashed cars. The Seine, overflowing its banks, drowning the Île de la Cité in muddy water.

I began to worry. What if Malcolm really had been sick? What if they'd had an accident? But they would have called. I picked up the phone on the kitchen counter. There was no dial tone. The lines had been brought down in the storm.

Daisy might be waiting at the train station with nobody to greet her. If Louise and Malcolm were somehow stuck, she would step off the train and find herself alone. Would a ten-year-old girl know how to navigate a foreign city, even one she'd visited many times before? I didn't know, and there was nobody to ask. Patrick would have known, but Patrick was not there. I was filled with fury at him for having flown off to Dublin and escaped. Why could I not escape, too?

There was sunlight coming through the window, overtaking the room slowly but steadily. I studied it, paralyzed by indecision. Perhaps I was worrying over nothing. Malcolm and Louise might have come back to the penthouse and left again this morning while I was sleeping my drunken sleep. They might be collecting Daisy from the train station right this minute.

I read Patrick's note again. It was a farewell, but Patrick was full of farewells. I had learned not to take his goodbyes too seriously. He had returned to me, hadn't he, in the end? He had not stayed with the girl — Mary McShane — at Montmartre. He had come to me, but I had rolled away from him. Was there still time to win him back? Could a case be made that I could still reasonably expect his affection if I pursued it? And to whom was I beholden — Patrick? Malcolm? Louise? Or only myself?

I checked the phone again, and this time there was a dial tone. The sunlight had reached the grandfather clock; it was almost noon. By one account, they might arrive at any moment — Louise and Malcolm, having successfully collected Daisy from the train. They might be pressing the elevator button, waiting to make their way up to the penthouse. I had to act now, or I might never get away. I hurried into the bedroom and threw my clothes into my pack. I ran a brush through my hair and washed my face. I pulled the shower curtain closed and hung up my towel. I brushed my teeth, then scrubbed the toothpaste out of the sink and made the bed.

I found paper and a pen and tried to compose a note. But I couldn't think clearly. Where would I say I was going? Where, in fact, was I going?

The phone began to ring. I stood listening to the sound. It seemed impossibly loud in the sunlit room.

I put Patrick's note in my pocket. I slung

my backpack over my shoulder. I pushed the elevator button, counting the rings of the phone. I shoved open the metal doors, stepped in and closed them again, and the sound stopped. When I entered the lobby, the porter was out front. If I went through the main door, I would have to walk right past him. I'd be caught running away. I turned left, down the hallway, and found another door. I shoved it open and stepped into a narrow alley, then onto the streets of the altered city.

Twenty-Six

The storm had touched down on the Brittany and Normandy coasts. It whipped the ocean into ten-foot-high waves, then swept east across France in a narrow band, reaching hurricane force when it blasted Paris. The Black Forest of Alsace had been hit like a hammer. Four thousand trees at Versailles were uprooted. A third of the forest at the Bois de Boulogne was destroyed. Chimneys collapsed and cars were hit by falling trees. Millions of homes lost power. Paris-area suburban rail services were suspended, and only a third of the métro lines within the city were still in operation. The airports at both Roissy and Orly had been closed for the early-morning hours. Thousands of travelers were stranded by the first total shutdown of the French national railroad.

I didn't know any of that, of course, when I stepped out of the building into the alleyway, then onto the street. I chose a direction at random and began to step through the debris. Patrick's scarf was flung around my neck and my boots kept coming untied. When I bent to retie them, the edge of my coat got soaked in a puddle.

I descended the stairs of one métro station after another, only to find there were no trains running. I reached the Seine and stood before it, watching its brown rage. It had overflowed its banks and was threatening to flood Notre Dame. I went on walking in a kind of stupor of wonder at the ravaged city. There was a general feeling of wreckage and tragedy, and I indulged myself in feeling at the center of it. I bought a sandwich at a café. I collected information about the storm here and there. Then I was at Gare Saint-Lazare and there was a train that could take me to Cherbourg, on the coast. I sat in grim relief that I was finally heading somewhere fast. The train hummed beneath me, its white noise obliterating the need to think about what I ought to do next.

At Cherbourg, there were no ferries to Dover, but there was a ferry about to depart for a place called Rosslare, which I understood was on the other side of the Channel. I reasoned that if it was on the other side of the Channel, it could not be very far from

London, so I bought a ticket. I would head back the way I had come and return to Victoria and spend Christmas alone. On the ferry, I sat down at the bar and asked the bartender how long the journey would take. She said we would land in Rosslare at noon the following day.

"That long to get back to England?" I said.

"Not England, love," she said. "Ireland."

"Ireland?"

"Rosslare. Are you not wanting Rosslare?"

Rosslare seemed as good a place as any, and I said as much.

"I hope you've booked yourself a sleeping berth," she said. But I hadn't. I'd bought the cheapest ticket available. I would have to sleep on deck somewhere. I would have to make do.

Standing across from me at the bar was a man. He had a cap pulled down low on his forehead and a dirty-blond beard and very full, very chapped lips. He had his foot up on the bar stool and a roll of duct tape in his hand. He appeared to be repairing his shoe. He bit a piece off and wrapped the tape all the way around the toe, then sat back down at the bar in front of his beer. There was an air of fortitude and certainty and cheerfulness in his broad face and body and a gentleness, too, in his very blue eyes.

A man like that, I thought, would take you in hand. A man like that would keep you safe from yourself.

Was it love at first sight? Not exactly. But it was a haven in the storm.

TWENTY-SEVEN

Do you recognize us, finally? Can you locate your parents at last in all this mess?

Parents. It's just a word.

It's a word whose meaning one does not think to interrogate until one must.

Now the story becomes more difficult to set down. Now it becomes necessary to distinguish between the lore and the truth. To disentangle the version of events that's made its way into dinner conversation over the years — becoming a matter of public record — from the truth. But is truth the same as memory? I offer you a memory. Has the memory been shaped by the waves of time, and by the history that has rushed against it since? Of course it has. What memories haven't?

Your father and I met on a ferry crossing from Cherbourg to Rosslare in the Irish Sea.

True.

It was Christmas Eve.

True.

We were both traveling alone.

Yes.

Your father was a gentleman. He offered me his sleeping berth.

Yes, he did.

I slept in that berth, alone.

There was one other man at the bar. A boy, really, about my age, an Irish boy with some quintessentially Irish name like Cathal or Manus. He had a sharp face and thin red greasy hair standing straight up from his head. He was trying to grow a beard that was not really taking hold. He was heading home to Wexford for the holidays.

The two men were sitting one stool apart. I listened to them talking. The man in the cap, an American, was saying he'd meant to spend Christmas in Nice, but he'd been unable to travel there from Paris because of the storm. It was fine with him, he said; he was sick of the French and had decided he'd like to spend Christmas where people spoke English. But he'd already spent the month of November working in a clinic in the English countryside, so he was heading somewhere new — Ireland. He had been overseas half a year, he said, and in two months' time he was expected to start a residency in family medicine at a hospital in San Francisco.

"A doctor, eh?" the Irish boy said. "You like sick people, so?"

"I like dogs, actually."

"Dogs?"

"I learned to breed dogs growing up," he said. "But you can't make much of a living that way."

"Which state?" the Irish boy asked.

"Wisconsin."

They finished their beers. The American took off his hat, and I was struck, again, by his beautiful blue eyes.

"I've always wanted to go to America," Cathal-or-Manus said. "Get out of feckin' Wexford."

After a while the blue eyes looked straight at me across the bar, and the American smiled.

"Are you ever going to come warm this empty chair?" he said to me.

I looked at him. I moved to the empty seat between the two men. He bought me a beer. He told me his name was Jonathan Gunnlaugsson. I couldn't pronounce it, so he wrote it on a paper napkin for me. I shoved the napkin in my pocket, where I had also put Patrick's note.

At some point we all took our beers outside. We sat on a plastic bench out of the wind and ate cheese sandwiches from his pack. The redheaded boy had a fiddle, and he began to play. The American and I struggled to talk over the fiddle and the roar of the sea. I told him I'd been to Paris with my boss and his wife. I told him my boss's wife was having an affair, and that the man she was having an affair with had come with us to Paris. I left out the bits about my own romantic entanglements. I was conscious that the picture I was painting was not entirely complete, but Jonathan was clearly a person of substance, someone I wanted to know, and already my interest in him was causing me to perceive the episode in Paris through a new lens. I had walked out of an unseemly situation; I wasn't going to walk back into it by setting the story between us.

There was a woman on the ferry with a small white dog. The dog was jumping up and barking and the woman was feeding it bits of a sandwich.

"That woman is rewarding the wrong behavior," Jonathan said. "The first rule of training is you don't reward with affection or food unless the dog is quiet and submissive. That woman thinks it's cute, the dog acting that way, but it's not cute and it doesn't make the dog happy. It doesn't make him settled."

"You're an expert?"

"Yes."

"A dog expert?"

"Actually, it's the same with women."

"Really? A woman gets affection only if she's calm and submissive?"

"That's right," he said. "If a woman wants to be loved, she has to be good."

I laughed. And he laughed. I felt I'd been taken in hand. And I felt, too, that the day was brighter and calmer than it had been just a few hours before.

He stood up and led me to the railing. The redheaded boy had stopped playing. Jonathan sent him inside with money to buy us all more beers. He told me he'd grown up on a farm in northeastern Wisconsin. He'd spent his summers on an island, Washington Island, where his grandmother lived and where his ancestors had first landed and settled when they emigrated from Iceland in the 1800s. They kept an old houseboat there. They lived on the boat every summer for the month of August.

"It sounds idyllic," I said, "but it probably wasn't, was it? Childhoods never are, are

261

they?" Where had I gotten this idea? From a book, probably.

"Actually, it was idyllic as far as child-hoods go. Except there was only my mother. No father. But my mother made it work."

"What happened to your father?" I asked him.

"They were never married. Then he died."

"Oh. I'm sorry."

"It's all right. I never really knew him."

"Why did you leave Wisconsin? If it was idyllic."

"That's what people do, isn't it? They leave so they can return."

I asked him how he ended up picking San Francisco as the place he wanted to begin his career. He looked at me, clearly decid-ing how much to reveal.

"Oh, you know, the usual thing," he said. "A girl."

"Oh," I said.

"But that's over. As far as I know."

I asked him for details. He told me they'd known each other when they were children. Then her mother had died, and she'd ended up in San Francisco, with relatives. That's where she was raised. But she came home every August, to Washington Island. She was "pretty and all that." She'd done well for herself, "under the circumstances." She'd wanted to get married, but he hadn't.

I told him how I'd thought I was heading to England, not Ireland. How I'd had no idea I was going to be on the ferry all night and hadn't booked a sleeping berth.

"You can have mine," he said.

"That's all right," I said.

"No, really. You can have it," he insisted. He said he would sleep on deck.

I studied his profile briefly, trying to decide if he was really handsome or not. His eyes were striking, but it was hard to tell about the rest of his face, because of the hat and the beard. He caught me looking at him, and before I could decide if this was a good or a bad thing, he stepped behind me and gathered my long hair in his hands and pulled it back off my face.

"England's that way," he said. "Ireland's this way. We're headed straight toward Ireland's Eye."

He was using my hair as a lever, holding it firmly, turning me gently. It was not so different from the way I'd stood with Patrick on another ferry two days before, and yet it felt nothing like that. The sky was dense with cloud, but for a moment there was a parting, and a final gasp of sunlight appeared, edging the clouds in silver and giving the misty rain the appearance of slow-falling snow. His hands were cool and dry on my neck and his body was grazing my back. I wondered why I had been so set on tall men. There were only three inches of height separating this man and me — if I turned around we would be almost eye to eye — and yet that felt exactly right.

He was talking to me, telling me about where he planned to travel next. Nepal, to trek, he was saying, then to a town in India he wanted to see called Varanasi. I felt the words moving in his chest and exiting near my ear, and I felt him let my hair fall through his hands, then gather it up again, smoothing it firmly off my neck and back from my forehead. His hands seemed to capture the whole of my head, calming and settling it, but exciting it, too. How was all that possible?

It seemed important to know how long we would be allowed to stand this way. Two minutes? Ten? And how would I know when those minutes had passed? It would not be possible to keep track of something as unimaginative as time while I stood with him this way, understanding, finally, about love. Understanding the impulse toward acts of bravery and abandon, devotion and sacrifice. It was not a matter of concentrated effort. It was not the carefully orchestrated pursuit it had been with Patrick. It was not the selfish oblivion it had been with Malcolm, either. It was not that fleeting suspension of thought, of everyday neuroses, followed by their sudden reinstatement — along with new burdens, new obligations. It was a tender, certain longing, not to press forward but to remain in his embrace. To resist a shift in the wind or in the position of his hands on my skin, his lips beside my ear, the hard pressure of his chest against my spine. To hold tight inside the cradle of meaning that was his body behind me, before the sun was swallowed up by the wet horizon. It was a moment that brought on a more or less permanent shift in my notion of the future.

But if he could do this with his hands, if he could form words, about a river in India, the Ganges, where the bodies of the dead were burned, if he was conscious and coherent enough to speak and move, then he must also be capable of letting my hair down and stepping away. That would be the very worst thing — if he were the one to end this before I did. I could not let it happen. I would have to stop it. I would have to be the one to step away.

But I couldn't. I didn't. I stayed there in his arms.

■ ■ ■ ■

What else do I remember? There was more beer. A flask of something stronger was passed around. Night fell and the ship passed through a squall. It rained harder and the ferry began to rock, quite violently, so that we could not stand on deck without holding on. I kept forgetting your father's last name — so many superfluous consonants! — and asking him to write it down for me. He kept reminding me he already had.

We moved inside, out of the rain. Cathal-or-Manus played the fiddle beside the bar. I sat next to your father on a bar stool. The curtain dropped, and I wanted the evening to go on and on; I forgot everyone and everything I'd left behind.

Do I remember descending the stairs to the bottom level of the ship? Do I remember your father, or the redheaded boy, beside me, as I entered the berth of the ferry?

No. I don't.

I do remember the berth itself, since I woke up there. A narrow bed along one wall. Plaid blankets. White pillowcases and white sheets, turned down. A small square window with an orange curtain. A bathroom just large enough for a toilet and a sink and a hose on the wall that served as a shower. I remember, vaguely, the idea your father had proposed, that he would find a place to sleep upstairs so that I could have the berth to myself. It was an oddly chivalrous and old-fashioned idea, and I'm not sure I believed he meant it, or that I wanted him to mean it. What I wanted, by then, after all the hours sitting with him, drinking and talking, after standing in his arms at the railing of the ferry, was to fall into bed with him and to have what seemed inevitable happen right away.

I sat on the bed beside him. There was kissing. His hand began to move under my sweater, over my back, and the kissing took on a life of its own. Or, rather, the kissing seemed to envelop the whole of life, the whole of what was necessary in order to live. Everything outside of it — a hand, for example, thinner, smaller, reaching down between my legs — was a distraction insignificant enough to ignore.

It was not your father's hand. It was the redheaded boy's hand.

How had it materialized between my legs? How had that boy come to be in the berth, and on the bed?

I don't know.

Maybe, as your father claimed later, I was slow to react. Maybe it took me a moment to differentiate the one hand from the other. To take in the substantial differences in size and temperature. Because, indeed, your father's hand was very rough and very cool and reasonably large, and the redheaded boy's hand was small and hot and smooth.

Perhaps it took me a moment to do the mental arithmetic. One plus one, plus one, equals three. One too many.

Then the redheaded boy coughed.

Your father stood up abruptly, knocking his head on a light fixture sticking out from the wall.

"Fuck," he said, holding his hand to the back of his head. Then he took in the fullness of the situation, namely, the redheaded boy sitting on the opposite side of me with a hand between my legs, and a confused look passed over his face.

"What the fuck is this?" he said, not to the boy, but to me.

I found I could not reply.

Your father picked up his pack where he must have stowed it when he boarded the ferry, slung it over his back and turned and pushed through the door.

I shook myself free. I stood up and lurched toward him. But it was too late. He was gone. I turned back toward the Irish boy, furious with him now. He stood and tried to embrace me. I pushed him away.

"This is not happening," I said to him. "You need to leave now."

I shoved the door open. He went through it. I never saw that red-headed boy — whatever his name was — again.

The many beers. The liquor from the flask. The exhaustion. The rocking of the sea. All of it caught up with me at once, and I spent the night on the bathroom floor, heaving into the miniature toilet. I finally slept, and when I woke it was nearly noon, and we were landing in Rosslare. I could not find Jonathan anywhere. I covered every inch of the ship, every level, inside and out. Passengers were disembarking and I was alone and of course I could not remember Jonathan's last name. Where was the paper napkin on which he'd written it? I checked my pockets, but there was only Patrick's note. I watched passengers walk down the plank toward the dock. When there were no more passengers leaving, I hurried back inside and searched the bar for the napkin. I dug through the trash, brushing bits of food and garbage off my hands onto my jeans. There it was, near the bottom. Just as

I unfolded the napkin, his whole name came into my head — Jonathan Gunnlaugsson — as if I'd never forgotten it at all. Only then did I realize it was not going to help me much, not in the short term, anyway. It was not as if I could type his name into a search engine and find a cellphone number, since there were no such things as search engines or cellphones then. Where, exactly, had he said he was going to spend Christmas? Somewhere in Ireland. That was all I had to go on, and it was not enough.

A terrible loneliness took hold of me, not only because I could not find Jonathan, but because it was Christmas. I didn't decide anything, really. I just did one thing, and when that was done, I did another. I took a DART train toward Dublin. The DART line carried on to Howth. I stepped off the little green train. I asked the woman working at the window about Hill House, where Patrick's family lived, and she told me it was on the first road to the left off the main street. I had not eaten anything, and I was not feeling at all well. Directly beneath the station, I found the Bloody Stream. I put my nose to the glass and peered in at the chairs upside down on the tables, and the long dark bar across the back, and the fireplace in the corner with no fire. I turned toward the village, but it was deserted. I checked one hotel, then another, but there was nothing open, and not a soul in the street.

I walked back to the station, then past it, toward the harbor. Thin white clouds were stretched across the sky. Hundreds of boats floated dormant in the marina, their empty masts like a vertical game of pickup sticks. The scene filled me with nostalgia. Not for a life I had led but for all the lives I wished had been mine. A childhood on Little Cranberry Island, in Maine. A life here with Patrick, sailing one of those boats. A life raising dogs on a farm in the Midwest, summers spent in a cottage in a cedar forest on the shores of a great lake, August on a houseboat.

I walked around the yacht-club grounds, which were slick and wet from rain. I sat on a bench. The moon had already risen. A crow called, shattering the silence and rising, dark and startling, into the sky. I felt the threat of evening in the changing light over the sea. A bleak little rain started up, growing heavier the longer I sat, crying now. Where were all the people I loved? I could feel them, flung about, the distance between us a crushing weight that I myself had put there.

I stared at the village beyond. There were houses built into the cliff. One of those was Hill House, where Patrick lived. I conjured an image of it — a roaring fire, the turkey cooking, Patrick holding court among his sisters with a drink in his hand. It disheartened me, this vision. It exhausted me. All the effort that would be required to ingratiate myself into it. But the sky was already bruising with the day's end, and I was without shelter. I had made a grave error, a series of grave errors, and these errors had set me down here on Christmas Day, alone, at dusk.

I fished an umbrella out of my pack and made my way up the hill. It was getting dark now, and the rain was drenching my feet and my calves beneath my umbrella. My legs began to feel very tired and my shoulders were sore from the weight of my pack. The road was narrow and steep. There were more houses built into the side of the cliff than were visible from the harbor. They were squeezed together, not nearly as grand as they'd seemed from below. Finally I saw it on the left, a blue mailbox with the words hill house painted on it, and a stone house with a steep shingled roof and small windows facing the street.

I touched my hand to my head. My hair

was dirty. My shirt smelled. My jeans were wet. I had no makeup on. But it was too late to turn back.

I knocked on the door. An old man opened it. I thought he was old, anyway, though he was probably no more than fifty-five. He had a wide forehead and deep wrinkles around his mouth and nose. A fringe of graying hair went all the way around his otherwise bare scalp. He wore an apron. At first, I thought he might be a butler of some kind. That is the extent to which I had Patrick's origins built up in my mind. I thought they would have "help" and a grand dining room for the dinner parties for which Patrick's mother had been so famous. In fact, the house beyond seemed modest, almost cramped, and it emitted a faint, dusky smell, along with the sounds and smells of home. Meat cooking. A piano being played. Voices. The clinking of glasses and pans. All at once I understood how far outside all of that I was, and how ridiculous I had been to have expected to step into it. I was wrong to have come.

Also, and more important, I felt a small gush of wetness in my underpants.

The man opened the door wider.

"John Ardghal, here," he said, extending his hand and shaking mine. "Now, then, ah, who might you be on this dark and stormy night?"

He was not a butler. He was Patrick's father, not what I'd expected, not a lost soul but a kindly one, very much present and alive. It was that kindness that made me lose my nerve. It was the curious, expectant smile taking over his broad, generous face that saved me from another grave error. Because if I'd said who I was, if I'd asked after Patrick, even though he was not there, because he was still stuck in Paris, I would have been invited in. I would have been given a drink and dinner and a bed. This gentle man would not have thrown a friend of Patrick's into the weather at Christmas, especially not a young woman alone — and if that had happened, I would not have walked back to the village and boarded a train back to Dublin. It was those two small interventions — the well-meaning face, the gush of blood in my underwear — that sent me into a future with your father.

"I'm so sorry," I said to Patrick's father. "I must have the wrong house."

I found a bathroom in the Howth station and changed my underwear and shoved in a tampon. I caught the last train back to Dublin. I stepped from the station and entered the first hotel I saw, a rundown bed-and-breakfast with peeling paint on its front door. I rang the bell on the desk. A small woman emerged. She informed me that I was just in time; Christmas dinner was being served in the dining room. And there was one room available with a single bed. The room was in the attic — it was not very nice, but perhaps it would do?

I said it would do just fine. I left my pack with the woman and walked into the dining room. Alone at a corner table — in a white shirt, with his hair combed back off what was indeed a handsome face, its beard shaved away for the occasion of Christmas dinner — was your father.

TWENTY-EIGHT

We spent the night together in your father's room. The bed was tilted, and when we woke up we were squeezed together on one side. There were two nightstands with yellow faded doilies and a chair with worn-out upholstery and a smell like wet laundry. It was a shabby room, a shabby hotel. But the shabbiness did not bother your father. He told me, that morning, that he liked to choose function over form, usefulness over aesthetics.

"Is that why you chose me?" I asked him. "Because I'm useful?"

He kissed me. "In your case I made an exception and went for beauty."

Later, I picked his towel up off the bed and hung it over the shower rod. I folded his sweater and set it on the chair. He allowed me to do these things, even though I had not allowed him to do what he'd wanted the night before. I had fended him off,

276

barely, not because I didn't want him, but because I was mostly sober and felt it might be prudent. He was old-fashioned in some sense; he would respect a girl who saved something for later. Also, there had been the matter of the blood.

He had asked me at dinner, point-blank, what had happened with the redheaded boy on the ferry, and I had told him everything I remembered, and assured him I hadn't let the boy touch me after he left. He seemed satisfied with my reassurances, and in my mind we'd put the matter behind us for good.

He said he was starving as soon as we woke up that first morning, and he insisted we eat in the dining room right away. Already the patterns were being set down that would over time lay grooves of wear on the floors and walls of our house and our hearts. Already the table that was to become our life was being laid. Already it was food first, love later.

After breakfast in the dining room, we returned to his room and got back in bed. I had taken the tampon out first thing that morning, surprised there had been so little blood, and pleased that there was no reason to continue to fend your father off. He put a condom on. We made love. I folded myself into the blanket of his body, and it was like folding myself into my future. I came, and he came, and we collapsed into each other, still kissing, and he held me in a way that made me feel everything was finally all right.

When he pulled out and looked down, the condom wasn't there.

"Oh, fuck," he said. "Fuck. I'm so sorry. I should have checked. I should have pulled out."

I found the condom inside me, and inside the condom, nothing at all. Whatever had been released had been released directly into me.

"Fuck," he said. "I'm really sorry."

"Don't worry," I said. "It's all right."

I wasn't just saying that. I believed there was no need to worry. I believed my period had come and gone in a day. I didn't keep track of that sort of thing very carefully, then. I didn't know about spotting in the middle of a cycle. And I didn't know sex could make you bleed, even when it was not your first time.

We ventured out of our room at some point. I told the woman at the front desk I would no longer be needing my room. I told Jonathan I'd pay for half of his, but he laughed at me.

"Don't be ridiculous," he said. "I have money."

"Then why don't you buy a new pair of shoes?"

"Oh, I will. I just haven't gotten around to it. And besides, I like these shoes."

We walked around Dublin. The rain was gone and the sky was clear and cold. I wondered about Malcolm. I wondered whether I would still have a job if I returned to London. It had all come to seem rather dim and distant — Malcolm, Louise, my desk at the office. It suddenly seemed far removed from this new life with Jonathan in Dublin.

Patrick, on the other hand, still felt acutely present. I was falling in love with your father, but my feelings for Patrick had not been left behind. All of it was rushing together, making a psychedelic mess of my heart.

We visited a cathedral. Jonathan dropped a few coins in the prayer bucket and lit a candle and knelt down on the cushion and folded his hands and told me faith was the center of his life.

"What do you mean by that?"

"What do you mean what do I mean?"

"I don't know. I didn't think someone like you would be religious."

279

"Well, I'm devout."

"Really?" I said. Here was a flaw, a flaw that might release me back into my irresponsible life. I felt a glimmer of relief, or hope, followed by a ringing of alarm.

Then he laughed. "Not really. I'm a recovering Catholic, like all the good Catholics of our generation."

"Oh," I said. "So am I."

"Would it have been a deal-breaker, if I had been some kind of religious fanatic?"

"Yes."

"You almost sound disappointed that I'm not."

"Maybe I don't want to fall for you. Maybe I want to keep being badly behaved."

"I'm not stopping you."

"You said you wouldn't love me if I wasn't good."

"I won't."

"Well, then, see?"

Over lunch he read to me from the guidebook. What did we want to see next? Dublin Castle? Trinity College? The famous prison? The factory where Guinness was born? He had a way of making the day, every day, feel festive and promising.

For three days after that we toured the city. On the fourth day, Jonathan consulted the guidebook again and decided we should take the DART train to "the charming seaside village of Howth."

I did not object.

We got off the train and decided to start with the castle. It turned out to be in the middle of a golf resort, but the structure itself was sufficiently dark and deteriorating to make it worth the trip. The sky was a stifled gray, and the wind was coming in fits and starts, stirring the branches of the massive oaks. Blackbirds circled over the stone battlements, and Jonathan read to me from the guidebook. The castle had been built in the fifteenth century and was still owned by the St. Lawrence family. There was a legend of a girl named Grace O'Malley, who showed up at the castle at dinnertime to find that the gates were closed, so she abducted the son of the castle's owners and extracted a promise that the gates would stand open forever after, and an extra place be laid at the table. And so the extra place was always laid.

"It's always a girl abducting the poor young boys," Jonathan said.

"I promise not to abduct you," I said.

"You've already abducted me."

We walked back to the village holding hands. I liked Jonathan's cool, dry hand in mine, and the solidness of his body next to me, and his lovely eyes and ready laugh. But that does not mean I was not on the lookout for Patrick. I had not mentioned Patrick again to Jonathan. I had not told him Patrick lived in Howth.

We wandered around the village. It had once been a small fishing outpost, but now it was a thriving Dublin suburb set down between ocean and wild hillside. There was a steady stream of cars driving up and down the main road. I dragged Jonathan in and out of shops. I lingered longer than I needed to. I couldn't help myself.

"Enough shopping," he finally said. "It's time for food."

There were taverns and pubs and inns all up and down the main street. Whose idea was it to return to the train station and eat at the Bloody Stream? Mine.

We ate clams, then oysters, because Jonathan insisted I expand my seafood repertoire, and there was no better place to do that than in a seaside village. I watched for Patrick. I thought of Malcolm. I studied Jonathan's face and compared him to the two other men who had captured some piece of my heart. He was nothing like Patrick, in appearance or demeanor. He was not like Malcolm, either; he had none of the deference or hesitation, but they shared a cheerfulness, and the sturdiness of thick-boned men.

There was a fire in the stone fireplace in the corner and a band setting up to play. I wanted to stay and listen to the band. I was not quite ready to give up yet. But Jonathan wanted to go back to Dublin and "experience my bodily parts." Those were the exact words he used, the ones he always used. It became a joke, over the years, a catchphrase that could pull us into the bedroom together.

Jonathan paid the check. We finally stood up to leave.

Then the door pushed open, and Patrick entered the pub. A girl followed him. She stood in the doorway, framed by the pearly light of early evening. It was the girl from Montmartre — Mary McShane.

They didn't see us. They sat at the bar. I pulled Jonathan by the hand and sat him down again at our table.

"That's Patrick," I hissed.

"Patrick?"

"The one who was sleeping with my boss's wife. The one who came with us to Paris."

"Oh," he said. "Would you like to say hello?"

"No," I said. "I don't know."

"Funny all of us ending up here."

"He lives here. In Howth."

"Ah, the plot thickens. Why didn't you say so earlier?"

"I don't know. It was kind of an awkward situation, I guess."

From behind, Mary's hair seemed even shorter and blacker than before, and Patrick seemed taller, probably because I'd already gotten used to Jonathan's height. Taller and flashier, a man people noticed. He was wearing polished black boots, jeans, a gray wool sweater and his black peacoat. Time had been taken to achieve this look of thrown-together elegance. Effort had been expended, effort Jonathan would have considered wasted. He'd said as much in a shop in Dublin when I'd tried on a dress I liked. He'd said that when you really thought about it, style was a completely arbitrary manifestation of culture. He said he preferred to be savage about the whole thing and wear whatever happened to be at the top of the pile.

Patrick shrugged off his coat. He lifted Mary's raincoat from her shoulders and laid it over the back of her chair. Blood rose to my face, not from the jealousy itself but from the shame of acknowledging its existence. Jonathan was the bedrock upon which to construct a life. Patrick was not.

Why, then, was I still under Patrick's spell?

"Let's leave," I said to Jonathan.

He looked at me. He looked at Patrick. Patrick turned and saw us and his face opened in surprise.

"Annie," he called out. He came right toward us. "We've been trying to find you. Where did you go? And why are you here?"

"I . . . we're touring."

"Never mind. It doesn't matter now. I'm only happy you're finally found."

"This is Jonathan," I said to Patrick. And to Jonathan, "This is Patrick."

Patrick did not introduce Mary McShane, who was hanging back, standing awkwardly by the bar. Patrick was looking at me closely. He took my hand and squeezed it. He searched my face. I thought he was about to make a declaration of some kind — a declaration of love, perhaps.

"You don't know, do you?" Patrick said.

"Know what?"

"The news," he said. "The terrible news."

He moved a step closer. He squeezed my hand more tightly. "I'm afraid we've lost Malcolm."

"We've lost him?"

"He had a massive stroke," Patrick said. "He died Christmas Eve morning. In a hospital in Paris."

TWENTY-NINE

Friday. Two more days until the girls are finally home from their week away with your father. I checked the weather in Wisconsin this morning. It snowed there last night. Here, on the other hand, it has turned unseasonably hot — hotter than it ever was last summer.

Last summer. That's where I've been this morning, in my mind. It's where I always seem to be when I am not explicitly somewhere else. Today I am inside an evening in mid-August, three weeks before your accident. It's a small evening, a small memory — more a memory of sound and touch than of images — one I could have captured even if my eyes had been closed.

I was in the kitchen with the girls. Dinner was in the oven. Clara was at the table making pencil drawings. I'd given her a good sketch pad and a set of pencils when she turned nine, and she'd been drawing all summer, making a study of photographs of people she found online, not their whole bodies, but individual elements. Knees and ankles. Chins and necks and elbows. Knuckles and noses. Braided hair. Eyes with precisely drawn lashes. Mouths full of surprisingly realistic teeth. Tacked to the bulletin board in the kitchen, the drawings were accumulating into a disembodied collage that was both bizarre and beautiful. Later, when you were in the hospital, Clara made a sketch of a human kidney she copied from the book your father published on the subject. It's still pinned up in the kitchen, not a piece of you, but a reminder of the piece you were missing.

I did not sketch humans, or their parts, when I was Clara's age — she must have inherited her fascination with the intricacies of the human body from your father — but I did like to draw. I drew the plain objects I found around me: teapots, vases, tables, bottles, a stack of dinner plates needing to be washed, a tin garbage can waiting to be dragged to the curb. I sketched labels for our jars of honey and our pickled vegetables and my father's home-brewed beer, and later, of course, I sketched lights.

That evening last August, Polly sat on the floor listening to a book on tape. I kept asking her to turn the volume down, but she kept complaining she couldn't hear, and turning it up again. She wanted to use earbuds, but I'd read they caused hearing damage in children, and I wouldn't let her.

I didn't hear your car, Robbie. I didn't hear the door open, but I heard the squeak of the piano bench as you sat down to play. I stood in the doorway of the living room. I hadn't heard you play the piano in years, and I listened for a long time before you knew I was there. I could see the top of your dark head, and though I could not see your hands, I knew what they looked like — I knew the precise way they curved when you played, and I knew how long your fingers were, and how well trained to transform the room with music, as you were doing now.

You stopped playing finally, and looked up.

"What was that?" I asked you.

"Nothing. Just fooling around."

"You were improvising?"

"I guess you could call it that," you said. "There's a piano in the house in Berkeley. I've just been messing around."

"It was nice."

"It was nothing complicated, but thanks."

"What brings you to the city?"

"I swam laps at the Y. I had a couple of

hours to kill. I hope it's okay I came by."

"Of course it's okay."

Polly came in and climbed into your lap on the piano bench. "Teach me," she said.

You placed Polly's thumb on middle C. I heard your father's car pull into the driveway. The dogs heard, too, and leapt to the front door to greet him. He stepped inside, ignoring the dogs until they sat, as he had trained them to do. Their tails thumped wildly on the floor while he patted them hello.

When you were three and we got our first dogs, I thought the training regimen your father imposed on the poor puppies was crazy. I thought it was your father's way of exerting absolute control over an element of our household — which fell by then mostly under my jurisdiction. But in time, I understood that well-trained dogs simply made him happy. Dogs he could walk on a city sidewalk without a leash. Dogs who would automatically sit at every crosswalk, and heel without ever being given a command. The elegance of it pleased him, the magic of shaping behavior with patience, and consistency, and gentle but unwavering discipline. It worked with you, to a certain extent, when you were small.

Your father had no real model for fatherhood. He had been raised by his mother in the seventies, and her philosophy had been that discipline ought to be shrugged off along with everything else her generation had deemed limiting. He'd spent much of his time with the family who owned the adjacent farm, breeding and training dogs. Dogs came naturally to him, as did very young children. Crying did not ruffle him. Tantrums did not deter him. He stayed the course. He taught you to follow the rules, and usually you did. Then you grew up. When you turned eleven, obeying your father ceased to make you happy, and our household was thrown into disarray. That was a difficult year. Then Clara was born, and Polly, and we were outnumbered, and your father softened. Or maybe it was only that Clara and Polly were girls.

Your father smiled at you and Polly now, and at Clara, who had set her sketch pad aside and joined you at the piano. He walked toward me, his wing tips making the sound they always did on the hardwood floor — the contented thud of another workday ending, and another evening in the life of our family beginning. He laid his lips on mine, and they made the smallish sound of a perfunctory kiss. If the kiss was perfunctory, though, the hug was not. He opened his arms and enveloped me. He crushed me against his barrel chest until the rest of the world was silenced. He always held me that way a little longer than he needed to, offering certain evidence that after the day apart, I was still loved. I closed my eyes and felt the coolness of his cheek against mine. I had dreamt again, the night before, of Patrick. I had felt the old stab of helpless longing. The longing had visited me on and off through the day, and it was only now, in your father's arms, that it finally departed.

Your father released me. Polly played another note. Clara took over at the piano and started to play chopsticks. You stood up.

"Are you staying for dinner?" I asked.

"No. I've got plans," you said.

"Anything exciting?"

"I'm meeting Emme for dinner in the Mission," you said, with the studied nonchalance you first perfected in high school.

I paused. She hadn't mentioned it to me that morning at the store. She had barely mentioned you all summer, though I knew you two had become friends of some kind. A tick of worry set off in my head, steady and even as a metronome. But I suppose I chose not to hear it. Because who was I to question you? It was not as if you were mar-

291

ried, or being indiscreet. It was not as if you were living with one person and wanting another.

I sit down at the kitchen table now, and listen for the story to start up again in my head. One of the dogs whines in his sleep. The other thumps his tail, as if in sympathy. I begin to make my pen move across the page. I try to be again the girl I was some twenty years ago, falling in love with your father with the same heart that was breaking as I said goodbye to Patrick. I try to stand inside my boots that evening at the Bloody Stream when Patrick told me that Malcolm was dead.

He filled in the details of the morning Malcolm died. He told me that right after he'd written his note to me, when he was just about to leave the penthouse for the airport, the porter downstairs had delivered a message from Louise with the news that Malcolm was very, very ill, and with a request that Patrick collect Daisy from the train.

Patrick told me he'd tried to rouse me. He'd shaken me and talked directly into my ear, but I'd remained passed out cold. On his way out, he'd asked the porter to inform me of the news as soon as I came downstairs. But of course the porter never saw me, since I left through the back door. Patrick had tried to call the penthouse late that morning, when phone service was restored, but I never answered. That was the call that shocked the phone into life just as I was making my escape.

When there was nothing left to tell me, Patrick embraced me, then held me at arms' length. He looked toward Jonathan who was sitting at the table taking it all in, and he embraced me again, long and hard, in a final farewell.

That night, after we returned to Dublin from Howth, I lay next to Jonathan in our shabby hotel room, listening to him sleep, feeling a thousand feelings, none that I could name. I slipped out of bed and dressed and crept down the stairs of the hotel, then walked the streets of Dublin alone.

I don't know how long I walked. I know I went into a pub. I know I drank until the pub shut. Would I never learn that this was the way not to gain clarity but to obliterate it? In my daypack was a notebook with lined paper and my little address book. I sat at the bar and wrote Louise a letter. I don't remember what I wrote, so I have no way to explain myself now. I can only speculate. I can only try to hurl myself back and ask what could possibly have possessed me to do such a thing. Maybe I stuffed in it all the feelings I couldn't put anywhere else. I felt at the center of the tragedy. I felt responsible, and the only way to shed that burden was to share it, and the only person I could share it with was the one person who would have been better off not knowing the thing I had to confess. But did I confess it? Did I come right out and apologize to Louise for consummating the flirtation that had been going on between her husband and me for months? Did I write that he had told me, breathlessly, that he loved me? Did I say that I suspected, given what had happened, that the breathlessness was not about love at all, but the result of too much blood pumping through his veins and pooling at the base of his brain? Did I tell her that he'd cried out when he came, and that I wondered, now, whether it was not in ecstasy but in pain, as his body began the protest that would kill him?

Did I — God forgive me — tell her about Patrick and me? Did I feel the need to set her straight on that score, too?

I hope I never have to know.

I send myself back to the bar in Dublin. I

fish an envelope from my backpack and scrawl out the address from my address book. I tell the bartender the whole story. He gives me two postage stamps he assures me will carry my letter to London. I walk purposefully out of the pub and stick the letter in the first mailbox I find. When I wake up in the morning next to your father, the incident is like one of your coma dreams last fall, a drama that felt very real but that I hoped, desperately, had played out only in my mind. I lay there trying to remember what message had seemed so urgent the night before, so pressing that I had to set it down and send it before Malcolm's body began to turn to dust.

"It's the last day of the year," Jonathan announced.

The last day of the year, I thought to myself, and too late to get the letter back. Confessions. For whose benefit besides one's own?

The last day of the year. The first day of heartbreak.

Not over Malcolm, I am ashamed to admit. I did not grieve for Malcolm on anyone's behalf, because I could not get a purchase on the idea that he was dead; I kept forgetting it was true.

I claimed the heartbreak for myself —
because I'd lost Patrick to Mary McShane.

I suppose unrequited love is the hardest
kind to shed because it is not really love at
all. It is a half-love, and we are forever
stomping around trying to get hold of the
other half.

We took a train from Dublin that last day of
December, then a ferry and another train to
London. We arrived late, and spent what
remained of New Year's Eve at the boardinghouse in Victoria. We shared a bottle of
champagne. We went for a walk at midnight.
I did not enjoy it, not even after the champagne. London was full of ghosts. Not just
Malcolm's, but Patrick's, too. And even
Louise's. In the archeology of my history, it
was time for the European period to be
buried under rubble and dust. It was time
to move on, and I did. The drama, the grief,
the residue of those unions was tossed away
in the name of migration and progress.

Or so I believed. Did I really believe it?

I really did.

Jonathan had a seat on a flight to Kathmandu. He wanted me to join him. So I
went. Why not?

I did not want to go home. I could not

stay in London. And I knew that it was only with Jonathan at my side that I might be able to fend off the ghosts and be happy. There was also by then a feeling between us, not a promise to stay together but the impossibility of imagining any circumstance that would allow us to part. I can't explain it any better than that. I'd never experienced it before. He claimed he had not, either. The future had grabbed hold of us, whether we were ready for it or not — and we knew only the half of it.

I had saved money working for Malcolm, and I insisted on paying for my flight to Nepal. We packed up my things and shipped my boxes home to my mother. I called her to tell her to watch for them, and I dumped out the rest of my news. My boss had died of a stroke. I no longer had a job. I had met someone in Ireland — a doctor from Wisconsin — and I was going to do some traveling with him. We were flying to Nepal to go trekking, then taking a bus to India. I thought the fact that he was a doctor would be some compensation, a salve to the wound of worry I was opening by removing myself farther afield.

"India?" she said. "But that's so dangerous, isn't it?"

"Not any worse than anyplace else," I said,

as if I were an expert.

She let me go. Not that she could have stopped me. Children will end up a world away, whether you want them to or not — unaware of the havoc being wreaked upon their histories back home. My mother shared news of her own. She'd decided to sell the rock-and-timber house and move with Ryan to a condominium in Burbank. And on the other side of the country, my father and Veronica Cox were engaged to be married.

We flew from London to Kathmandu. There had been an uprising in Nepal, and there weren't very many tourists about, most having taken heed of the advisory recommending against travel into the country. Your father said it was the best time to come; we would have the Himalayas to ourselves. What did I think of the idea of trekking? I thought it would be an adventure, and I liked the idea of an adventure. I thought it would help me purge the ghosts.

We spent a few days in a small hotel in the center of Kathmandu. A ten o'clock curfew had been imposed on the city, and when we walked home from dinner at night, there were soldiers with guns standing in the city square. At the hotel we made friends with two Canadian girls and an Australian man. They'd bought a ball of hash on the street. We smoked it on the roof of the hotel. I took two hits and looked out over the darkened rooftops of Kathmandu, but I felt sick, not high.

"Take another hit," your father recommended. "It might actually make you feel better. Cancer patients take it, you know, when they're on chemo."

So I took another hit, and a few more after that, and he became my accomplice.

We took a bus to Pokhara. We stayed in a guesthouse, then set out on our trek. Jonathan said we wouldn't need a Sherpa; we could carry our own packs. I made it six days, hiking seven or eight hours a day, stopping at dusk to find a house to sleep in. The Nepali people who lived on the trails took in travelers, giving them food and hot tea and a bed for a tiny fee. Once we spent the night in a house on the edge of a ravine, with a majestic view of Annapurna, for the equivalent of fifteen cents. We watched women picking something in a field. We showered under a bamboo tube sticking out of the river. Jonathan washed my hair. It was not so much romantic as practical; my shoulders were so sore from carrying my pack, I couldn't lift my arms above my head to scrub shampoo into my hair. What did we talk about, during all those hours of all those days? Not much, I think. I was concentrating on not feeling sick — we thought it was the altitude, or the food — and Jonathan was concentrating on making sure we didn't get lost, but we got lost anyway.

We were crossing a mile-wide dry river valley with cliffs rising on both sides. It was a high desert between mountains, astonishing in both its desolation and its beauty. There was a cold wind blowing down the valley from the mountains. We thought the valley was dry, but it wasn't. There was water flowing, little rivers, seven or eight of them, down the center of the cracked earth. Each time we reached one of these rivers, we took off our hiking boots and tied them to our packs. We waded across barefoot, rolling our pants up to our thighs. The rivers got deeper and faster, until we were wet to our waists. Beyond the final river was a high cliff. On the cliff we could see a narrow path twisting its way up the side of a rock face. How were we going to get up there?

"We'll find a way," your father said.

Why did I expect him to know everything? Because he acted as if he did. It was one of the things I loved about him, all the time we lived together. He had an answer for everything. He somehow knew it was more important to be reassuring, to seem to be in command of the situation, than to be right. And he was always willing to give in when he was found out to be wrong.

The water in the river was waist-high and very cold. My feet were freezing. Then the water was rib-high and thick with current, and I struggled to keep my feet on the ground. Your father stopped, midstream. There was a little dot of black on the path high on the cliff — a man — yelling in a language we did not speak. But he made himself clear enough, motioning with his hands for us to go back, go back; we had come the wrong way. So we forded the seven little rivers again, taking our boots off and putting them on again seven more times. I was furious with Jonathan by the end. I wanted to be rid of him. I wanted to be alone.

In the distance was a smudge that grew into a shape as we moved toward it. It was a shack, smack in the middle of the bare river valley. There were three women in colorful Nepalese dresses sitting in front of the shack. They smiled and bowed and sat us down on the floor outside the hut. They gave us lemon tea. Your father shrugged. Then he smiled. He opened his arms to encompass the valley, and the mountains, and the brilliant colors that had begun to ravage the sky as the sun set. He was not going to let me stay angry with him. Already he seemed to have mastered me. Already he knew how to insist I be the best I could be. I grinned, though I tried not to. We drank our tea. We climbed the cliff back to the town in which we'd begun our day's journey. We fell into a single bed, tangled up in each other, and slept for fourteen hours straight.

The next morning I woke up queasy. Your father decided I had giardia. He thought it would be a good idea to get me back to civilization. There was one flight a week, out of a town a day's walk north. We made the walk. We took a plane to Pokhara, where your father found me medicine. He promised I would feel better in a day or two. We found a bus that would take us to Varanasi, across the border in India. At some point during that journey, your father's pack was stolen from the top of the bus. We bought him new clothes at a roadside town. He looked regal, during our difficult time in India, in the white sari of the highest caste. He had not lost his passport, thank goodness. He could still prove who he was.

THIRTY

Varanasi. One of the oldest continually inhabited cities in the world. The place considered by Hindus to be the holiest city, the final resting place, built on the shores of the River Ganges, the river Ma — mother of all rivers — as if named for the revelations we received there.

You've seen the photos, Robbie. You've heard how I fell in the river and a dead body floated by. You've heard it all except the bits we left out.

I remember the city as buildings like painted shoeboxes crushed together, rising in pastel splendor beneath an orange sky. I remember obelisk towers with spires and haunting music playing at all hours, music free of melody and constructed out of an alien scale. I remember the river, of course, and all the life and death it held in its body and on its shores.

I continued to feel queasy. We decided it

was a virus; it would run its course and I would get better in time. We rode on a raft to the center of the river to witness a cremation ceremony one morning at dawn. I remember the dark seriousness of our guide's face in the gray morning, the glow of his skin as the sun first appeared in the sky. From the river we watched people gathering on the stone steps of a temple on the shore. We watched little boys and girls brushing their teeth, scooping river water into their mouths to rinse, and women beating clothes against the stone steps. A dead cow floated by. It looked like a rubber cow, blown up. We heard music, and the ceremony began. The gray sky gave way to pink. The people on the steps, in their orange gowns, were singing and dancing a slow, ceremonial dance. The air smelled of burning hair. I felt sick. I leaned over to splash some water on my face, thinking it might shock the queasiness out of me. Did I fall, or did I jump? I don't know, but I ended up in the river. My mouth filled with river water. I gasped and gagged. Your father lifted me out of the water and wrapped his jacket around me, not tenderly but brusquely.

"Why did you do that?" he asked me.

"I didn't do it on purpose."

"It looked like you did."

The guide began to row us in. He maneuvered around another raft in which three boys were poking at something in the water with a stick — an object, wrapped in gauze.

"What is it?" I asked.

Your father leaned in to look. "A dead body," he said.

A corpse, incompletely cremated, floating right in the spot I had just gone underwater. I threw up in my lap, all over my wet clothes. But it wasn't the dead body that had made me sick. It was a new one — yours, Robbie — taking me firmly in its grip and not letting go until the fall.

You are thinking about the chronology now.

You are thinking about what you've been told. The pieces dropped here and there at the dinner table over the years. We met in Ireland. We trekked in Nepal. We traveled in India. We ended up in San Francisco. We bought the house, and the following year you were born.

Except it wasn't the following year. It was that year. In January, we went to India. In June, we got married. In July, we bought the house. In September, you were born.

We agreed that if you ever asked, if you made your calculations and found a discrepancy, if you came upon our marriage certificate, for instance, and noticed that we were married in the year of your birth, we would tell you the truth. You never asked, though. And I have wondered of late whether it was only to save us from embarrassment. Some reticence you inherited. Some resistance to putting people on the spot. A natural tendency toward restraint. An ability to put the comfort of others in front of your own.

I wish you *had* asked. I wish we'd come clean years ago. Then these revelations surrounding your conception and birth would not be huddled together in secrecy, ready to pounce on you all at once.

We had planned to travel to Agra and Jaipur and then Goa. But I was too sick. I felt my sickness was somehow tied up in the city, Varanasi. Its filth and crowding and its fetid river, where corpses floated and little girls brushed their teeth at dawn. Where there was endless, formless music rising out of the heat and humidity and coalescing into a single dirty song.

We lay in our filthy room that night on the sagging bed under the slowly turning fan.

"I want to go home," I said.

Jonathan turned on the lights. He looked at me, lying in a fetal position on the bed.

"You don't look good," he said. "You look green."

"I feel green," I said. "Actually, I feel black."

"Maybe . . . you couldn't be pregnant, could you?"

I looked at him.

"We've been so careful."

"But that first time . . . when it slipped."

"But I had my period."

"Still."

He scoured the city and found a drugstore that sold a Western home-pregnancy kit. We stood together in the seedy bathroom down the hall from our room. There were spiders everywhere, and ants. There were dark stains in the bottom of the sink.

I peed on the stick. We watched the line form, then darken.

It's astonishing to me, now, how shocked we were. Astonishing that we had not known all along.

"Holy shit," he said.

"I can't believe it," I said.

"I'm really sorry about this."

"It's not your fault."

"What do we want to do?" he asked me. Not what did I want, but what did *we* want, together. I was grateful to him for putting it that way, because all alone, I had no idea

307

what I wanted.

"Go to a clinic, I guess. Get it taken care of."

"All right," he said. "But not here. Obviously. We need to get back to the States."

Three days later, we were in San Francisco, staying at a motel south of Market. Your father found a Planned Parenthood clinic near City Hall. He made us an appointment for the following day. In the morning, we went to a diner for breakfast. I ordered a hamburger, even though it was only nine o'clock in the morning. Beef and bread — those were the things I'd discovered I could keep down. Jonathan ordered eggs and corned beef hash. I ate the hamburger. The nausea briefly receded.

It was a glorious winter day, bright and cold, with white sunlight glinting off the windows of the skyscrapers. In the back of the cab to the clinic, I rolled the window down for air. The wind blew my hair around. I held it back with one hand. Your father reached for my other hand and held it in both of his. But his hands were trembling, and that was the thing that finally made me sad and afraid.

When the taxi stopped, Jonathan opened the door for me. He took me by the hand

and led me along the sidewalk. We passed City Hall. Did I think he might say something then? Was I secretly hoping he would suggest that instead of going to the clinic, we turn in to that mass of stone and do whatever it was people did — procure blood tests and marriage licenses and the strength to be faithful and true? If that hope existed, it existed alongside the wish to get the whole thing over with so I could continue with the business of being healthy and normal and young.

The sun was high and full on our faces. The wind was cold. The sky was an aching blue. It had rained the night before and we could taste the residue of water in the air. We stood holding hands on the sidewalk, and it seemed to me for a moment anything might be possible. We might, the two of us together, be capable of beauty and bravery and unfounded optimism. He felt it, too, I think, right then — the possibility of an alternate path.

At the clinic, we went to the window and gave them my name. They didn't ask for his name, only his money. It was my ordeal, apparently. It was my child. Did I think of you as a child? At least a part of me did. I may have worked hard to shrug off my Catholic training, but I had not been entirely successful. Inside me, very much alive, were reminders I would have preferred right then to forget. Bloody posters held up by protesters in front of clinics. Words, warnings, debates. The tricky question: When does life begin? Trying to reason it out is like trying to imagine what existed before the universe. There is a point at which human intelligence falls short. It's one of the reasons I hate an election year. All those debates. All that certainty. It seems so frail to me. It seems pointless, and even fraudulent, to pretend to have answers to unanswerable questions. I could not persuade myself that the life inside me was not a life. I could imagine a baby readily enough. A fetus that, uninterrupted, would grow eyes and eyelashes and limbs and fingers and toes. It would open its eyes and they would be blue, like your father's.

On the other hand, there were all the things I had put in my body since the night the condom slipped — hash and liquor and dirty river water — that might have given you brain damage. I felt an intolerable rush of guilt and regret. You had begun with the potential to become a perfectly formed being, and now you were impaired. Was that a reason to terminate you? Such a terrible word, *terminate.* A word from a brave new world in which only the flawless are allowed to be born. And here I was, your mother, your protector, the one to introduce the possibility of flaws. Now I was about to heap sin upon sin. I was about to pay for my appetites with a tiny life.

But maybe none of this is true. Maybe I wasn't thinking any of that. Maybe I was thinking that if I kept you, your father would marry me, and I would become a doctor's wife. I would never have to go home again. And where was home, anyway? A condominium in Burbank directly beneath the flight path of an airport. What was the future there? A degree from a community college. A career like my mother's career. A life like my mother's life.

On the other hand, a doctor's wife. What did I imagine such a woman might look like? What would she do with her days? I imagined walks across the city in expensive clothes. I imagined tennis, or possibly sailing. Long lunches, during which I would drink iced tea and stare out at the boats in the bay, battling the wind under the Golden Gate Bridge. I'm not sure my vision included a child at all. Or if it did, it was a stylized version, a cartoon baby with bright eyes and round red cheeks, stashed away somewhere while I conquered the city.

I sat in the clinic and began to imagine a bargain. In this bargain, I would promise to be good. I would give up drinking. I would stop being impulsive and selfish. I would stop thinking of Patrick. I would be faithful to Jonathan in mind and in deed. Instead of oblivion, I would seek equanimity and purity of purpose. I would strike out on a new path and forge a new kind of life. I would save the child inside me from termination, and in exchange for my goodness, that child would be born free of imperfections, with all his fingers and toes and mental faculties intact. It's not so different from the bargain I made again last August, when I spewed out my confession and broke your father's heart. I faced my sins, and promised to be good, and hoped to be forgiven.

In the clinic that day, I didn't say any of what I was thinking out loud. I sat next to your father and filled out the forms and turned them back in at the counter.

We didn't have long to wait. They called my name and I took a step forward. I gave your father a weak smile.

He stood up. He took me by the elbow and sat me down again. He spoke in a low, tender voice, the voice I had until then heard him use only in bed. "You know

312

what?" he said. "I think we could handle this."

"Handle what?"

"Having a baby. Getting married. All that."

"Really?"

"Yeah, really."

"But do you want to?"

"I do. I really do. If you will."

We left the clinic. We took another cab, back to the diner. I ordered another hamburger, but it was too late. The interval between meals was too long, and I was too sick now to swallow. I sipped a glass of water. Your father ordered a pastrami sandwich and wolfed it down. There was a red vintage gumball machine next to the hostess stand. He stood up and put a quarter in it and turned, but nothing came out. He tried again, but again, he had no luck. The hostess had disappeared, so he walked back to the kitchen and returned with a screwdriver. He pried off the red metal lid and set it on the ground. I watched from the booth as he burrowed down with his hand, pulling out prize after prize, each encased in a clear plastic capsule with a blue top. Finally he held a prize up to the light, then slipped it into his pocket. He screwed the lid back on the gumball machine. He returned to me and bent down on his knees beside the booth and fished the plastic capsule out of his pocket. He popped the blue lid off. Inside was a ring.

He asked for my hand. I gave it to him.

"That's the wrong hand," he said.

"Oh," I said. "Sorry."

I extended my left hand. The cheap metal band of the ring was painted a bright gold. There was a stone — an imitation diamond. It was very large. The band was not solid but open on one side, so the size could be adjusted.

Your father slipped the ring onto my finger. He squeezed the band hard, until the metal was pinching my skin. We laughed a little, a high, private laugh at the absurdity of it all. He lifted my hand up and kissed the ring. He leaned in and kissed me on the lips. He pressed his forehead against my forehead.

"Will you marry me?" he whispered.

He kept his forehead crushed against mine, and his face was so close to my face, it was as if I swallowed the question as soon as he posed it. I felt our held breaths as the words burrowed down inside me, where you were burrowing, too, so small but so certain, and where, right beside you, an answer had already been waiting.

"Yes," I said. "I'll marry you."

■ ■ ■ ■

PART II

■ ■ ■ ■

THIRTY-ONE

Saturday morning. The girls will be home from Wisconsin tomorrow. Before they arrive, I'll hide everything again in the hatbox, then I'll return it to the hall closet. Between now and then, I wonder, can these artifacts carry the story? They say a picture paints a thousand words; do you need so many more words than that?

The hatbox came into my possession when I purchased an off-white silk pillbox hat with a little veil in the spring of 1990 at a bridal store on Union Street. It was a bizarre headpiece for a young bride, in retrospect, but I suppose I felt a full white virgin veil would be too much, given my condition. Taped to the inside of the hatbox, still, is an envelope in which the store clerk placed the receipt for the hat. I've never looked at it. I've never needed to, because I remember how much it cost — seventy-eight dollars — much more than I wanted to spend, but an extravagance I allowed myself because I had money left over from the check my mother had sent me to buy a wedding dress, which I managed to purchase at a secondhand shop.

The hat has long since been given to Goodwill, but the hatbox has endured. It's like the keep in Canterbury, the place for things that need to be hidden from invaders. The first thing I put in it, as I recall, was the sealed envelope in which I'd placed the notes from Patrick. The second was the toy ring in its clear plastic shell — fished from the gumball machine the day your father proposed — which he promptly replaced with a cubic zirconium, another placeholder, he promised, until he could afford a real diamond.

What came after that?

A wedding. A wedding certificate. A wedding photo.

The photo is of the whole wedding gathering, posed informally in front of your father's mother's cabin on Washington Island, Wisconsin, no more than twenty people, half in shadow, half in sun, crowded around the two of us sitting on a chair made from cedar logs, me with my arms folded across my ribs. I stare at it now as if seeing it for the first time. My dress, with its empire waist, in cream-colored silk. The bouquet of wildflowers picked that morning from the field next to the house. My hair pulled back, the pillbox hat pinned on my head, the veil obscuring the green of my eyes. My ears below the hat adorned with the little pearl earrings that had belonged to my mother. My arms trying to conceal my six-month bump. The dark suit your father wore, the one he'd bought himself when he graduated from medical school the spring before. The cedars towering over us in witness. The lake in the distance, roughed up by wind. Jonathan's mother, who died when you were a baby, smiling her wild smile. Her cheekbones like small round apples, her gray hair plunked haphazardly into a bun and stuck through with chopsticks. The faint smell I can remember coming off her of incense and patchouli. Her friends gathered behind, old hippie ladies dressed in denim and burlap and gauze. My mother smiling a set Jell-O smile in her lime-green suit, her shoes dyed to match. A half-dozen of your father's friends from high school and college and medical school — hearty, clean-cut, intelligent boys drinking the local beer. I hadn't invited any of my friends from home. It was too far to travel, and I was embarrassed that I was pregnant.

There were no fathers in attendance. Jonathan's father had never married his mother or been part of Jonathan's life in the first place, and when Jonathan was ten, he'd died. I had not invited mine.

As a wedding present, Jonathan's mother, Catherine, gave us fifty thousand dollars, an amount that astonished us both. It was money she'd inherited from her own parents but never spent.

"Buy a house," she said. "A tangible asset. You can never go wrong with a tangible asset."

There is a copy of the check in the hatbox. And there is a copy of the cashier's check I received from my father a week after the wedding. Not a wedding gift, but the balance of the money he owed me, plus a little extra. My father had signed the check, but I wondered if it was not his money, but Veronica Cox's.

At first I hadn't informed my father of the wedding at all. I could not bear to imagine what he might think of an idea as outrageous and outdated as getting married because of a pregnancy. Had I not been informed that my generation had been liberated from that particular last resort? Why was I hell-bent on repeating history when history itself had provided a way out? What was the point of the protests and upheavals of his generation if the next one was not going to make use of hard-earned progress?

I had no good answers to the questions I projected onto him. It would not do to claim I wanted to be a doctor's wife. It would not do, either, to describe the way I was drawn to Jonathan, and he to me. Or to explain the bargain I'd struck in the clinic on that bright winter day. It would not even do to tell my father I was in love. Which I was quite convincingly, and still am, though Jonathan no longer believes it, and my love may no longer be returned.

Why did I expend worry about what my father might think? After all, he was the one who had disappointed me. He was the one who had dodged rehab and abandoned his family. He was the one who had let the IRS suck my life savings away and promised to send a wire to London but never did. He was the one who let Christmas come and go without a word. He was the one who was about to marry another woman. I knew all this to be true, but I could not feel its truth inside me. All I could feel was the awfulness of shattering the vision he'd had of my future, even though that vision had never been especially well defined.

I finally did send him a letter explaining

that I was getting married and having a baby. I'm not sure I actually invited him to the wedding. Probably I was afraid that if I asked him to walk me down the aisle he would say no, he couldn't make the trip from Maine. Or he would say yes, then not show up. Or he would show up and try to talk me out of it. Or he would come and be generous, and kind, and false.

So I didn't ask. And he didn't come.

Then he sent the money, and I sent it back. Why make a copy of the cashier's check, and, more important, why send it back? It wasn't that I had forgiven him; I had never had the fortitude to hold it against him in the first place. I thought I was doing a brave and noble thing. I thought the gesture of sending the money back would be received in the spirit in which I'd intended it, and that it would end the estrangement that had sprung up between us. Instead, it seemed to set that estrangement in stone.

There is also, in the hatbox, a photo of our house, pasted onto the real estate flyer I plucked from a sign in the front yard that summer, when we stumbled into the San Francisco housing market with your Grandma Catherine's money: "A striking classic Eastlake row house (ca. 1885) on a tree-lined block in Noe Valley notable for its many handsome Victorian homes. The house's façade includes a prominent columned portico, bracketed cornice, stairs with bold balustrades and newel posts. The floor plan is excellent and filled with light. 1800 square feet. Offered as is."

There are three birth certificates in a single envelope, yours on top, with the grand name we chose for you — Robert Jonathan Gunnlaugsson — which right away in the hospital seemed too grown-up for a person so small, so we nicknamed you Robbie. There are, in that same envelope, three photographs, one of each of you, the official hospital photographs taken when you were born. Yours is the only face red from crying, presumably over the failed effort to feed during the first, difficult day of your life, when you refused to latch on.

This was unexpected. I had not even known it was possible a baby would not be able to breastfeed. We struggled in the hospital bed together, and your father lay on a cot under the single window in the hospital room in a pool of light, a magazine open over his chest, apparently fast asleep.

"Oh, dear," the lactation consultant said, when she had pinched and squeezed and prodded. "Your nipples don't come out easily, do they, hon? And does baby always have his tongue up on the roof of his mouth like that?"

From what pool of experience did this nurse expect me to draw an answer to that question? This was, after all, my first child. He had been born four hours ago. I was twenty years old. Was there not a note to that effect on the chart at the end of the bed?

"I wonder if you wouldn't mind nudging my husband over there on the cot," I said. "Maybe he can help us out."

She looked at Jonathan, asleep in his pool of light.

"Oh, hon, let's let him rest. He's had a long night."

She bent down and arranged my arms across my body, palms up, then she placed you in them and turned your tiny jaw toward my left breast.

"Will he suffocate?" I asked, suddenly afraid.

"He won't suffocate, hon."

Your mouth was in the right place but nothing was happening. You were not sucking because you were asleep. Another nurse arrived. She ordered me a breast pump and breast shields. The pump was to be attached

326

to each breast for fifteen minutes every hour to train the nipples into the right shape. In between pumping sessions, I was to use a syringe to feed you sugar water from a tiny glass bottle so you wouldn't get dehydrated. She didn't want you having a bottle of formula or even water, because your mouth would form to the nipple and get in a bad habit. She put the apparatus over my breasts and turned the machine on. It made a sound like a sick farm animal, a sound like the end of life, not sustenance for it. When she took her leave, I spent some time staring at you. Your lips trembled in your sleep. You made little frightened noises, like the noises you made last fall, when you relived your coma dreams. Your face was all gentle curves — your arched brows, the sweep of your cheeks, the round lobes of your ears, the deep, squashed slope of your nose. You had wild dark hair sticking straight up from your head. Behind your closed lids were blue eyes, but they didn't stay blue; they changed to a green just like mine.

Those moments watching you sleep were the first of many moments, many hours, many days, when time shocked me by changing — the minutes passing slowly and the days creeping forward, as if in conspiracy, but the years moving too fast. There was boredom, as I had never known it, alongside intense joy. Those were the bedfellows I was to carry with me through your early years, while your father went to work and came home again.

What I felt for you, then as now, was love like a kind of pain. Hot in my throat. Burning my eyes. I lay in the hospital bed and kissed your cheek hard. I was in a hurry to know you, to find out who it was your father and I had made, but I could see that I would not be able to rush you. I could see, also, that I would always be afraid; I would never again be free of worry, and that worry was necessary to keep you safe. Somehow this revelation felt like a blessing, not a burden or a constraint. How long did I stare at you that first day? So long that I worried you might have become dehydrated.

You opened your eyes, finally. I shifted you into one arm and reached for the bottle of sugar water. I opened the bottle with my teeth. I set it on the tray and it tipped over and spilled. You started to cry. Your father materialized beside the bed.

"He still won't latch on," I said. "Can you try to find another bottle of this stuff?"

"Um, okay. Where would I find more, do you think?"

"I have no idea, Jonathan," I said impatiently.

He stood with his hands in his pockets and surveyed the room. Then he buzzed the nurse.

"Bring us a bottle of sugar water, would you?" he said. "Actually, bring us a six-pack."

I handed you to your father. He laid you on the bed and unwrapped your blankets and changed your diaper and swaddled you expertly. Had he been listening, or watching, from his cot in the corner? Or maybe this was something he had learned in medical school?

"What I'm wondering . . . ," he said, but he didn't finish. He hung the DO NOT DISTURB sign on the outside of the door. "Those nurses are kind of bullshit."

"No kidding," I said.

"It's really a mechanical issue."

"If you say so."

He told me to sit up straight, and he squared my arm off at the elbow. He lifted my breast in his hand and pinched my nipple. "Hold it here," he said, "upright."

I did as I was told. He laid you in my arms. He held you against my stomach and turned your tiny face toward my right breast with the heel of his hand. You opened your

329

mouth and I felt a pinch of pain and a tingling, then your lips sealed over the nipple like a plug fitting into a drain and I watched you swallow.

Your father smiled. He had not been asleep on his cot. He had been listening. He had been waiting for the right time to intervene in the care of his newborn son.

I smiled. Then I cried. Did I thank him? I don't know. I don't remember. But I was grateful.

Your father never looks in the hatbox. He's not sentimental. He never prays, either, as far as I know. I didn't pray, until last fall. I don't set out to pray now, but sometimes I find my hard hope crossing the line. In the hatbox are three baptism certificates in a single envelope, one for each of you, my reasoning being that it couldn't hurt to usher you all into the world of faith, even if we didn't actually believe. And it made my mother so happy.

There is also a photocopy of a pamphlet from the Centers for Disease Control and Prevention that I found in the San Francisco Public Library when you were not quite a year old. I was ready to wean you by then. I was ready to sever the cord that tied what I ate, and drank, to you, but I was also terrified. Terrified to think that my body would be my own again, and that I could do with it what I wanted. I longed to be irresponsible, and free, but I was also stapled in place. I was madly in love with your bright cheeks and your ready smile, and I was ever conscious of the bargain I'd made in the clinic before you were born. Everything, it seemed, my whole new life, with its burdens and its joys, depended on my holding up my end of that bargain.

In the pamphlet from the CDC, three definitions are highlighted, the ones I must have felt were most relevant. "Normal drinking" in women was a single drink a day, and no more than seven in a week. "Heavy drinking" was a habit of more than one a day. "Binge drinking" was four or more drinks on a single occasion. I did not highlight the definition of sobriety. I suppose I thought it would be easy enough to remember what that meant. After all, I'd been entirely sober for more than a year and a half.

A simple set of definitions from which one could derive a simple set of rules. That was the straightforward formula I relied upon to turn me into a grown-up, a normal woman. I followed the rules. I developed new habits, and the habits stuck. Not just drinking habits, but other ones, too. I learned to cook, and I put dinner on the table each night. I made it a habit to take you for a long walk across the city every day — at first in a sling, and later, a backpack. I read a half-dozen books on child-rearing, and made a point of mapping out the hours of our day so you could have regularly timed meals and naps.

I did not go to bars. I had no more than one drink a day. I found that if I was not going to have more than one drink, it was hardly worth drinking at all, and most days I didn't. Not drinking became a habit that no longer required resolve. Over the years, it was just the person I became, and I can count on two hands the times I've consumed more than three drinks in a single sitting in the entirety of my marriage.

And then, in a single fortnight last year, I drank too much twice. It is a period I long to banish from the book of our history, but of course I can't. First, I let the flight attendant refill my glass again and again on the plane that carried me to London, and to my foolish indiscretion. Then, on the night of your accident, at the fateful dinner with Emme, I refilled my own glass too many times.

I haven't had a drink since that night,

when you flew from Emme's car and nearly died. I wasn't the one to put you in the car or drive it, but my lips were loosened by wine, and Emme's temper was loosened by my words, and the memory of that dinner clings to me like a hangover that won't end.

A photograph has accidentally slipped into the CDC pamphlet on alcohol abuse. It's the official race photo marking the first time you completed the Sharkfest Swim, across the bay from Alcatraz, when you were fifteen. I study the photo — your tanned skin, your wide smile, your arm raised in victory — and I remember how changed you were from the year before, when you had been a more careful, deliberate boy, conscientious to a fault, often worried and much too thin. Then you went away to camp that summer, and you swam across the frigid lake every morning and earned yourself a prize. You returned home with broadened shoulders and a plan to swim across the bay. Your father's relationship with you changed. For a long time, I think he thought he could train you. He could control you with his hands, or his words, like he controlled the dogs. But now he could see, we could both see, the foreshadowing of the man you would become, a man who would take direction mostly from himself.

While you were gone that summer you were fourteen, Polly was born. You didn't seem especially interested in her when you returned, at least not until she could talk. You had been more interested in Clara. I'd tried so hard for so long to get pregnant with Clara; perhaps you couldn't believe a baby finally conceived in vitro on the third try would indeed be the same as a regular baby. She was, of course. Then three years later came our splendid surprise — Polly — who was conceived without our even trying.

The hatbox is almost empty, now. The artifacts that remain are newer and cleaner, but still heavy with meaning and intent.

There is a photograph of the inside of the store my father took for the commercial real estate company that has let me the space for fourteen years. The photo documents the damage the claw-foot tub made when it fell through the floor in the hours before, or after, or perhaps at the exact moment of your accident. The tub was made from a single-piece casting of volcanic limestone and resin, already very heavy and made heavier by water the night of the accident. The subfloor beneath it, weakened by a leaky pipe, was further weakened when the tub overflowed. The subfloor collapsed, and the tub crashed through the ceiling, crushing the arc light, with its diamond bulbs, which had been displayed directly below. The water went on running for a day and a half, flooding most of the store.

You never saw the damage. You never knew who started the flood, or at least you never knew from us. And if you were told of her plan, the night it happened, the telling was wiped clean by the memory loss from your accident and coma. There was no reason to tell you during your rehabilitation and recovery. I'm not even entirely convinced there is a reason to tell you now.

Three more artifacts are all that is left.

The photo Mitch took of us at Christmas.

The letter I received two months ago, on Valentine's Day, from an elderly English gentleman. The one that was not the beginning of the story, but that teased out the hidden plot. The one that contained the words that made it necessary to write down all these other words.

And finally, the photograph I took at Gold Hill on the Fourth of July, of you and Emme, holding the greased watermelon between you. The only photo we ever took of Emme and the last one taken of you before your accident. A keepsake that might have told us a few things, if we'd had any idea where to look.

THIRTY-TWO

The Fourth of July. Three quarters of a year ago now. You had not even been home from Northwestern a month. One of Jonathan's authors had invited us to his neighborhood pool, in a place on the peninsula neither of us had ever heard of called Gold Hill. I might not have wanted to go if I'd known that seven months later, your father would move out of our house in the city to take over that very same author's house and make Gold Hill his home.

But I didn't know, and I agreed with your father that it would be good for all of us to get out of the city and spend the day at a pool in the sun. There were going to be field games and pool games and a bake-off, and your father insisted on baking a cake with the girls that we could enter in the contest. It was his brainchild, but your sisters provided the hard labor. It took them most of the evening the night before, and all of the morning of the Fourth. When it was done, I wondered what had taken so long. It appeared to be a simple thing — a round, tall, multilayered cake with plain white frosting. But Clara explained there was a secret. They had dyed and stacked each layer, so that when a piece was cut and laid flat on the plate, it would be a miniature replica of the American flag.

We'd assumed you'd be spending the Fourth with your Berkeley roommates, but you surprised us by saying you'd like to come along with us instead.

The store was closed for the holiday, but I stopped in to pick up ten do-it-yourself papier-mâché lamp kits I'd promised to deliver to a client that morning. Emme emerged from the bathroom upstairs with a towel wrapped around her head.

"Sorry to barge in," I said.

"No worries," she said.

I asked if she had Fourth of July plans. She said she had "nothing set" for the day. She seemed subdued. Her voice was very quiet, and I felt sorry for her. This was not the first time I'd seen her like this, but I'd also seen her just the opposite — vibrant, expansive, flirtatious. The male customers were drawn to her when she was in that mood, and I told myself it was good for business.

"Come along with us," I said, immediately regretting it. "We're in search of the sun."

"That would be lovely, actually," she said. "Really lovely."

"Good," I said, forcing a smile. "We'll swing by here on our way out of the city and pick you up."

The weather as we left the house was typical for a San Francisco summer — foggy, with a cold wind — and it seemed absurd to pack bathing suits, but we did. We put the dogs in the backyard and piled into the Suburban and drove to the store. We waited out front in the car, talking of savages and stories. Then Emme joined us, and you looked at the book in her bag, and the conversation turned to Zen koans and happiness. When we arrived at Gold Hill, our jeans and sweatshirts felt like suits of armor. It was not even noon, but already blazing hot. The sky seemed to me tired out by the heat, the blue nearly sucked out of it. In the parking lot, a bike and pet parade was in progress. Kids were riding around in a wide circle while the national anthem played; dogs wore red and blue and white streamers and had flags tucked into their collars. Polly cried because we had left our dogs and our bikes at home.

The girls changed into their suits and took their place along the edge of the pool, where dozens of kids were sitting with their feet in the water, waiting for the games to begin. How pale your sisters' skin was compared to those bronzed suburban children. How uncertain they'd seemed tiptoeing over burning cement to the edge of the pool. How tentative they were, at first, diving into the water when the coin toss began. But soon enough they were plunging and resurfacing, side by side, smiling and showing us the coins in their hands. There was a relay race, parents versus teenagers, and an inner-tube race, and a contest to see who could dive over a rope held in front of the diving board.

Now and then, I watched Emme out of the corner of my eye. She had a red cover-up tied tightly around her, only her pale shins exposed. She was on her back, laid out on a chaise with her eyes closed and a white sun hat pulled down over her face. Every so often she looked up and surveyed the scene with an expression — how to describe it — a kind of semidetached malaise. As if she were not quite sure how she'd found herself here, in this alien landscape, and not quite sure how to conduct herself within it.

Then the greased-watermelon race was announced. The idea was to dive in the pool and chase after a watermelon that had been coated in peanut oil and tossed in the water. The first swimmer to push the slippery fruit out of the pool was the winner. There were categories, ten-and-under boys, ten-and-under girls — which your sisters sat out — sixteen-and-under boys and girls, men, women and, finally, coed pairs of any age.

"You two should give it a go," you said to your father and me.

"No way," I said.

You looked at Emme. It was as if she could feel your gaze on her face, and her eyes opened.

"How about it?" you said to her.

She stared at you intently, then at the pool. Finally, a smile crept into her face and transformed it. "Why not?" she said.

She reached her hand out and you pulled her up. She dropped her cover-up to the cement. Her skin was paper-white against the strings of her red bikini, and her hair was very, very blond. Her body was lean and long, but with curves in the right places. She moved across the pool deck with a languor, an unabashed sexual energy that made me feel like I was watching porn. Who knew that beneath the many layers of cloth-

341

ing she always wore in the store — the sweaters and skirts and tights and scarves and boots — she'd been hiding this model's body? She smiled at you sideways, her face utterly changed from that of the woman who had been stretched out so sullenly all afternoon.

"They're beautiful, aren't they?" I said to Jonathan.

"What's beautiful?" he replied.

"The two of them," I said. "Robbie and Emme."

He nodded, and we watched you stand side by side in swim-racer position at the edge of the pool. You dived together when the race gun went off. Your dives were smooth and synchronized, as if you'd choreographed the show in advance. Emme kept up with you, stroke for stroke, and you reached the watermelon in the exact same moment, a body's length ahead of any of the other dozen pairs in the race. You passed the watermelon between you expertly as you kicked to the side. Then you shoved it, with your four hands, up over the side of the pool.

It was all over in less than a minute. Your sisters went wild. I took only one photo of you that day. I took only one photo of you all summer. I snapped it as you and Emme stood together after your victory, the watermelon held between you.

They say people who are bipolar see colors differently when in a manic state. What did Emme see when I showed her the photo a few days later? What did any of us see? The colors, the curves, the important straight lines? You in blue trunks with your dark skin, brown hair, green eyes. Her white skin and slender hips beneath the strings of her red bikini. The oval of watermelon, the roundness of her breasts, the hardened muscles of your swimmer's arms. The long, narrow torsos. The splayed feet. The second toe larger than the first. Your slender fingers nearly touching her slender fingers, your four thumbs, your two sets of lips, smiling, lovely as the summer hills behind you — layer upon layer like a tiered yellow cake.

The girls joined in field games. An egg toss. A three-legged race. A water-balloon battle, children chasing one another under the high, hot sun.

Sparklers were handed out. A band set up beside the pool. Barbecues were lit. Picnic blankets were spread on the grass. Card tables had been arranged in the shape of a *U* and covered with red-white-and-blue-checked plastic tablecloths. All day we'd watched as people entered the pool area, carrying baked goods in their arms, setting their confections tenderly on those tables. The area was roped off, and the children, your sisters included, stood close, pressing their bodies against the ropes intended to contain them, until one of the judges warned them to stand back.

What was laid out on those tables was not just an assortment of baked goods. It was the wild ambition — and care, and time, and effort, and love — of ordinary people, in an ordinary suburb, and it moved me as no art gallery ever had. There were brownies and cakes. There were tarts and pies. There were doughnut pops dipped in colored sprinkles, patterned in stars and stripes. There was a two-foot-tall cookie shaped like the Liberty Bell. There were Rice Krispies treats cut like watermelon wedges, dyed pink and green. There were cupcakes made to look like sunflowers, each leaf of each flower intricately carved out of yellow frosting. There was the cake that had come from our own kitchen, which, when sliced into pieces, formed miniature American flags.

I held Polly against my hip as the winners were announced. The cake your father and the girls had made was overlooked. I exchanged an uh-oh look with your father. He had a hand on Clara's head, as if to protect her from the shower of disappointment. But your sisters handled it rather well. There was a consolation prize, and they knew it. They knew that in a moment the ropes would come down and they would be allowed to fill their plates so high, the colors and flavors of one sweet would become indistinguishable from the next.

I wondered, a little desperately, if there weren't some way to preserve all that effort and beauty. But there was not, and in the matter of an hour every single confection had been devoured, or demolished, or discarded, the crumbs left on the checked tablecloths like the rubble of a ruined city.

When night fell, the band played. We drank cold beer in the hot night. The kids danced. They threw their bodies around on the sloping lawn between the band and the pool. Jonathan and I sat beside each other and watched fireworks explode over the neighboring towns. A slow song came on. He dragged me onto the dance floor. I leaned into him. His skin was cool and clean from swimming. I felt as I had so often felt in his arms, as if everything really would be all right. It was one of the times, last summer, that I thought only of him.

Then I looked over and you were dancing

with Emme. Your hips were moving together. Your noses were an inch apart. There
was no good reason, yet, for the alarm bell
that rang in me, and yet it did ring, and the
sound was long and loud.

THIRTY-THREE

The trip to London in late August was a last-minute inspiration. A few weeks earlier, after an early-morning rush with so many customers in the store that Emme and I could barely keep up, the whole city took itself off to the Giants game, and we did not have a single customer for two hours. I gave Emme the rest of the day off. I sat in the quiet and sketched ideas for new lights. I had been in the field across from our house the day before, with Clara and Polly. I had photographed them as they leapt back and forth over the branch of a pine tree that had fallen in the shape of a perfect arch. I remembered that I had seen a contemporary floor lamp in that same shape at a lighting show in the spring. The arc had been fabricated out of steel. Six pendant lights had been attached to it, the beams directed downward, perfect over coffee tables, or dining room tables where there was no wiring for an overhead chandelier. It had been listed for thirty-five hundred dollars. I guessed the manufacturing cost was mostly in the arc-shaped steel base, since the lights themselves had been nothing special. But if you replaced the plain pendants with something more remarkable, like the samples of faceted diamond-shaped bulbs that had arrived in the store from a Swedish designer the week before, the light would be truly distinctive. And if you swapped out the metal, with, say, the branch of a pine tree already bent into an arc shape, most of the cost would be eliminated.

I hauled the pine branch to the store, and the following weekend, I constructed the light. Emme was at a Zen retreat center in Santa Cruz, and your father and the girls were away on a two-night father-daughter camping trip. I had the store to myself. I holed up after closing on Friday and worked on the light. I made three trips to the hardware store for supplies. Once, returning, I noticed a man walking past the store, and for a heart-stopping moment, I thought it was Patrick. But it was only Michael Moss, from the lingerie shop, heading home.

I worked long into the night, then thought perhaps I'd sneak upstairs and sleep in the bed in the loft. But I opened the sliding doors to find a mess so disastrous it was both disturbing and fascinating. There were brochures and books and papers covering almost the whole of the bed. There were gum wrappers and panties and bras and jeans and T-shirts and sweaters and scarves. There were books on Buddhism and meditation and yoga and a few California travel books. There were brochures for meditation centers — not only in California, but all over the world. I picked up a few and flipped through them. I fought the urge to tidy up, and finally forced myself to slide the doors closed. I slept at home and returned to the store early to continue with the arc light, seized with the pleasure of solitude and work. I sunk the branch in concrete inside a half wine barrel that I painted brick red. I crafted hoods for each of the diamond bulbs out of old baking tins and painted them green. I hung the lights, with their forested hoods, a foot apart from one another on the branch, on three-foot-long wires I painted gold. The shape, the colors, the vintage and organic materials, the brilliant diamond bulbs — all this added up to a quirky but elegant light, and I was pleased.

When Emme returned from her weekend

away, she stood up close to admire what I'd made.

"They're fifteen-watt halogen bulbs encased in clear glass," I said. "I thought the diamond shape was a nice twist on an ordinary bulb. And it casts a different kind of light."

"I agree," she said, tapping her finger lightly on each bulb. "But you mustn't sell it. It's too beautiful. And it's powerful, too: The geometry of the diamond held in meditation allows a higher understanding of the soul."

I never did put a price tag on the arc light. Instead, I moved it to hang over the table on which I displayed our vintage lamp collection. At least that way it was casting light on products I might indeed sell. I emailed a photograph of the whole display to the Swedish designer of the diamond bulbs, asking if he was interested in posting it on his website as a unique application of his lights. He responded the next day with an invitation to display the arc light in his booth at the biggest architectural lighting show of the year, in London, in a week's time.

I sat at my desk and read his email again and again. It was not practical for me to skip town for a week, given my responsibilities at the store and at home. Nor was it practical to ship a wine barrel of concrete and a ten-foot pine branch overseas. But I could not stop thinking about it. Perhaps I could find a babysitter for the girls. Perhaps Emme could help at the store. Perhaps I could build a new light when I got there. I could use local materials and assemble the arc light in a few days, as I had done here. Decorative branches were all the rage for interiors. I could simply order the organic material wholesale. It did not need to be pine. It could as easily be oak, or birch. It could even be fabricated, not a real branch at all.

I told Jonathan about the offer. Right away, he said I must go, as I should have known he would. He said I deserved it. He said it was not fair that he was the only one who ever traveled for business. He would handle Clara and Polly — he could work from home — and Emme could hold down the fort at the store.

"Just go," he said, over and over. "Go."

Was there treachery in my accepting his generosity? Perhaps there was, since London was the last place I knew Patrick Ardghal to have lived. But I wouldn't have known where to begin looking for him there. Or, at least, I wouldn't have known where to look that I had not already looked. That summer, I had searched the web exhaustively for Patrick Ardghal, and though many other Ardghals had turned up, Patrick had not.

I called my mother.

"Just go," she said. And then, "If you do go, would you be home by Labor Day weekend?"

"Yes," I replied. "Why?"

"Well, I might be coming for a visit. We both might. Your dad and I."

"Dad?"

"Yes."

"How did this suddenly come about?"

"He and Veronica Cox got a divorce."

"They did?"

"Yes."

"Why?"

"She's still drinking. He's not."

"Oh."

"Looks like he'll be packing up and heading out on a road trip. He says he's going to come all the way to the West Coast."

There was a silence. "I hope you know what you're doing," I said.

"I'm not doing anything."

"You're doing something."

"Is it such a crime to want to be friends with the man who is the father of your two children?"

"It's not a crime. It's just . . . dangerous."

"Oh, it's not dangerous. It's important, is what it is. It's important he comes to see his grandchildren."

"He's never even met his grandchildren."

"High time," she said.

"Was it his idea, or yours?"

She sighed. "Does it matter?"

I called your Uncle Ryan, who was living in Venice Beach, working four days a week selling pharmaceuticals. He answered on the sixth ring. He said he was just in from surfing. His life seemed to me shallow and empty, or shallow and alluring, depending on the day. I did not really understand our relationship. We could go months, or a year even, without speaking, but the distance between us collapsed as soon as I called and he picked up the phone. I was always the one to call. I was the older sister, after all.

"Have you talked to Mom?"

"No," he said. "Why?"

"Dad's coming out west."

"He is?"

"For the record, I think this whole thing is a disaster waiting to happen. She wants to bring him for a visit."

"Really?"

"You'll have to come see him if he visits San Francisco Labor Day weekend. You'll come, won't you?"

"I'll think about it," he said. "Tricky getting away." He changed the subject. "How's Robbie? Does he want to come down? I've got a new long board he can try out."

"I'll ask him. He's got the job at Berkeley. And he's been hanging around with this woman who's working in the store and living in the loft. I'm not exactly clear on the nature of their involvement."

"Is she hot?"

"Yes."

"They're not shacking up or anything, are they?"

"No, they're not shacking up."

"Good. He needs to keep it loose."

"Loose. Yes. I agree with you."

"Amazing," he said. "We agree on something."

"We often agree. Don't we?"

"Sure we do. Absolutely. Anyway, Annie, the thing to do is not think about Mom and Dad. Just worry about yourself."

"Easier said than done."

"Seriously, try it," my little brother said to me. "Try it this once."

So I tried it. I put my parents — and my children and my husband — out of my mind, and thought only of myself. I ordered an artificial branch and a wine barrel from a British wholesaler, then I packed my clothes and got on a plane to London.

Thirty-Four

It was my first flight without my family in more than twenty years. Appropriate, since I was traveling to the first and last place I had ever lived alone. On the train from Heathrow into London, where I would be staying in a hotel near Hyde Park, I was jet-lagged and suffering the aftereffects of wine I'd consumed on the plane. I had not meant to drink so much. It was not the sort of thing I did these days. But being by myself seemed to liberate me from my obligations. I felt the way I had coming to London the first time: I was alone, and unwatched, and might as well do as I wanted. Now that the flight was over, I was full of regret. I wondered how I would survive seven whole days without your father and the girls. But once I settled in, I enjoyed myself. I did not really miss home until the end.

I arrived in London on a Tuesday, and I was not scheduled to start work on the arc light until Thursday. My hotel was on Park Lane. The room was furnished in deep reds and golds. There was an upholstered chair by the window and an ornate reading lamp and heavy damask drapes pulled closed. The bathroom was spectacularly clean and appointed with tiny fragrant soaps wrapped in pink paper. There were gorgeously thick white robes folded on a shelf in the bathroom. How different this space was from the plain blue room in Victoria I'd lived in two decades before.

I could hear the wind sweeping across Hyde Park. I pulled back the drapes and there, surprising me somehow after all the time that had passed, was the London evening sky I remembered, tender pink and etched with white clouds. I went out and walked straight to the river. It was summer but not warm. I did not feel lonely, but I felt the memory of loneliness. It rained. I had no umbrella. I had never carried an umbrella then, either. Had I changed so little?

I walked to Embankment Station, where I stumbled upon a memory of being pressed against something — a wall, a bench, the glass partition inside the tube — and kissed by Patrick. It was not that the kisses themselves had been so remarkable, but there was a texture of abandonment in them, and in him, a way he had of giving himself over to a moment, that I remembered.

I decided to take a sunset river cruise. Waiting to buy my ticket, I was distracted by a baby in a pram. The baby was small and dark, its face poking alertly from its hooded suit, its dark eyes glowing. The mother was small and dark, too, the father paler, flushed red in the face. There was an older couple along, the woman's parents, visiting from out of town.

"Fourteen quid for a single journey?" the young father kept saying. "That's ridiculous. We could get a taxi for a tenner. We could get the bus. Why don't we catch a bus? We could get the fifty-eight."

The baby coughed. The mother glared straight ahead. Her parents milled about at a distance, keeping quiet.

"Fourteen quid," the man said again, igniting an old feeling in me — a clutching feeling about money. I fished a twenty-pound note from my wallet for my ticket. It used to panic me to spend a bill like that. It used to trigger a personal indignation at the price of things. A quick shock in the morning that the twenty pounds was gone. The run home from the tube station at Victoria after work, the sweat on my forehead as I imagined missing the free dinner. The inescapable mental calculations: This meal cost two hours of work; this skirt, a half a day; this journey on the tube, outside zone one, nearly an hour. This night of drinking, a half a day's work. I used to go to pubs alone to drink. There are worse confessions in these pages, but the thread that came loose the night of your accident was first stitched into the fabric of my life in those pubs, and I wish it hadn't been. I wish I hadn't wasted that money, drinking pint after pint, and obliterated all those hours, and set down a habit that returned briefly, last summer, and inadvertently might have obliterated you.

Fourteen pounds for a single journey along the river? I didn't like this pale man, but I had to agree with him that it was too much. They turned around without buying a ticket. I bought mine and boarded the boat. The rain had stopped, and the sun came out suddenly. The sky became pale gold. The sun glinted green off windows. It glinted off the river, too, flooding the city with an aching beauty. At the edge of the river were birch trees huddled in patches of dirt, the trunks like bleached bones strung upright in the light. They had missed it, this moment; perhaps it would have been worth their fourteen quid after all.

From the boat, I stared at river things: long houseboats painted black and brown or blue and white. The bleached, then blackened, brick of the Tower of London. The gray clouds moving swiftly overhead. Yellow brick tenements rising above the moss-green walls that contained the river and its tides, tides as far up as the point where the river ceases to be tidal and becomes an inland body unattached to the sea.

The next day, I took the Docklands Light Rail to Canary Wharf. I wondered who'd ended up engineering it — this massive station that connected the glittering new buildings to London proper. It should have been Malcolm. It would have been Malcolm if he had not died. Standing there, I came face-to-face with the unwelcome finality of death. What can you do with it? It stops you cold when you think of it; it leaves you no out. So I took the light rail back into London and tried to put Malcolm out of my mind.

I walked the route I had sometimes walked from the river to Victoria. Each landmark was familiar: Westminster Abbey, Westminster Cathedral, Victoria Station. I tried to find Victoria House, but the neighborhood was so changed, I did not see anything that looked like the building in which I had once lived. I walked back to Victoria Station. I stood inside its vast white halls. I watched a young woman standing alone before the board, looking up, holding on to her suitcase. The train schedule flipped over in its white letters. She could go anywhere. She could simply board a train and end up somewhere else. As I had done once, with Patrick.

It was not yet noon. I had all day. I'd be back by evening. Why not?

I bought a ticket and boarded the train. I spent the day walking around Canterbury, as Patrick and I had done. I tried to find the place we'd stayed. But all the bed-and-breakfasts looked the same. I did not spend the night this time. I took a train back to London to the hotel on Park Lane and collapsed into bed.

I went to the exhibit hall on Thursday, where a small room had been assigned to me for two days to assemble the arc light. I did not end up building an exact replica. The branch was faux, for one thing. The diamond bulbs the Swedish designer wanted me to use were yellow instead of clear glass, and for hoods, I had shipped over a half-dozen antique copper colanders, instead of

361

the baking tins I'd used the first time. I worked for two days straight, and by Friday afternoon, I was done. I turned off the overhead lights and plugged in what I'd made, and the ceiling and the walls absorbed the new pattern of light. The effect was startling, better than I'd hoped — and I sat for a long time taking it in. Then I was free to do whatever I wanted until the following morning, when the Swedish designer was to help me move the light into his exhibit.

I decided to walk back to my hotel. The exhibit hall was not far from Bond Street, and suddenly the area was very familiar. I wandered around until I found the street where I'd worked for Malcolm on the Docklands bid. It had gone upscale, with posh stores and little cafés, and the sandwich shop on the corner had become a Starbucks. I found the building and stood outside and looked up as dusk took hold. I felt that stopping again, the stopping of death, and I went on walking.

The exhibition was a success. The arc light showcased the Swede's diamond bulbs beautifully, and both consumers and retailers expressed strong interest. I sketched' a version of the light I thought could be made easily, manufactured en masse, shipped and assembled on-site. The Swede was impressed, and we struck a deal. He would manufacture and distribute; I would help market, and take a cut.

He invited me to join him and a colleague for drinks when the show closed Sunday, but I declined. It had been a rewarding two days, but I didn't want to spend any more of my time in London doing business. I wanted, I suppose, to leave room to linger again in the past. And I wanted to talk to your father. I called him as soon as I was back at the hotel. I told him all about the show, and the deal I'd struck. He did not say he was proud of me, but I could tell he was by the tenderness in his voice. Or maybe that was only him missing me, as I suddenly missed him. He gave me a report on the girls. He told me you'd come for dinner and he'd made steaks and you'd spent the night. He told me everything was fine, and I should enjoy my last day tomorrow.

I ate by myself in the hotel restaurant. I felt loneliness like I hadn't felt in years. I felt it in the endless wine list, and in the menu inside its stiff red jacket, and in the indifferent city below me, flickering with light. I lay in the hotel room bed, later, unable to sleep. I wished, quite badly, that I was already home. I wished your father was beside me, so I could press my body against his coolness until the night was put to rest.

On the last full day of my stay, I slept late and had an early lunch. Then I set out walking. Steady rain was falling straight down out of a bland white sky. Water was pooling in the gutters, washing up over curbs.

I came to the former site of the Photographers' Gallery. I sought it out that afternoon and found it, though I'd decided, before I came to London, that I would not. It was still a gallery, but full of paintings, not photography, and it was now called Oxford Fine Art. I asked the woman working inside if she knew what had become of the photographic gallery that had been in this building in the late eighties. She said it had moved a few years ago, to a new site not far away.

She gave me directions. I walked slowly. I stood outside for a long time, then I went into the gallery and climbed the stairs and found a café. It had natural light, which the old café had not had, but it was as white and sterile as the old café had been. It had black counters against the wall and four round tables and a few benches with white legs and the same black laminate surface.

I ordered a coffee. I spoke to the man working at the counter. He told me they'd been in this site four years. He said he liked the old furniture better, but the wooden tables had been too long for this room so they'd had to be sold. On one wall was an enormous black-and-white photograph of a single tree. I was not impressed by it, but I sat on a hard white stool and drank my coffee and stared at it anyway.

I closed down memories, one by one, ticking them off like items on a to-do list. The exercise made me tired. Tired to remember that I had tried so hard, back then. Tired of wondering why that photograph of the four of us at the White Cliffs had arrived in my mailbox. Tired of trying to remember that Malcolm was dead. Tired of thinking of the sad past, and of the way I had behaved, and of Patrick.

I finished my coffee. I went to the counter in the print shop and picked up a brochure to take home as a keepsake. Clipped to the brochure was a business card. THE PHOTOGRAPHERS' GALLERY, it read. OWNER AND CURATOR: PATRICK ARTGAL.

I stared at the name. It was a different spelling. But could it, might it, still be Patrick?

"Patrick Ardghal?" I said out loud.

The man at the counter looked up. "Do you need to speak to him?" he said. "I believe he's in his office downstairs."

There were people behind me, talking about the photographs on the walls. Shadow and color, depth and perspective. There were other voices, too, leaking in from the street, voices full of laughter and boredom and fear. But the only sound I heard, walking back down the wooden stairs, was the sound of my own heart.

I knocked on the door. Patrick himself opened it. He stood for a minute staring at me, then he shouted out, "Annie Black, is it really you?"

What sound then? A gasp as he embraced me, and I discovered that I had long ago given myself permission, if I ever found him again, to find out what would happen next.

THIRTY-FIVE

The girls are finally home from Wisconsin. Your father delivered them this afternoon. I had to bite my lip to keep from crying when they stepped out of the car. They seemed older, and taller, if that was possible in a week's time. They gave me a quick report of their vacation. Yes, they'd skated on the lake. Yes, there were cousins their age. Yes, they'd had fun.

I didn't want your father to leave. The sun was out, and I told the girls they could play in the field across the street. It wasn't really a field. It was a rare undeveloped eighth of an acre in an overdeveloped city in which you used to spend hours, when you were little, searching for pill bugs and bottle caps and broken glass. Clara worked on her cartwheels while Polly looked for flowers.

"Any news about Robbie?" your father asked.

"No," I said. "Nothing. How about on

your end?"

"Nope."

A silence hung between us. I felt blame inside that silence, so strong it was as if it were physically embodied and resting squarely over my head. To lay blame. It's a strange expression. To lay it at someone's feet, like an offering? To lie inside it, suffocating? To fall in a pool of it and drown?

Perhaps blame is the way the universe organizes itself around tragedy and loss. Without blame, suffering is random, and that kind of randomness leads to madness.

Polly presented herself in front of us, then dragged us across the dirt to a clump of flowers with bright-yellow blossoms.

"See what I found? See how they face the sun?" Polly said. "That means they're sunflowers. Sunflowers face the sun all the time in the day even if the sun moves."

They were not actually sunflowers — they were prince daisies — but I wasn't going to correct her.

"Where did you learn that?" I asked her.

"From Emme-and-Emme."

Your father gave me a look.

"That's weird," Polly said, bending down. "These two aren't facing the sun. They're facing away. They must be sick."

"Maybe they think there's another sun,"

your father said.

Polly looked up in the sky.

"That would be very bad," she said. "Because then the sunflowers would keep turning and turning, and they would get a pain."

I picked her up and held her on my hip. Clara came and stood beside us. The four of us looked up at the single sun in its corner, poking between the clouds. Is that what I did last summer — see two suns in a single sky and forget which way to turn for sustenance? It was dangerous, doing that. It was possible to drop seeds at the wrong time, in the wrong places, failing to grow the expected future. It was possible to rush forward, looking back, and break your neck.

Thirty-Six

I see that there is nothing left to do but to set down what happened next in London, last August.

Patrick stood in the doorway of his office at the gallery and shouted my name. He lifted me up and embraced me. There was a feeling that no time at all had passed, that I still knew him well, and that he knew me, that we were both still young in spite of our altered exteriors.

He gave me a tour of the gallery. We had a beer in the pub next door. We exchanged personal histories.

He had never married. He had never had children. He had lived with many women, but so far, he hadn't fancied the few who'd wanted to marry him, and the ones he'd wanted to make a go of it with had unfortunately wised up in the end.

He struck me as fundamentally changed. He seemed humble and modest. I asked him if he'd finally discovered humility.

He laughed. "Hard to support my old bravado in the face of such dismal results."

He was still taking pictures, but he'd given up trying to make a living from it. He was content running the gallery, trying to discover and nurture the talent of others. At some point, he said, it would be necessary to move home to Ireland. His father was still alive, but not in good health.

We took a walk beside the Thames. For the first time that week, I didn't notice the weather, or the time, or the color of the river. I noticed only Patrick. He said we ought to pop into the Tate. There was a new installation by a Polish artist he wanted to see. We'd just make it before the museum closed for the night.

The exhibit was a simple, enormous rectangular structure that took up most of the first floor of the museum. The outside was steel and wood, painted black, and the inside was darkness. The exhibit was called *How It Is,* taken from the Samuel Beckett novel of the same name. Patrick read the placard posted on the wall out loud: " 'How shall I move forward? you might ask yourself, as you stand at the threshold, confronted by the darkness ahead.'

"Dramatic, isn't it?" he said.

"Or melodramatic."

"Shall we have a go anyway?"

"Why not?"

We entered the structure and were suddenly enveloped in an astonishing darkness. It was darkness like you never find in nature. Darkness like you never find anywhere. Darkness like a gateway into a different world. I walked slowly, taking small, uncertain steps. I could hear strangers floating by us, heading out of the blackness as we headed in. I became dizzy, thinking I had a long way to go to get to the end. But the room was shorter than it seemed, and the end was there before I expected it, a sudden velvet wall at my fingertips.

"Ah, the wall," Patrick said.

"It's a little far-fetched, don't you think," I said, "calling this art?"

"It depends on your definition of art, I suppose."

"What's your definition of art these days?" I asked him.

"Perhaps whatever stands in the world with no other purpose than to move us."

"Shouldn't it be more than this emptiness, though? Shouldn't it be beautiful?"

"It doesn't necessarily have to be beautiful," he said. "Everything can't be beautiful like you."

It was the first time he had ever told me I was beautiful. We stood touching the velvet wall. We were alone, together, in the dark. I could hear his breath. I could smell him, and the smell was familiar and intoxicating. Then I felt his hand moving over my hand against the velvet wall. Hesitant, like those steps we'd just taken in darkness.

I turned my hand over so that my palm was pressed into his palm. I offered him that encouragement.

Our fingers became entangled, and after that, our lips.

The first kiss.

The first kiss in more than two decades, anyway.

Was it, too, familiar?

It was not. It was as if kissing the same person, Jonathan, for so long had made kissing another set of lips faintly ridiculous. It was like playing truth or dare or spin the bottle. After all the buildup, it was a performance for which I was inadequately prepared. The insistent lips. The darting tongue. The pressure of his hand on the small of my back. Was this all it would be? Was this what I had been waiting all these years to experience again?

But it did not end with the kiss. He ran his finger along the edge of my cheek. He lifted my chin — I don't know how he found it so easily in the darkness — and kissed me again. This time more intently. He slipped his hand inside my sweater. I let him.

We went to dinner at a restaurant in Covent Garden. The table was in the center of the room under too-bright lights. He ordered wine. Food was delivered. Crusty rolls. Crab cakes. Sashimi. It sat on the table between us, barely eaten. We drank the wine. I couldn't remember, afterward, what we talked about. I could remember only that his features were familiar, but that it was as if I had never really seen them before. The angular face. The wiry hair. The large ears. The silver chain around his neck. The neck itself — thin and pale. But mostly, his hands on the table. Elegant hands. Too soft. Too tender. Lacking in vigor, somehow. Not at all like Jonathan's hands.

Jonathan, whom I loved. Jonathan, whom I wanted. His body in my bed. His hand in mine. Forever and ever and ever.

Was it to be only about bodies, after all?

Skin. Lips. Tongues.

Hair. Faces. Fingers.

Ears. Hands. Breath.

Like Clara's sketches, the disembodied

parts that somehow represented the whole.

What you can stand and what you can't stand. The material you wish to pull from the bucket of love again and again.

But what you can stand, for the duration, is not the same as what you want right now. It is also not the same as what you wish, for reasons that remain mysterious, to offer up.

He excused himself and pushed his chair back and went to the bathroom. I watched him walk away, struck by the narrowness of his waist and the new stoop of his shoulders. Struck by how he seemed to have grown older over the course of the few hours we'd spent together that evening. Was it wanting that had aged him? Wanting and not knowing whether this time he was going to get what he wanted?

While he was in the bathroom, I began to eat the barely remembered food. I found I was ravenous. I ate the crusty bread. I devoured a crab cake dipped in thick sauce. I downed my water, then his. I found myself joyous at the return of everyday appetites. I didn't touch my wine. I didn't want it now that I saw I no longer needed Patrick to love me.

He sat back down. He seemed sad. It was not because of me. I knew that. It was because he was a lonely man staring down the second half of life.

"Would you like a coffee?" he asked me.

"No, thanks."

"I won't have one, either, then."

"Your choice."

Then we were outside walking again. He stopped abruptly after a few blocks. "Would you like to come up?"

"Come up where?"

"Here. My flat. This is where I live."

The sensible thing to do was to kiss him goodbye and return to the hotel on Park Lane, but I already knew I was not going to do the sensible thing. It was not like before. I was not hungry for Patrick's love. But I was hungry for something — for both getting it and giving it. I was hungry for one night.

I let him take my hand and I followed him into the lobby, then the elevator. He pushed the button and the doors closed. He pressed me against the wall and kissed me with something of his old abandon, and my body responded. It was not just my body; it was the whole of me moving forward. It was as if the terms of our indiscretion had already been negotiated by history, and according to those terms, I would make to Patrick an offering of my years of wanting him. In that way, the wanting would be reinterpreted in

the record of my life. It would be no longer
a foolish intemperance, but a permanent
and valuable gift, and I would finally be able
to grant myself a pardon for having indulged
it for so long.

The elevator opened. He fumbled with the
key to his flat. He made a tense little joke.
Inside, he lit candles and put on music and
pulled me into bed.

Clothing was removed. I never looked at
his body. He insisted on examining mine,
naked, from every angle, by candlelight.

"So beautiful," he said. "Still so beautiful."

I tried to look inside myself for the gift I'd
glimpsed in the elevator, but the terms
seemed already to have changed. I found no
pardon. I found only hard bones and hard
breath and lust. My own lust, I discovered,
had a selfish, conscious quality. It was as if I
could predict my actions, and their effect,
in advance. The licking and sucking. The
hard kissing, then the soft kissing. The
thrashing. The noises I made. The noises he
made in return.

I suppose it was very good sex. Yet it
seemed vaguely theatrical, on both our
parts. It was hot, but immediately afterward,
I was left cold. Whatever novelty had existed
between us years before had vanished into

this — a story we'd witnessed in a hundred
dark theaters on a hundred big screens.
Persuasive enough, but you never really
forgot it was a fiction. You never really forgot
it was all happening for the benefit of an
audience, even if that audience was only the
body locked on to yours. I willed myself to
come, then lay beneath him listening to him
moan, and gasp, in just the way I remembered.

Afterward, I knocked a water glass off the
bedside table and it shattered on the concrete floor. The floor had an abstract mural
painted on it, all sharp edges and angles
and primary colors, and it was as if the
points of the mural themselves had shattered the glass.

"I'm so sorry," I said. "I'll sweep it up. Do
you have a broom?"

"Leave it," he said. "I order you not to
abandon this bed."

But I insisted. I found the broom in the
kitchen. Naked, I swept up the shards. It
has always amazed me how far broken glass
can fly — and how often you find a sliver
long after you've swept the mess away.

"That's good enough," he said. "I'll use
the Hoover in the morning."

But I was bent on finding every piece of
glass. On whose behalf was I being so

diligent? Perhaps only my own. Perhaps I was thinking of the soles of my own feet, waiting, even as I swept, to set themselves in motion and flee.

"You know," he said, "I never stopped thinking about you. Never in all these years."

"I find that hard to believe."

"Well, it's true. Such a mistake, letting you get away."

"You didn't let me get away. You dropped me for Mary McShane."

"Mary McShane?"

"The girl from Montmartre. With the tambourine."

"I know who Mary is," he said. "But it wasn't like that between us. She was more like a sister to me. More like a little broken bird that needed a resting spot for a while. She's married. Big family. Settled in Howth. She's gotten a bit — how shall I put it — plump."

"Oh," I said. "I thought . . . I always assumed —"

"No. Never."

Then I asked the question I'd been waiting to ask. I asked if he was the one responsible for the photograph of the four of us at the White Cliffs ending up in my mailbox in June.

He looked at me with wide eyes. "My God," he said. "You got one, too?"

Thirty-Seven

As I left the hotel on Park Lane for Heathrow in the morning, the weather was brilliant and clear. I was quite the opposite. I was filled with regret, not only for the night with Patrick that had just ended, but for the indiscretion with Malcolm so many years before that Louise had apparently wanted to remind me of with a photograph. But why? What was the message she wanted to impart? Not the same message for both of us, presumably, since Patrick's copy had been treated differently from mine. Both had been subjected to solarization, the reexposure of the print, the same trick Patrick had used on his photographs years ago. But in mine, it was Malcolm and me cast in silver light. In Patrick's, it was Louise and Patrick.

Stepping from the taxi at Heathrow, I was unsteady on my feet. I had had very little to drink the night before, but I felt as if I had a hangover. I was sick to my stomach, and I felt sullied. I had given away the one impeccable element of my life — the faithfulness of my twenty-one years of marriage.

I bought gifts at duty-free. Aftershave for you. Cuban cigars for your father. London Underground pins and stickers for Clara and Polly. A purple burlap bag with a big ribbon to carry it all home in.

At home, I presented my gifts, and two days later, I told Jonathan. Not everything, not the whole truth and nothing but the truth, but the critical point: I had had sex with another man. Why did I tell him? Why punish him? Why cause him to recoil from me, as if I were a snake he'd found hidden in his bed? Why throw up between us terrible silences, terrible hurt? Why threaten the bedrock upon which I'd built my life?

I operated on impulse, without premeditation. It was as if once again, the terms of indiscretion had already been written, and I could not move forward with my life keeping this secret from your father. I was muddled and unhappy. I had lost track of my place in the world, and the only way to get it back was to have Jonathan put it back for me. I told him because I wanted what everybody wants — to be known. To know oneself, and to tell the whole story of that self, and to be loved anyway.

Someone else, too, helped tip the scales. Polly.

I was tucking her in the night after I'd returned from London. She was telling me the baked ham I'd made for dinner had been "too ham-ish," and the weather had been too "warm-ish."

I nuzzled her neck. I nestled her tender, hot body against mine. Then I remembered, again, what I had done, and I felt a constriction in my face. She ran her hand down the center of my cheek. She touched the crease between my eyebrows and the fine lines at the corners of my mouth.

"This is what happens to a mommy's face when it gets old-ish," she said. She pressed her finger gently against the lid of my left eye, then my right. I was trying hard not to cry. "And this is what happens to a mommy's face when it's sad-ish."

I closed my eyes against the tears I finally could not keep from coming.

"Love, love," she said. "So much love."

It was exactly what I'd said to her every night of her life. Even the intonation was the same. And here it was, word for word, coming back to me. That was the way it was supposed to work, with love.

I rubbed Polly's back until she was nearly

asleep. Then, seeming to remember something, she said, "Mommy, what does it mean, breaking your heart?"

"Breaking your heart?"

"How can you break it if you can't see it?"

"Oh, it doesn't really mean breaking. Not like an arm or a leg or a nose. It doesn't bleed. People say you have a broken heart if someone, or something, has made you really, really sad."

"Oh!" she said. "I would never, ever, ever break your heart. And you would never, ever, ever break mine."

"I'd try not to," I said. "I'd try not to make you very, very sad. But I might. Without meaning to. That can happen. Between mommies and kids. Between mommies and daddies, too."

"But then you'd say you're sorry."

"Yes," I said. "If I broke your heart, or Daddy's heart, I would definitely say I was sorry."

I offered only the most relevant details. I told Jonathan I'd run into Patrick at an art gallery. I had to remind him who Patrick was — the man who had been having the affair with my boss's wife, in London, before we met on the ferry. The one who had come along to Paris. The one we bumped into in the pub in Howth. The one who had told me Malcolm was dead.

"I remember," he said finally.

I told him about the beer in the pub and the exhibit at the Tate. I told him about dinner. I told him about spending part of the night in Patrick's flat. I didn't go into any specifics, but I said we'd used a condom, which we had. I told him about the broken glass. I told him the whole thing had been pointless, but that I supposed I'd had to get it out of my system. I admitted that I'd always been hung up on Patrick on some level. I told him I did not love Patrick and maybe never had, and that I never needed, or intended, to see him again.

I didn't tell him about the photograph. I didn't say that someone — Louise — had sent one to me and one to Patrick. I didn't explain how Patrick had stood up out of bed and retrieved his copy from a drawer in the desk in his flat, and that I saw that it was indeed the same photograph — the White Cliffs, the chalk down — but differently exposed.

I didn't tell Jonathan that Patrick said he hadn't heard from Louise in years. Last he knew she'd remarried and moved to Paris with Daisy.

There were other things I left out when I made my confession. I left out all the nights with Patrick in the blue room in Victoria, and I left out the morning with Malcolm in Paris. I left them out because I had left them out then; I didn't want your father to think I'd been lying to him since the beginning. And it was all ancient history now, anyway.

Of course it is upon the rubble of ancient history that the present stands.

Later, I found Jonathan on his knees in the garage blowing up a camping mat.

"What's that for?"

"I think you know what it's for."

He couldn't bear to sleep in the bed with me. I did not try to talk him out of it. I let him recoil into himself. I let him shrink from me into an impenetrable silence. I stepped around him, on the mat on the floor beside our bed, when I got up to go to the bathroom in the night.

The next night, I said, "You'll get a crick in your neck sleeping on that. Let me give you a pillow, at least."

"That's all right," he said. "This thing has one built in. I can just blow it up if I need it."

"All right," I said. "If you insist."

Then he said bitterly, "You know, it's not as if I haven't had opportunities over the years."

On Saturday, the night before the dinner that preceded your accident, your father lay down on the camping mat again, on the floor. I lay alone in the vastness of our bed and stared at the ceiling for a long time. I could tell he wasn't asleep from the sound of his breathing. I got out of bed and lay down next to him. He didn't touch me at first. I didn't touch him, either. Then, abruptly, he rolled over on top of me.

It was as far from making love as the act cán be. His body over me seemed not so much hungry as violent. He never in fact hurt me, but I kept having the feeling he was not trying to possess me, or pleasure me, or even pleasure himself, so much as to violate me. He wasn't tender, or conscientious, or accommodating, as he had always been before. He didn't hold me afterward. But that night opened something between us that had not been opened before. And even though afterward he seemed not like my husband, but like a man I'd picked up in a bar who would never love me, I found myself wanting more of it. Wanting again that animal thing that had happened between us atop the camping mat, without speech and without love, but that seemed to be trying to drag those things out of us.

There was no time for more, though, because the following day was the Sunday before Labor Day, and my mother arrived, and my father was delayed, and Emme came to dinner, and the store flooded and the car flipped.

THIRTY-EIGHT

The Sunday before Labor Day — you don't remember it, so I will fill in the details.

Emme had agreed to continue to manage the store for a week after I returned from London so I could spend time with the girls and have the holiday weekend to visit with my mother and — perhaps — my father. Sunday morning, I prepped the dinner. I marinated the steaks. My mother arrived in the afternoon. We took some trouble with the table setting. I wondered what my father would think of the house. If it had been eccentric when we bought it, it had become even more so over the years, as I'd swapped out the original lights with fixtures from the store. Anything that wouldn't sell, or that I couldn't part with, I brought home. The lamp with its base made of teacups and teapots. The milk-bottle chandelier. The sconces made from white birch twigs and tiny low-voltage teardrop bulbs. The jam-jar pendant lights, like the ones I'd first seen in the penthouse in Paris.

I tried to see it as my father, a stranger, might see it. When I looked at it that way, it seemed to me less a house than a museum of salvaged light. And of course there were Clara's sketches, disembodied human parts patched together on the bulletin board like postmodern art.

You arrived at five. My mother hugged you. You said, casually, "Emme might stop by later. After dinner."

"Oh," I said. "Okay."

You'd barely said a word to me about Emme that whole summer, and she had barely said a word to me about you. I hadn't pressed either of you for information. I hadn't wanted to pry. But I made a mental note to let you take me for a drive sometime soon. It was always in the car, during those sideways conversations, that you had told me important things when you were growing up. Maybe a drive would get you talking now.

You kissed Clara and Polly on the tops of their heads. You helped yourself to a beer and joined your father out back at the barbecue. The doorbell rang. I felt a constriction in my core as I walked to answer it, certain it would finally be my father.

But it was Emme, not "later," but in the here and now, in time for a dinner to which she had not been invited.

I had grown accustomed to her getups, but I was taken aback that night in spite of myself. She wore gold fishnet tights beneath an obscenely short A-line cocktail dress constructed of sheer lace and sequined gold leaves that looked to me like drapery fabric. On her feet were red fur high-heeled ankle boots, and around her neck was what looked like the decorated mane of a lion, a necklace made of gold goose feathers and heavy beaded silver jewels. But the real shock was her hair. In the twelve days since I'd seen her last, she'd cut off her gorgeous blond waterfall of hair and dyed it a brown so dark it was almost black. It was barely shoulder-length and teased up into a wild fuzz around her face.

"You changed your hair," I said.

"Yes!" She flicked her head from side to side like a model, then she stuck out her hip and struck a pose, smiling broadly, her face so changed inside its new frame as to be almost unrecognizable. All her features were called out anew — the straight, narrow nose and round pink cheeks, the huge eyes beneath the long lashes, the plump red lips, the slender white neck choked by the goose-feather noose.

The girls had not seen her in a month. They circled around her as if she were a friendly alien, touching her dress with the tips of their fingers, touching her tights, her boots, her necklace, her hair, and then climbing into her lap when she flopped down on the couch and crossed her legs.

At least we had gone to a small bit of effort in our own appearances. I'd combed the girls' hair and had them change their clothes, and to impress my father, perhaps, or to ingratiate myself upon your father by offering a small reminder of the body he'd ravaged the night before, I'd changed out of jeans into a sweater dress that clung to my waist, and I'd pulled on my high-heeled boots. My mother looked elegant in black pants and low black heels and a green wool sweater that called out the color of her eyes. She wore a pearl necklace my father had given her when they were still married.

I offered Emme a glass of wine, which she declined, announcing giddily that she couldn't drink alcohol because it interfered with her medications. This was the first I'd heard of her "medications." But how much did I really know about her? I never liked to become enmeshed with the people I was obliged to pay to be part of my life. It seemed mercurial or false, somehow, when there was always the chance the situation would turn. Not that I had any intention of firing Emme. As uncomfortable as she sometimes made me — with her mood swings and her clothing and her entanglement with the environmentally correct lingerie man next door, not to mention her relationship with you, whatever its nature — I had come to rely on her at the Salvaged Light. She could handle the store on her own. She was careful with the merchandise and the money, and she was exceptionally good with customers, especially the men. I had eased off asking her to babysit the girls, because as much as they loved her, and as much as she appeared to be fond of them, I had decided she was not the model of young womanhood I wanted nesting inside their malleable frontal lobes.

The phone rang, and my mother answered. It was my father. They spoke briefly. She put her hand over the receiver and said that he wanted to speak to me, but I could not bear to hear his excuse — a flat tire, a change of plan, an emergency back in Maine — for what I was certain was, in fact, plain cowardice. I shook my head.

"Don't even tell me," I said, when she'd hung up.

"It's all right. He's still coming. He got on the Pacific Coast Highway below Eureka and it took longer than he thought, then the car broke down."

"Of course it did."

"He's in Bodega Bay, wherever that is. It's the alternator, apparently. With the holiday weekend, it's been hard to find a garage with the parts and the manpower, but he's found a mechanic in Petaluma who will do the job tomorrow. He says he'll sleep in the car tonight, and get it fixed in the morning, and see us sometime tomorrow afternoon."

"And he's calling us now?"

"Well, you know your father."

"And of course he had to take the scenic route. He couldn't stay on 101 like a normal person."

My mother shrugged. "We didn't exactly tell him we'd planned a big dinner tonight."

"But he promised he'd be here this afternoon," I said.

I decided, for the thousandth time, that until he was standing on my doorstep, I had no intention of believing I was ever going to see him again.

Jonathan had come into the house and was watching the exchange. How I wished he would take me in his arms, as he would have two weeks before. I could sense, in his face, the battle raging inside him, and I could see the moment that his pride, or hurt, or anger, or simple pain won out — who could blame him? — and he turned away to tend to the grilling of the steaks.

We sat down to eat. Emme was, that evening, as I'd never seen her before, almost dancing as she walked, or hopping, darting here and there, talking very fast about I don't remember what, picking the girls up and swinging them around, touching Jonathan's shoulder — flirtatiously, I thought — when he brought in the steaks, and practically hanging on you. She took for herself the seat I had set for my father, between you and Polly. My mother was directly across from her, next to Clara. Jonathan and I faced each other at opposite ends. I drank too much wine. Not like me. Not like me, at all, to overindulge for the second time in two weeks. I was not myself, I suppose, and in that I was not alone. I did not drink so much that I failed to keep track of the drinks of others — namely, yours, since your plan was to drive back across the bridge that night, and the city was, as usual, swamped in fog. You had four beers in four hours. Inside the legal limit, perhaps, but outside my comfort zone.

I myself had three and a half glasses of

wine. The vehemence the wine unleashed in me set off a domino effect as devastating as if I had been not only drunk, but the one behind the wheel of Emme's car. It was not the predictable, linear sort of effect one gets with actual dominoes. It was more like the elaborate constructions you used to make out of blocks and marbles and plastic tubes and pulleys and levers and ramps when you were young. Rube Goldberg machines, I think they're called. Architectural masterpieces that required every single curved and straight block, every groove, every angle and turn to be placed so precisely, the ball would roll smoothly on its intricate journey each time, finally coming to rest with a satisfied thud.

That Labor Day weekend dinner was an architectural masterpiece of its own — a tragic chain reaction of wine and words and chemistry and history and madness that sent the car flying down the Pacific Coast Highway sometime in the night with you in the passenger seat and Emme at the wheel. It must have been my angry mention, over dinner, of my father choosing that route, instead of the more practical 101, that put the idea in Emme's head. My anger and my righteousness became essential connecting pieces that nudged Emme's hand, later, toward the faucet of the tub in the loft of the store, ultimately overflowing the tub and sending it through the ceiling, smashing the diamond lights below. And that nudged her hand again, however unintentionally, on the steering wheel of the Volvo, hurling the car over the side of the road and nearly sending you into oblivion.

What had set her off?

We had eaten dessert. My mother had taken the girls upstairs to get them ready for bed. You and Emme and your father and I were alone at the table, still lingering over the pie, and in my case, wine. I referred again to my father having the gall to take the Pacific Coast Highway when he must have known it would double the time of the journey and make him late. I went on with my ancient complaints. His selfishness. His narcissism. His habitual tardiness. His lack of interest in the people who mattered most — my three children, his own flesh and blood, who had gathered around this very table in his honor. In my mind I was contrasting him to Jonathan, who sat at the other end of the table, clearly uncomfortable with my rant. Jonathan was as reliable and unselfish as I believed my father was not, but he was also inclined to give people the benefit of the doubt until they proved him wrong.

"Why don't we wait to throw the book at him until he's here to defend himself?" Jonathan said.

"I'm not convinced he's going to be here," I said. "Ever."

I meant that when I said it. I really believed I might never see my father again. That he would vanish somewhere between Petaluma and the Golden Gate Bridge. When he did arrive the next day, I wasn't there. I was at the hospital, then the Mermaid Inn. So he was greeted by my mother. Did they embrace? Was it as easy for her to have him there as it was for me, when I finally did come home? Was it as if they had never been apart?

You and Emme sat quietly at the table through my rant about my father, but Emme stood up abruptly when I stopped speaking, knocking over your half-full beer. Her eyes were suddenly blazing, and she was leaning toward me with both hands open, as if she intended to strangle me.

"You bloody fucking cunt," she said. "At least your bloody fucking parents are bloody fucking alive."

The three of us were shocked into silence, and instinctively I put my hands up to defend myself. Emme pulled back and stood upright again at her place. She was gripping the edge of the table with her hands, and for a terrifying second I thought she was going to overturn it. I wish she had. There was nobody on the other side. The wine, the beer, the dessert plates, the forks and knives and candles would have been pitched onto the hardwood floor, and that mess might have been enough for us to recognize the extent of her mania and detain her until we could get help.

But you stood up and gripped her shoulders and turned her body toward you.

"Emme. Calm down."

"Fuck you," she said.

"Look at me."

"Fuck you."

"Emme. Change the channel."

"I can't."

"You can."

"I can't. I can't think of anything else."

"You can," you said to her slowly. "You can think Zen."

Zen. It was like the word that ends the spell. The kiss that turns the witch back into a princess. Or so it seemed right then.

She looked at you. Slowly, she let her forehead fall against yours. It reminded me of the moment, some twenty years before, when your father had proposed. There was a potent silence, and I felt we were invading a deeply private exchange. Then you put your arm around her and led her outside.

Later, it was like the episodes from my childhood of my father's drinking. I felt the evening more like a dream than a memory, the visuals both bright and tangled, the characters both themselves and not, the meaning clear one moment and lost the next. I could remember her leaning toward me and using that word, but I refused to fit the scene into the movie of my civilized life. I lay in bed unable to sleep. Jonathan lay next to me. He had generously rolled up the camping mat for the night. Was he only pretending to sleep while he mourned his own dead parents, and my inability to appreciate my living ones? Were the things I'd said about my father so mean and small as to justify such rage? I didn't think so. Had I mistreated Emme in the store? No, I had not. Had I underpaid her? Or expected too much? Or been ungrateful for her hard work? Had I judged her, or belittled her, or bossed her around? I hadn't. I'd been fair, even generous, if a little remote as the summer progressed.

I thought of the mess she'd lived in in the loft. I thought of her mood swings. Were these signs of a serious mental disturbance I'd somehow overlooked? Maybe it was as you posited when you returned from delivering her back to the loft: She was an orphan, jealous of our family life.

Your father and I had peered out the window after you'd led her from the house, and watched the two of you walking down the street. Not hand in hand or arm in arm, just walking beside each other like friends.

Then I went upstairs to find my mother, who had heard the commotion and taken the girls into Clara's room and closed the door.

We put the girls to sleep. My mother followed me to my bedroom. My hands were shaking. She sat me on the bed and made me take deep breaths, which brought on tears. She handed me tissues, and when I was calmer, she raised her eyebrows at me.

"I hope he doesn't end up with that one."

"Yeah," I said. "No kidding."

You returned, after an hour and a half, alone.

"She's all right," you said. "I walked her back to the loft. I didn't think she should drive a car. And I figured I may as well walk off the beers."

"What was that all about?" I asked you. "Why does she hate me so much?"

"She was saying some crazy shit," you replied. "I don't think it was about you. She's got a chemical imbalance going on. Her parents both died, so I guess she feels envious of our family. She knows she has to go see someone right away, though, an actual psychiatrist who can assess the medications she's on. Meditation isn't going to do the trick this time."

"She takes the meditation that seriously?"

You looked at me, surprised. "Yeah, she's into it," you said. "I am, too, incidentally."

"You are?"

"Yeah."

"Why did you never say so?"

"I don't know. You and Dad are so . . . anti all that."

"We are?"

"Anyway, the good news is she was sleeping when I left her. I think she'll be all right." You handed me her car keys. "I got her to give me these. I guess she'll want them back in the morning."

"That was a good move, Robbie," I said, as I hung the keys on a hook by the door.

Then you reached for your jacket. "You're not going back to the loft, are you?"

"No," you said. "I'm going back to Berkeley."

"Alone?"

"Yes, alone."

"She might go find you there."

"She's never even been there, Mom."

"Why not sleep here?"

It was not that I was worried you were still tipsy, though I myself still was. It was that I wanted, very badly that night, to have all my children safe under one roof.

You slipped one arm into your jacket.

"Grandma's on the fold-out, but you can have Polly's room," I said. "I already moved her in with Clara."

You looked at me. You hung your jacket back on the wall.

"Okay," you said. "You win."

"Do you want me to change the sheets?" I asked you as you followed me upstairs.

You shook your head and told me I was crazy.

"I'm not the only one," I said, and we shared a quiet laugh. I was certain that laugh contained a mutual measure of relief. Because clearly this woman did not belong in our lives. Her outburst over dinner was affirmation that it was time for her to move on, go home to New York, find a way to get better. I would not have to dismiss her, or evict her, certainly. She would see for herself the situation was untenable given her feelings for me, whatever had brought them on.

You grabbed a sleeping bag out of the closet and laid it on top of Polly's sheets, saying you didn't want to stink up her bed.

I smiled, because you seemed so like your father just then. So considerate, so oblivious to your own bodily comfort, so invested in family. You flopped down in all your clothes and I shut the door behind me. I had no reason to doubt you were there, where I'd left you, when the phone rang in the morning.

Thirty-Nine

Stories don't like to end when you want them to, do they? Loose ends aren't easy to snip with scissors or tuck inside a hem. They tempt you. They want you to keep pulling until there is nothing left to keep you warm.

April is almost over. The plum tree across the street, which, a few weeks ago, was blooming a flamboyant pink, has already shed its color. My mother called, as she always does on Saturday mornings. She said she had news. I felt a hitch in my chest, thinking it must be news of you.

"What is it?"

"It's about your father," she said.

She'd been keeping me abreast of their communication since he'd left in January. He'd been pestering her to come to Maine. He'd been telling her she'd love Little Cranberry Island, and that there was more work than he could do alone, with the garden and the goats. But she'd put him off. She hadn't wanted to leave with you still missing. On the other hand, aside from a few emails, I hadn't heard from my father at all.

I could tell from her voice that something had changed. It was a voice I remembered from long ago — thin as blown glass.

"Let me guess," I said. "He's off the wagon."

"No."

"What then?"

"He's met someone."

"Who?"

"A woman."

"You've got to be kidding."

"No."

"Where?"

"AA," she said. "A widow with a home on the water in Northeast Harbor."

"Northeast Harbor," I said. "So she must be wealthy."

"She must be," my mother said. Then, "Apparently he's proposed marriage."

For a minute, I couldn't say anything. I was shocked. Not only by the news, but by the strength of my own feelings. Somewhere, deep down, I'd believed my parents would get back together. I'd hoped for it — a reassembling of my original family — without even knowing that was what I'd been doing.

And my mother? What had she hoped for? What was she feeling now? I don't know, because she never said. She kept whatever was in her heart locked away, where it couldn't interfere. She forgave him, I suppose, for so quickly finding someone new to love. And I saw that I would have to forgive him, too. If I expected to be forgiven myself, I would have to forgive indiscriminately from now on.

I set out for a walk to shake off the news. The sky was bright blue and there were flowers blooming everywhere. I found myself outside the store. The key was still on my key chain. I opened the door and flicked on the lights. There was a stack of mail piled up in a white plastic bin by the door. My bookkeeper had been fishing out the invoices and checks, but the rest of the mail, months and months of it since your accident, lay unopened in the bin. I flipped through it. I came upon an envelope from London, postmarked a month earlier. I pulled a photograph out of the envelope.

Memory is fallible. Does a photograph tell the truth any better? Or is a photograph an equally unreliable artifact? It was nearly a year ago that I'd received a photo in the mailbox I'd thought was from Patrick and misinterpreted entirely. This one actually was from Patrick.

It wasn't just one, I realized, after a minute. It was one, blown up, and a dozen more in the standard size, every single one a photograph of me. In all the photos my hair is in a thick dark ponytail nearly to my waist, half hidden, as is my face, by a wide-brimmed straw hat adorned with a simple black ribbon.

I thought at first they were the photos Patrick had taken the day we went hat shopping. I could recall no other time I had worn a hat. But he had not taken photos of me in the shop. He had taken them outside, when we were walking in the rain, and I wasn't wearing a hat then.

I looked more closely. In the background were clues. Horses. A racetrack. The stands. The white-clothed tables of a dining room. The elegant red-velvet seats of a train compartment.

There was a note from Patrick, explaining. That fall, before Malcolm's death, when Patrick was living in the cottage in Richmond, Malcolm had asked to borrow a camera. He'd taken some photos with the camera, not quite a whole roll. He'd returned the camera to Patrick with the roll inside it. Patrick had promised to develop the film, but he never had. Then Malcolm had died, and the roll had been filed away in Patrick's haphazard filing system, undeveloped all this time.

Patrick wrote that since he'd seen me last summer, his father had died and left him the house in Howth. He'd sold the gallery and was moving back to Ireland. He was cleaning out his darkroom, purging more than twenty years' worth of debris, including dozens of rolls of old film. He'd come across a roll labeled MALCOLM CHURCH. Out of curiosity, he'd developed it, and this was what he'd found.

The photos must have been taken the day Malcolm and I took the train to the races. But where did the hat come from? And where was the posture I remembered myself taking back then — aloof, annoyed, self-absorbed? I couldn't find any evidence of that sentiment in these photos. Instead, I saw in my shadowed face something startling. I was gazing at the camera, and at the photographer, who can only have been Malcolm, with what appears to have been a look of love. Was it possible I had loved him — Malcolm — after all?

I closed my eyes. I dragged the memory of that day out of the darkness of time. I stepped through it, in my head, blurred image by blurred image, until finally, I saw it. A shop next to the stands at the races that sold sundries and snacks. Nuts. Gum. Cigars. Sunglasses. And hats. Finally, I located myself.

I am standing inside the shop, with Malcolm. We are at the counter. He is buying me a hat to keep the sun off my face. He is placing it on my head. He is leaning in to kiss me, and I am not only letting him, I am kissing him back. The hat is falling off. We are laughing, and he is reaching for it, and setting it tenderly, again, on my head.

The hat never made it back to my room in Victoria that night. I must have left it on the train. But how can I be sure? How can I be certain I'm not manufacturing a memory to match the evidence? You can't rely on memory. You can't rely on ancient artifacts, either, to tell you a story you can live with. You can rely only on the sculpture of your life you carve out of the available material, the one that stands by while you muddle your way into your future.

Patrick's note said he thought I might like to have the photographs, so he'd included copies but kept the originals for himself. He wrote that he'd enjoyed our night together more than he ought to have, that he was thinking about me more than he should, but that he certainly understood why I had not been in touch, and he would forgive me if I chose not to communicate with him again. He wrote that he was tempted to tell me he had always loved me, but it wouldn't be true. "It was the tragic mistake of my younger self," he closed, "that I did not."

He signed with the single loopy *P*, unchanged all these years.

I placed the photos and the note back in the envelope and stuck them in my purse. I walked home, flooded with feeling. I pulled down the hatbox and buried the envelope at the very bottom, where I need not find it again.

FORTY

When you finally woke from the coma, your memory of the accident was lost. Emme had disappeared. There was nothing to tell us what happened after I closed the door to Polly's room that night except the evidence left behind. We found your iPhone on top of the sleeping bag on Polly's bed. There was a cryptic text conversation, initiated by Emme, at 2:19 that morning:

"Going for a drive."

"Not a good idea."

"Need my keys."

There was a log of a forty-second call from you to Emme at 2:26.

Your jacket was still hanging where you'd left it. Your truck was in the driveway. Clearly you had left Polly's room in a hurry, and had not expected to be gone long.

The disaster at the store — the tub crashed through the ceiling, the water running for two days, flooding the downstairs

— wasn't discovered until Tuesday, when Michael Moss arrived at his store after the long weekend and noticed water pooling around the door of the Salvaged Light. He tracked down my home number and spoke to my father, who had indeed arrived, having driven straight from Petaluma to our house as soon as his car was repaired. My father drove to the store and waded through the ground floor, then climbed the waterfall of the stairs to the loft and turned off the faucet that was still in the wall and still running. The tub itself had fallen through the floor, taking with it the subfloor, the ceiling and the pine branch with its hooded diamond lights. We were lucky there wasn't a fire.

There wasn't much to learn at the site of the accident. The car was totaled. It was confirmed that the forty-year-old passenger-side seat belt had not malfunctioned, but had ripped at the buckle. There was no evidence of tampering. Emme had been given a blood test on the scene, which showed a zero blood-alcohol level, along with a medical exam at a hospital in Santa Cruz. She was released, uninjured except for a small cut on her forehead that did not even require stitches. Separately, a helicopter had flown you to Stanford and the doc-

413

tors there had sunk you into unconsciousness, so you could be intubated and your organs could rest. We made our frantic drive. We slept at the Mermaid Inn. We waited. We evaluated our fitness as organ donors. On the afternoon of the fourteenth day of your medically induced coma, your father met privately with Mitch and learned that if an organ was needed, it would have to come from me. On the fifteenth day of your coma, the propofol was tapered, and you were expected to begin to wake up. But you didn't.

The days that followed were the worst of our life. I can barely force my fingers to remember them, and set them on the page. I can barely make my mind's eye watch again as Mitch moved around your hospital bed, then took us aside to tell us that in his opinion, the doctor had made a mistake. I can still feel my heart beating in my chest, like one of Polly's birds, as Mitch explained the situation and your father mastered his doubt, and I didn't, and your father nodded his assent, and Mitch sprang to action and saved your life.

Three days after Mitch ordered your medications to be increased, then very slowly tapered, you opened your eyes. The respirator was removed, and you took a breath. The following morning, on your twenty-first birthday, you looked at me and smiled. Within a week, you were transferred from the trauma center to a regular room, officially on the road to an exceptionally rapid recovery. By mid-October you were moved from the medical center to an adjacent rehabilitation center, just a block from the Mermaid Inn.

We were ecstatic. You, on the other hand, appeared deranged. You were plagued, long after you regained consciousness, by memory loss, and by what we learned were officially termed "coma dreams" — relentlessly vivid dreams experienced not as dreams at all, but as if they were waking encounters. We learned that there is no clear-cut medical explanation for their intensity and tenacity, but they are experienced by the vast majority of coma survivors. It can take weeks, or months, until the feelings associated with these dreams subside and the patient is no longer afraid to fall asleep.

You didn't realize you were actually awake for two weeks after you emerged from the coma. You asked me often whether something you were sure had happened the day before had actually happened. Most often it had not. And most things that had in fact happened you didn't remember at all. You didn't remember meeting my father for the first time. You didn't remember a visit from your three roommates from the house in Berkeley. You didn't remember the belated birthday celebration we held in your hospital room, or the homemade cake on which the girls had frosted an enormous pink smile.

"Because we're so happy," Polly said to you.

"We're so happy you woke up," Clara said.

"Mommy said it was like your brain got lost," Polly said. "And then it got found."

You can see why we couldn't bear to tell them, just a few months later, that your brain seemed to have become lost again, taking you with it.

You screamed out in the night. Sometimes you tried to get up and walk around in your sleep, and an attendant had to sit with you to keep you from injuring yourself. We continued to take turns staying at the Mermaid Inn. When it was my turn, I set my alarm for five, so I would be at your bedside at the rehab center before you woke up. Sometimes, when you opened your eyes, you looked at me blankly, not sure whether I was real or not. It seemed to help if I squeezed your hand. It helped if, instead of asking you about the dreams, which only sent you back inside their terrorizing images, I asked you to name the emotion you were feeling.

Dread. That was the word you used most often.

Terror. That was another.

You told me about the one dream that came again and again.

"It was the night of the accident. Emme was driving the car along Highway One. We'd just passed Pescadero."

"I thought you didn't remember that night."

"I don't. But my dream does."

"Okay," I said. "Keep going."

"Dawn was coming. I could see its hard orange edge hitting the tips of the cliffs to the south. I wanted to pull the car over to watch it. Emme refused. She wanted to drive right toward it — into the center of the sunrise. She started driving very fast. When the sun finally crept over the edge of the mountains, it was so bright I knew we'd made a mistake. We hadn't driven into the sunrise. We'd driven into the center of a light-source machine. We'd sacrificed ourselves to the synchrotron, and we were about to be burned to ashes by a light ten billion times brighter than the sun."

■ ■ ■ ■

"Sadness," you said, once, on a morning your eyes were puffy and red, as if you'd been crying in your sleep. "I felt so sad in my dream, I thought I was going to die of it."

Sad was a word I hadn't heard you use in years. I felt as I'd felt when you were a child: I wanted to throw myself in front of your pain to stop it. But I couldn't, because the pain was coming at you while you were asleep.

Then, during the second week of December, when you'd been at the rehabilitation center for nearly two months, you woke in the morning and I asked you to name your feeling, and you told me you felt normal.

"What do you mean 'normal'?"

"I feel the way I used to feel every morning," you said. "I feel hopeful."

The next day you felt normal again, and the very next day after that, you began to ask us about getting your college education back on track.

"Sure," I said. "We could figure out some online courses."

"We'll have to talk to Mitch," your father said. "But maybe you could even go back to

Northwestern this spring. Plenty of excellent doctors in Chicago, after all."

"No," you said. "I mean . . . not Northwestern. I mean the institutes. As planned. Japan. Then Oxfordshire."

I don't have to be too detailed about how things went from there, since you were awake, and your memory was working, and once again you were pulling the strings of your own life. You persuaded us to help you make arrangements to travel to Japan. We began the necessary preparations while you were still in the rehabilitation center. You were walking better every day, albeit with a cane. Your concussion had resolved. Your ribs and your lung had healed. Your kidney was functioning at 100 percent, eliminating any need for dialysis, or a transplant. The nightmares, and the waking remnants of your coma dreams, had subsided.

Mitch was the one to give you a clean bill of health.

Then it was nearly Christmas, and you came home. We planned a celebration Christmas Eve. My mother and father cooked for days. My mother found my good china, and the good silver, and place mats and candles and the cloth napkins and the gold napkin holders. She and the girls made

419

a centerpiece of pine and fresh flowers. They hung mistletoe. Your Uncle Ryan played the guitar. Your father made a fire. My father kissed my mother. Your father did not kiss me, but I was certain he would forgive me in time, so I didn't despair. I'd insisted Mitch join us for Christmas Eve. I'd wanted him to share in the joy of your homecoming, since he was the one who'd orchestrated your recovery. He knocked on the door, and presented us with an extravagant bottle of champagne.

You were upstairs, resting. I called you to come down. You stood at the top of the stairs in a bow tie with your cane in your hand. You cleared your throat. We all looked up. You took a clumsy step down one stair, leaning heavily on the cane, then pitching forward a little as if you were going to fall. Ryan leapt to his feet, ready to catch you, and the guitar that had been in his lap banged to the floor.

But you'd planned this. You smiled, and spun the cane around and let it drop behind you — a Willie Wonka gesture that delighted the girls — then you walked down the stairs, not even holding on to the railing. We all stood and applauded. I leaned heavily into your father, next to me. I looked over at my mother, who was smiling, and then at my own father, who was crying, same as I was. We all sat down to dinner, and Mitch popped the bottle of champagne.

After dinner, I managed to arrange everybody in front of the fireplace for a photo. At the last minute Mitch snatched the camera from me and I slid into his place. The photo is there in the hatbox, evidence that all the people I love best in the world were once in the same house, at the same time, healthy and whole, celebrating the season together.

We sent you off to Japan in January, a little worried because you seemed not quite yourself, but you insisted you were ready to go. We waved goodbye and smiled through our tears as you passed through security at SFO. You arrived safely in Japan. You moved into your room at the institute — and here, on the other side of the world, your father moved out. The girls went to Gold Hill for one weekend, then a second. I began to think about repairing and reopening the store. I returned to the preoccupations that had been shut out by your accident and everything that followed — chief among them the question of how to save my marriage and put our family back together.

Valentine's Day came. I'd stashed a box of chocolates in your suitcase before you left. I'd bought the girls stuffed teddy bears with red silk hearts and baskets full of their favorite treats. I'd spent a long time at the drugstore trying to find a card I could give your father. But he did not like Hallmark holidays, as he called them, and there was no card that said what I wanted to say, perhaps because I did not know exactly what that was.

I opened the mailbox. There was a Valentine's card for me from my mother. I stood on the lawn and opened it, and the uncomplicated message of love it contained made me cry. Then, at the bottom of the stack, was another smooth white envelope, smaller than the one that had arrived in June, with a return address in Paris I recognized right away. It was not a Valentine card; it was a handwritten letter from an elderly English gentleman I'd never met, but in whose apartment in Paris I'd unwittingly drawn in blood, tissue and bone the map of two families' futures.

FORTY-ONE

7th February 2012

My dearest Mrs. Gunnlaugsson,
We have never met, but after much deliberation, I have conceded to the duty of writing to you in the matter of my grandniece, Marguerite Greatrex Church, whom you may know as Daisy Church. You may also know her as Emme Greatrex, a name she adopted in her professional endeavors in New York City.

Since the tragic and untimely death of her mother, my niece Louise Greatrex Church, in September of 2010, Daisy has not been well. At the time of Louise's death, Daisy and her mother had been estranged for nine years. The estrangement appears to have compounded Daisy's grief and has ultimately garnered her a psychiatric diagnosis of "rapid-cycling bipolar disorder."

She may have been ill for quite a while. Perhaps since the sudden death, when she was ten, of her beloved father, Malcolm Church. She had been prescribed antidepressants for some years, and took them faithfully, but the diagnosis of depression appears now to have been incorrect, and the medication that had been prescribed likely contributed to the onset of the rapid cycling Daisy suffered under.

Which brings me to the point of this communication. Some months after Louise died, Daisy returned to Paris to consider the future of her mother's possessions. At that time, she found a wooden box that held her mother's lifetime correspondence, as well as various keepsakes. It did not amount to much, I'm afraid, as Louise was not a sentimentalist, but for our purposes here, there were a few relevant items. There was a roll of film, which Daisy developed in a darkroom here in Paris (she is quite a capable photographer), and a letter from a person who shares your name and, I presume, your identity, dated 30th December 1989, bearing a postmark from Dublin, Ireland. You may or may not recall the nature of that letter, and it is of no account now, since Daisy destroyed it after she read it, except that it caused Daisy considerable upheaval, particularly, it seems, the use, in the letter, of the word "ecstasy." The discovery of that letter, along with the roll of film, sent Daisy into what the doctors suspect was a "hypomanic episode," which, in turn, at some point last summer, escalated to full-blown mania.

Suffice it to say that when she arrived in San Francisco last spring, and mailed you a letter, her mental health had been compromised. As the summer progressed, it continued to deteriorate.

I understand that Daisy presented herself at your place of business, where you generously offered her living quarters and employment, and that your son, Robert, became her close acquaintance. I also understand there was an unfortunate flooding of your store, an incident for which Daisy takes full responsibility, and the memory of which, I assure you, is cause for deep regret on her part. She tells me there was also a horrific accident in a car of Daisy's possession that occurred while Daisy was driver and your son her passenger. I have been informed by Daisy that your son was very seriously injured, and for that the both of us send our most profound regrets. She wishes for me to reassure you that she had no intention of injuring your son. In fact, she seems to have been deeply attached to him, though she has not offered any details to me as to the particular nature of their involvement. This was Daisy's third serious automobile accident, and we have agreed there is no need for her to operate a vehicle again in the foreseeable future. It is my hope that your son has recovered fully, and if this is not the case, I offer my gravest sympathies.

Daisy's behavior the night of the accident, along with her disappearance, must have seemed from your vantage point unforgivable. I hope my letter will serve as a starting point for a reassessment of that sentiment. She came straight from San Francisco to me, in Paris, and I assure you she is currently receiving the best possible psychiatric care.

In short, I hope you will forgive Daisy for the damage to the business of which you are proprietor, and most important, the injuries, both emotional and physical, your son suffered at her hand. I assure you she has forgiven you for what she perceived as your role in her father's death. I do not mean to suggest her perception is reality, but perception is often loath to give up its stranglehold on the mind when it comes to the strange bedfellows of love and death.

Yours, faithfully,

Arthur Greatrex, Esquire

Forty-Two

Daisy. An Anglo-Saxon word that means "Day's eye." The flower so named because of the way it opens at dawn. Also a translation of the French *Marguerite,* and used as a pet form of Margaret. The name Malcolm and Louise used for their daughter when they were alive, but not the name she chose when she left Europe and reinvented herself — and not the name you will hear when she visits you in your dreams.

Emme. One syllable. Like the letter.

Grief. One syllable. Like a great black wave.

I sat at the table on Valentine's Day with the letter in my lap and it came at me — grief — catching me in its curve and twisting me inside its history. Then, a day later, when I showed the letter to your father, and he in turn presented evidence of his own, that wave of grief shoved me under and took my breath away.

Grief for your father, for his predicament.

Grief for Malcolm, more than twenty years after the fact. And for Louise.

Grief for you, on many fronts. Because the woman you fell in love with last summer was not who you thought she was, and your father was not who you thought he was, which makes you not who you thought you were — and me a stranger, and an enemy, for making all of that true.

And finally, grief for Daisy, whose own grief over the loss of her parents I'd opened anew. What would I have written in that letter? What would I have apologized for or explained? What burden did I transfer to Louise — and then Daisy — only because at that moment, I did not have the strength to carry it myself? Every idea I have is a reconstruction. After all, experiencing something is not the same as remembering it. A memory is by its nature a revision. I don't know what I wrote in that letter beyond the single clue I've been given — the word *ecstasy.*

I reread Arthur Greatrex's letter many times. I tried to imagine her — Emme, Emme-and-Emme, Daisy, Margaret, Marguerite Greatrex Church — that final night, after she'd screamed at me and left our house and you'd walked her back and taken her keys. Before you climbed into her car. I tried to claw my way inside her brain as she put the plug in the drain and stuffed a towel in the clean-out and turned the faucet on full blast. As she descended the stairs, the lights from the geometric cutouts casting blue triangles on her red fur boots. Was it madness — or was it plain, bald want? She wanted her parents back, and because she could not have them, what she'd wanted instead was some small revenge. The mania had given her a reckless invincibility, as drinking used to give me, a reckless certainty that she could, and should, get what she wanted at any cost.

And maybe the next thing she'd wanted, after flooding the store, was her car. Or maybe that was only a ruse. Maybe what she really wanted was you.

I picture her storming the twelve blocks of sidewalk in her red fur boots and her gold-leaf dress and her goose-feather choker. I see her standing in the gloom outside our house, texting you upstairs in Polly's room. I hear the sound of your phone next to your ear. I watch you rise, and read, and text her back, and drop your phone, inadvertently, on Polly's bed. What happened next? Did you find her inside the house, snatching the keys, and know you had to follow her? Did

430

you step outside to save her and somehow sacrifice yourself?

I believe Arthur Greatrex, Esquire. I believe she never intended to hurt you. I believe that what she felt for you was not a sinister emotion but a tender one — drawn from the bucket of love.

I went to see your father in Gold Hill the day after I received Arthur Greatrex's letter. I brought the letter and the photo taken in front of the White Cliffs that I'd received in June. The photo Daisy herself had printed twice in a darkroom in Paris, then reexposed one print to achieve the desired effect, then reexposed the other for a different effect. One copy went to Patrick. The other to me.

Jonathan put on his glasses and read Arthur Greatrex's letter. When he finished, he took his glasses off and rubbed his eyes and handed it back to me.

" 'Ecstasy'?" he said.

"I know," I said. "Horrible. I have no memory of it. I don't know what possessed me. I'm just thankful she destroyed it. If I had to read it, I might die of shame."

He looked at me steadily. "I think it's time you told me the whole story."

So I did. I told him everything I'd left out.

431

The morning on the satin sheets with Malcolm at the penthouse. The ongoing affair with Patrick in London. Montmartre, when Malcolm had felt dizzy climbing the stairs. How we'd met Mary McShane at the top. How I hadn't returned to the penthouse with Malcolm. How I hadn't known it was to be the last full day of his life.

I ended with the letter I'd written in the pub in Dublin while Jonathan slept at the bed-and-breakfast, the letter that included the word *ecstasy*. I slid the photograph of Malcolm and Louise and Patrick and me at the White Cliffs toward him. He stared at the photo intensely, saying nothing. He stood and picked up a photo of you off his mantel, from one of your high school swim meets — an action shot, right at the start of your dive. He laid the two photos side by side on the table. He leaned back in his chair with his hands clasped behind his head. He stared up at the ceiling, as if the words that needed to be set down between us were written on the exposed beams.

"Well," he said. "That explains some things. But not quite everything."

"What do you mean?"

He took a deep breath. He went to his desk in the corner and pulled out a folder and slid it across the table toward me. The document on top, which I had never seen before, was titled "Information for Families: Tissue Typing for Kidney Donation." It explained tissue typing in lay terms, describing how a child inherits three antigens from each parent, but cannot inherit a number that neither parent has, and how a parent might not necessarily have a blood group compatible with his or her child. There was a final paragraph titled "A Special Note on Paternity Testing": "It is important for a male relative to understand that tissue typing is similar to what is sometimes called 'paternity testing.' We ask that you consider this carefully, and before you agree to the test, we would want you, as a family, to decide who should be told if the results are unexpected."

I read that paragraph, and finally, after all this time, I understood.

He'd known. All through your ordeal, and your release, and Christmas at home, and your departure. He'd been taking that folder out and studying it at night, I imagine, the way I'd been studying the contents of the hatbox. No wonder he hadn't been able to forgive me. No wonder he'd moved out.

"There are only two cases in the medical literature," your father said. He formed quote marks with his fingers. "Two cases of

433

'unexpected discovery of misattributed paternity in kidney donor pairs.' " He gave me a meager smile. "At least Robbie and I are not entirely alone in our predicament."

I sat in a stunned silence. Was that silence an acknowledgment that I had always known?

I don't know. I know that I had not been engaged in a cover-up, as your father must have suspected. But perhaps I had experienced a "distortion in thinking," to use a phrase borrowed from the clinical literature of addiction. I had not lied, but I had not seen.

I closed my eyes. I sat alone at my end of the table, remembering. The flash of lightning. The roll of thunder and the hammering rain. The bout of undeserved pleasure on white satin sheets.

"It was Malcolm," I said.

"How do you know?"

"Because I know."

"That means Daisy is —"

"Robbie's half sister."

This time it was your father who closed his eyes.

"We don't know what went on between them," I said, when he opened them. "It might have been nothing."

"It might have not been nothing, too."

"Mitch told you? When you met about the tissue tests after the accident?"

"Yes."

"But you chose not to tell me until now."

"Yes."

"Does Robbie know?"

"No. I didn't tell Robbie. Though I wish I had. At first I thought it could wait until he was better. And then I thought it could wait until he came home from overseas. I didn't want to spoil his year. After everything that's happened. After how hard he's worked, first to win the grant, then to recover. And anyway, it was your story to tell, not mine. I didn't even know what was what or who was who. And I was too angry, and too disgusted, to tell you what I knew. What I thought I knew."

"What did you think you knew?"

He balanced his chair back and stared at the ceiling again, avoiding my eyes as he spoke. "All these months I thought it was that kid from the ferry. That skinny red-headed kid with the fiddle. I thought he was Robbie's father. What was his name? He was from Wexford."

"Cathal," I said.

"No, not Cathal. It was an *M*. Maurice. Morann. Something like that."

"Manus."

"Yes. After I left the berth that night, didn't you two —"

"No!" I said. "Nothing happened. I didn't let him touch me. I never lied to you about that. You have to believe me."

"Why should I believe you?"

"I don't know."

"How do you know it was Malcolm? How do you know it wasn't Patrick?"

"I know it's not Patrick."

"How can you be so sure?"

"I just am."

"You didn't use protection with Malcolm?"

"He said . . . He said it was all right. I thought that meant . . . I don't know. I don't remember. I trusted him, I guess."

"Well, maybe he was in love with you."

"I don't know," I said, though I did know Malcolm had been in love with me.

"Maybe he wanted to father a son."

"Stop. Just stop. Please."

"All right. I'll stop. The important thing is we need to reach Robbie. We need to tell him the truth. You need to tell him. From the beginning."

"All right," I said. "I will."

But five days later, when we tried to reach you at the institute in Japan, we discovered you were no longer there.

FORTY-THREE

The medical establishment ruled out Jonathan as your biological father. History implicated Malcolm. But history is a human creation, and so is memory, and so is the science of medicine. And humans are only human. We wanted absolute certainty. We wanted hard evidence. So the day after your father and I confessed to each other at Gold Hill, we went to work. We had everything we needed to know about your DNA from the tests conducted after your accident. We had everything we needed to know about Emme's, too, it turned out, since her blood had been drawn and added to her medical record at the hospital in Santa Cruz. We ought not to have had access to that record, but we had connections in high places. Mitch made some phone calls, then summoned your father into his office. He left a particular patient's record on his desk, where your father could see it, then he stepped out of his office to attend to the important matters of life and death.

We sent you an email on February 20 — the day after we reviewed the results of the sibling DNA tests, six days after I read the letter from Louise's uncle — asking you to call us. We received, right away, an out-of-office reply from your Gmail account. The subject line was a Zen proverb: "When you seek it, you cannot find it."

We called the administrative office of the institute and were told you had withdrawn for the semester. We spoke to the director, who told us in excellent English that he was terribly sorry, he had assumed we had been fully aware of your withdrawal from the program. We grilled him about the circumstances of your leaving and were told it had been cordial and deliberate, and that you had withdrawn for reasons of "health and well-being."

We retraced our steps. We walked through the summer, and the accident, and the coma, and the double-coma, as we thought of it, and your recovery. Then Christmas at home, and sending you off to Japan, and the few cryptic emails we'd received from you there, the first telling us you'd arrived safely, the second that you were settled into your living quarters, the third that the coursework was unfortunately more conventional than you'd anticipated. We second-guessed every decision. We walked back along the thread, trying to find the beginning, but we came up short.

We were tortured by the question of why and where you had gone, and also by the deplorable but seemingly inescapable corollary: Who was to blame?

We did not blame you, of course, after all you'd been through. I did not blame your father, either; in my mind, he was a victim, too. I would have blamed myself, except that the thing that would have alienated you from me — the secret I'd kept from you, unwittingly, all your life — was not yet known to you. So I was inclined to blame a temporary insanity brought on by a return of the coma dreams.

Your father was hell-bent on holding the professor at Berkeley, whom you'd been studying under, responsible. The physics God, Dr. Ivan Karinsky, who also happened to be a Zen master and interested in the intersection between science and enlightenment. Your father was told by the physics department that Dr. Karinsky was on sabbatical in India. Your father would not relent until he was given contact information —

in, of all places, Varanasi. We spoke briefly with Dr. Karinsky over the phone, but all we learned was that he did not know your whereabouts, and that even if he did, he would not be at liberty to disclose them, given that you were legally an adult. He added that it was your prerogative to seek healing wherever you thought you could find it, and that if indeed you had embarked on a spiritual journey, our trying to find you would only drive you further away. His response infuriated us both. It was all I could do not to tell him that clearly he was a person who had never raised a child.

I contacted Arthur Greatrex in Paris to see if he knew anything, but he assured me he did not. He wouldn't allow me to speak to Emme directly. I went so far as to ask him to put his hand over his heart and promise me that if he learned anything at all, he would contact me immediately. Like the gentleman he was, he gave me his word.

I went to speak to Michael Moss at the Green Underthing. A long shot, I knew, but I sensed he had in some way been in competition for Emme's affections. What did I think? That he'd slain you in a transcontinental duel and hidden your body? Or that he'd locked you away so he could win the fair lady's hand? He looked at me like I'd

440

lost my mind and told me he'd never even heard of you, and he hadn't heard from Emme since before she flooded the store. He softened, it's true, when I told him you were my only son, and that you and Emme had been involved in some way, and that now you'd disappeared.

Mitch came to see us, but he could offer nothing more than a reassurance that there was no reason to expect your health would fail. You did not need dialysis. Your kidney had astonished us all by healing completely, as had your concussion and your lung and your ribs and your knee, though you would probably continue to walk with a slight limp for the rest of your life. We assured him we were not concerned about the limp, and he assured us he knew that; he was only attempting to give us the fullest possible information.

We grilled the administrators at the institute in Japan again and again. We contacted the research center in Oxfordshire. We scoured the Internet. We checked with all the hospitals; we enlisted the support of the U.S. Embassy; we worked with the travel authority to establish that you had not left Japan, at least not on a plane or a ship using your own passport. We contacted all of your friends, and all of your ex-girlfriends,

441

and all of your professors and mentors. We started a Facebook page to publicize our search. Your father flew to Japan. After ten days he returned, having exhausted all leads. He'd seen the dormitory room in which you'd slept before you disappeared, but the room had already been stripped clean and assigned to someone else.

So, again, we lie in wait. In our separate houses. In our separate beds. We go through the motions of daily living. We parent your sisters as best we can. Your father keeps his business running. I open the door of the Salvaged Light now and then and try to make order out of the wreckage.

To lay. To lie. A lay. A lie. It's a versatile but tricky word, isn't it? To get the lay of the land. To lay down the law. To lay blame. To lie low. To lie down on the job. To let it lie. To lie down and . . .

Not once, in all the time you were in the hospital, not even when you moved from the first coma into the second, did I imagine your death. Oh, I considered it often enough when you were growing up, as every mother does. When you were a baby, and you slept too long, I imagined that the fumes from the chemicals required by law to make your mattress flameproof had entered your lungs and killed you. Every time you rode your bike, I imagined a neighbor backing his car out of his driveway and running you over. Like all mothers, I lived in a land of imagined disaster in defense against a real one. I worried, I predicted, I prevented — except the time I didn't. And now I can't, because I don't know where you are. I try not to think of you drowned, shot, lost, crushed beneath a train — but sometimes my imagination runs wild.

FORTY-FOUR

Yesterday. The second to last day of April. It poured rain. The power went out. I found some flashlights and candles and waited for your father to deliver your sisters back home from a weekend at Gold Hill.

"April showers bring May flowers," Polly shouted as she and Clara rushed into the house.

Jonathan stood in the doorway.

"Come in out of the rain," I said to him. "The power's out."

"I think there's a lantern in the garage," he said. He disappeared and returned after a long while with the lantern in hand, already lit.

"Have the girls eaten?" I said. "Have you? Do you want something?"

I opened the refrigerator, forgetting that I would not be able to see what was inside. Your father brought the lantern over and I grabbed what I could. I cut up apples and cheese and found some peanut butter. I set out crackers. I found a bottle of wine, and your father let me pour him a glass. I opened a bottle of Pellegrino for myself.

The wind howled. Your father made no motion to leave. He built a fire and we sat around the fireplace. The girls showed us routines they were learning in their hip-hop dance class after school, though without music, since there was no way to amplify it.

When it was bedtime, we put Polly in with Clara so she wouldn't be scared. Jonathan read to them by candlelight. When they were asleep, he and I sat down again by the fire.

"I need to talk to you," he said.

"Okay."

"I went to see Mitch."

"Oh?"

"I wanted to find out if he knew anything about Robbie."

"But he doesn't. He said so. More than once."

"I know. But."

"But what?"

"Something wasn't adding up. I don't know. Christmas Eve."

"What about Christmas Eve?"

"We had words."

"You and Mitch?"

"About Robbie. About what he should or should not be told, and when. We argued, but we didn't resolve anything. What I didn't know was that sometime that night, after our argument, Mitch took Robbie aside and told him what he knew."

"What he knew about what?"

"What he knew about the tissue testing."

"Oh, my God. Are you joking? He told Robbie you weren't his father? Why would he do that? He had no right. He had no jurisdiction."

Your father raised his hands in a gesture of helplessness, but his face was pinched with held-in fury.

"He says he's sorry. He says to tell you it was an awful mistake. He says he had way too much to drink that night. Apparently, he's retained a private detective, on his own, to try to find Robbie. He feels responsible for Robbie's disappearance."

"He is responsible for Robbie's disappearance!"

I was on my feet, now, pacing the room. "Remember he told us he was giving us the 'fullest possible information'? Remember he said that? Weren't those his exact words? He went on and on about the limp. The limp, for Christ's sake! So that's why Robbie disappeared. That's why he was acting

446

so strangely when we put him on the plane to Japan. That's why he was so remote."

"Yes."

I closed my eyes, remembering. "What I don't understand is why Robbie didn't tell us he knew. If he'd only come out with it, we could have put a stop to all this."

"He must have been asking himself the very same question," your father replied. "Why hadn't we told him? Why would we send him off for a year, still in the dark? He must have been asking himself right up until he boarded the plane for Japan. He must have thought that at any moment, we would come clean. And we didn't. You didn't, because you didn't know. I didn't, because I just couldn't bring myself to. I withheld the truth, which was the same as lying. I undid a whole lifetime of trust."

I could hear your father talking, but I wasn't really listening anymore. I was caught up in my own turmoil. "I can't believe Robbie's been alone somewhere, dealing with all this. It's been festering. And Mitch knew. And he didn't tell us. How long have you known?"

"Since . . . for three days."

"Three days. Jonathan!"

I walked across the room, away from him. I stood by myself for a long time, breathing

447

in and out, trying to get my heart to slow down. Your father was sitting on the couch with his head in his hands. He lifted his face, and I could tell by the light of the lantern he hadn't slept. I didn't know in how long. I stared at him, and tried to remember. I tried to remember that half a lifetime of knowing each other, and loving each other, still rested between us. It was right there, in the air, a whole history of standing side by side, facing the world.

I was finally able to move toward him. I held the lantern to his face and saw that he was crying.

I took a deep breath. I stood there a minute longer, then I set the lantern down and sat silently beside him. I put my hand on his shoulder. He didn't shrug it off. We sat and sat that way, saying nothing.

I held the lantern up again. I wiped a tear from his cheek.

"You poor man," I said.

"I don't need your pity."

"It's not pity."

"What is it, then?"

"I don't know."

"You shouldn't pity me. You should blame me. It's my fault Robbie's disappeared. I knew I wasn't his father and I didn't tell him, but he found out anyway."

"Jonathan," I said to him softly. "You're still his father. You're the one who raised him. And it's not your fault."

"Whose fault is it?"

"It doesn't matter. That's the one thing that doesn't matter."

And saying it, just like that, I saw that it was true.

I pulled his face toward my chest. I held him there, against his will, feeling his tears soak my T-shirt. There was nothing I could say. No words that would describe for him the hard, heavy, certain thing that had come into my chest when I'd seen the tears running soundlessly down his face. It was not forgiveness for him. It was not forgiveness for Mitch. It was forgiveness for myself.

It had been a relief to learn that it was not my indiscretion with Patrick last summer that undid us, but the one from more than two decades before, with Malcolm. How much easier to blame the impulsiveness of youth than the wanton self-indulgence of a grown woman. But maybe even that wantonness was forgivable. We are only flesh and blood. We are only chemicals mixing and circuits firing, sometimes in disarray. We are, every last one of us, plagued by useless want. The night with Patrick had been a small indiscretion, I saw now, in the sprawling story of our life, and finally I knew that blame had no role to play. It was time to shed it. It was time to step from its fetid pool. It was time to begin the business of healing, so that when you were found, your parents would be whole.

I kissed the top of your father's head. He turned his face toward mine. I kissed his lips, and he kissed me back.

"There's something else," he said.

"What else?"

"I've been seeing someone."

"You have?"

"Yes. But I'm not seeing her anymore."

He didn't appear to intend to say anything more about it.

"Who is she?"

"Why does that matter?"

"Is she the realtor?"

"What realtor?"

"Never mind. Just tell me."

She wasn't the realtor. She hadn't painted the girls' nails. She was someone the girls never met, and I'd never met, but we might have if we'd been paying attention, since your father first ran into her at the pool in Gold Hill on the Fourth of July. He didn't pursue her that day. He'd barely spoken to her. He didn't get in touch with her until he had moved out in January. They'd known each other growing up. She was the woman he'd been in love with before he met me. The woman who'd wanted to marry him. The woman I had in some way stolen him from, who, all these years later, was threatening to steal him back. There's the past again, keeping its foothold, wreaking its havoc.

"Was it serious?" I asked him.

"It was not nothing."

"Were you in love with her?"

"Back then, or now?"

"Now."

He looked at the ceiling. "Yes," he said.

What force in that single syllable. I felt it hit my chest, a sudden blow. It was like the electricity going out — whatever came afterward was not going to be business as usual.

"Is that why you took the girls to Wisconsin?"

His face colored. "I saw her only when they were with their cousins. I never brought her around. I never even mentioned her."

"Are you still in love with her?"

"No. I don't know. She's not coming back here. She's staying in Wisconsin. I don't expect to see her again."

"All right," I said after a long time. "Thank you for telling me."

"You're welcome."

It was very late. Twice, then a third time, the lights struggled on, whirred for a moment, and shut down again.

"Let's go to bed," I said.

I stood up, lifting the lantern off the coffee table and blowing the candles out. I walked toward the stairs, the lantern casting its dim light as Jonathan followed me and we moved together through the familiar house in the unfamiliar darkness. When we reached the bedroom, I turned off the lantern. Your father took my hand and led me to the bed. It was a feeling like the feeling of walking forward into the darkness at the Tate, walking into oblivion to claim love. Only this time the love was of a different order.

When I woke up, it was nearly eight, and Jonathan wasn't there. His car wasn't in the driveway, either. I stood for a moment at the window and felt the stab of the morning's beauty, clear after the night's rain, high clouds turned electric white by a brilliant morning sun.

I called his cellphone. "About last night," I said.

"Never mind last night," he said. "I shouldn't have let that happen."

"Why not?"

"Because."

"Because why?"

"Just because."

I waited for him to say more, but he was silent, and I could not bear the sound of it, so I hung up the phone. I sat on the bed and waited for him to call back. I looked at the place next to me where he had spent the night. I laid my hand, in his absence, on the white sheet.

He'd said he did not expect to see this other woman again, but what is life if not fueled by the unexpected? A rush of blood came into my head. I stared at my hand on the sheets, and at the wedding ring on my finger. I had been married to Jonathan for more than two decades, but I had not even had the new ring, with its old stone and its three new stones, for a year. I had slipped it on my hand just as our troubles began, and it seemed, right now, like terrible bad luck to keep wearing it. I took it off and stared at it in my open palm. With my other hand, I touched the inside of my wrist. I ran my hand along the bare flesh of my arm and felt again what I'd felt the night before. I was naked. I was human. I was fallible. I deserved to be forgiven. We all did.

I opened the drawer of the bedside table

and dropped the ring in. But it seemed too risky, too tentative a place to leave it. I found an envelope in the drawer and placed the ring in the envelope and sealed it and walked to the hall closet and pulled out the step stool and lifted down the hatbox. I fished out the photo of the White Cliffs of Dover and stared at it. I had not been able to make sense of it last summer, because I'd been asking the wrong questions. I'd been asking who I was, and who I had been, instead of who you were or might become. I had not been experiencing our shared history as a case to be cracked, or a puzzle to be solved, but instead as inside the arc of an already-finished story, a fairy tale shaped out of hope and inexperience — and, of course, love. I picked up the photo taken at Christmas, the one that captured our whole family together. Even petrified memories, it seemed, even buried fossils, could degrade over time. You stood at the top of the stairs, took a step, dropped the cane and made us all clap and laugh and cry. After dinner, Mitch graciously lifted the camera out of my hand and snapped the photo. But before the evening ended, he'd told you that Jonathan was not your father. He'd saved your life and captured our happiness, then he'd compromised both.

I replaced the two photos and laid the envelope with the ring inside it in the hatbox. There would be time, later, to concern myself again with the question of my marriage. After all, who knew better than I how to salvage a lost thing and give it new light? But for now, I decided to let it rest.

I put the lid on the hatbox, then for no good reason at all, I lifted the lid off again and slipped my hand into the envelope taped to the inside, which held the receipt for the pillbox hat with its beaded veil that I'd worn on my wedding day. I felt the paper with my fingertips and pulled it out. But it wasn't the receipt from long ago. It was a clue, one that appeared to have been placed there quite recently — for me alone to find.

FORTY-FIVE

Mother's Day. The girls won't be home until this afternoon. There will be no breakfast in bed this year without your father here to orchestrate it. No tray delivered to my room laden with scrambled eggs and fried potatoes, and a flower from the yard in a bud vase, and a chocolate in gold foil. I don't care about any of that, but I can't help nursing a secret hope that this will be the day the phone will ring, and I will pick it up, and I will hear your voice. Or the front door will make its familiar groan and you will be standing on the step with a bouquet of grocery-store flowers in your hands. You will walk into the house. The dogs will pounce. I will take the flowers and thank you. I will say that I am sorry. I will begin to tell you the truth.

The Deep Forest Meditation Center, sixty-five miles north of Yangon in Myanmar, the country formerly known as Burma. That was the clue that had been left in the hatbox. Or at least that was what was printed on the flimsy business card I pulled from the envelope taped to the inside. I stared at it a long time before I remembered that I had seen that name on a brochure in the squalor of the loft, the weekend I built the arc light, when I thought I might sleep in Emme's bed.

Here she was — Emme, Daisy, Marguerite — making another invasion.

I found the website. I called your father and read to him from its home page:

"The Deep Forest Meditation Center is a sacred retreat intended to allow residents to walk the Buddha's True Path to Spiritual Liberation. The generosity of Dhamma supporters in Burma and throughout the world promise that all meditation instruction, room and board and travel for worthy candidates are given freely in the spirit of meritorious deeds. Residents' stays begin with a mandatory hundred days of silence, including no contact with the outside world. Stays can continue as long as many months or years, or even a lifetime commitment."

"Do you think Emme is there, even though her uncle said she was in Paris?" I asked your father.

He said nothing for a minute, and I could almost hear the machinery of his brain doing its work. "No," he said. "I think she's where he said she is. But I think Robbie is in Myanmar."

It was like the maternity ward all over again — your father seeing something I was too close to see, and stepping in to save us.

Your father dialed the number and conferenced me in, and that one phone call was all it took to inform us that you were indeed at the Deep Forest Meditation Center in Myanmar. You could not receive our call, we were told, since you had committed to one hundred days of silence. But a message could be delivered to you, letting you know that your parents were trying urgently — desperately — to reach you.

Did I thank your father? I did. I thanked him until I was sure he knew I was grateful.

Forty-Six

May 20. The day of the annular eclipse. I was in the backyard with the girls. Your father had joined us for an early picnic. We ate hot dogs and corn on the cob on a blanket on the lawn and, at five o'clock, the yard was folded in a strange blue half-darkness. The girls sat on a blanket, not seeing the change, oblivious to the universe's important event. We had forgotten all about our plan to make viewing devices out of cardboard and foil.

"It's the eclipse," Jonathan said.

We all three instinctively looked up at the sky.

"Don't look directly at the sun," he said. "It's not safe."

He ducked into the garage and found a pair of welding glasses. Clara and Polly looked through the glasses, then I looked. The sun was a circle of light around the moon. It reminded me of the halo effect in the photograph of the White Cliffs. Light and shadow. Shadow and light. The things that had been exposed the least now exposed the most.

"It's the first annular eclipse visible in the continental United States since 1994," Jonathan said. "The moon's diameter appears smaller than the sun's."

I left him with the girls and went inside for the pie I'd bought for dessert. The computer was open on my kitchen desk, and as I had come to do so many times each day, I checked my inbox for word from you. Then I checked the home phone for messages. Then I checked Facebook, and my cellphone for a voice mail or a text.

Then. Then.

The Skype icon on my screen began to flash, and the screen opened, and Skype made its unmistakable sound for an incoming call. I hit the answer button, and on the screen of my computer, like the first sighting of the sun, was your face, nearly hidden inside a wild helmet of hair. You looked like a prophet, or a savior.

"Robbie!" I screamed out.

"Hi, Mom," you said, smiling.

I called out for your father. He came running, just as he had almost nine months earlier, when I'd held a burning phone in

460

my hand.

You'd taken passage on a cargo boat that had never asked for a passport. The boat took you from Japan to Thailand, then you traveled overland into Myanmar. You had sat in silence for one hundred days. At some point, you had been slipped a note informing you that your parents were trying urgently to reach you. Now it was 101 days, and here you were.

I was watching your face closely as you spoke. I was watching it for signs of the as-yet-unanswered question: If Jonathan was not your father, who was? It was a question that was mine to answer, but that you didn't ask, which was a relief, because I didn't want to answer it while you were still a world away from us.

You told us you were not going to dedicate your life to walking the Buddha's true path to spiritual liberation. One hundred days had been enough. You hoped to pick up where you'd left off and spend the fall studying in Oxfordshire. Before that, you wanted to travel, not in Asia but in Europe. You planned to buy a Eurail pass and do some backpacking.

"Excellent plan," your father said.

"I have money," you said. "All my savings

461

over the years."

"Don't worry about the money," I said.

"How did you . . . how did you find me in the end?" you asked.

"There was a clue," I said, "in the hat-box."

"Oh, that."

"Was that you?"

"I barely remember putting it there. It was right after I came home from rehab. I walked past your room, and I saw your wedding photo on the bed. I'd never seen it before, so I just walked into your room and picked it up. There was a hatbox sitting there, full of papers and folders and photos. For some reason I had the card in my hand, and all of a sudden it was like I wanted to get rid of it. But it was like I'd memorized it, too. It was the coma dreams all over again. Something you want out of your mind but that won't leave you. I wasn't planning anything then. I just stuck the card in there. I don't know why. Then, when I got to Japan, I kind of fell apart. Before that, even, I was . . . Ever since —"

Your father finished the sentence for you: "Ever since Christmas Eve."

You looked at us steadily. "Yes. Ever since Christmas Eve," you said. "In Japan, I just couldn't deal. I couldn't sleep. I'd just lie there. I felt like I was going crazy. I had to do something. And I kept remembering the silent retreat center in Myanmar, so I just decided to go there. I'm sorry about disappearing."

"It's all right," I said.

"Consider yourself officially exonerated," your father said. "But where did the card come from? How did you know about that center?"

"I don't know. It could have been given to me during the time that I don't remember."

"It must have been Emme," I said.

Your face colored brightly inside your frame of Jesus hair.

"You're probably right," you said. Then you cleared your throat. "Speaking of Emme . . ."

And you told us that your first stop in Europe was going to be Paris, since you'd been in touch with Emme, and she was living there with her uncle.

Emme. Like the letter. Like an eclipse. A force of nature that keeps coming around, taking out the lights.

FORTY-SEVEN

June has arrived. For the second time in less than twelve months, I find myself on a plane to Europe. I made sure to book my flight so that it would land a half-day ahead of yours. You don't know I'm coming, and it's critical that I find you before you find Emme.

I take a folder out of my bag. I set the folder on the gray flip-down tray in front of me to study the evidence. A copy of the results of your tissue tests, and of your father's, and the explanation of what those results mean. The record of the DNA tests that were garnered from Daisy's blood, then compared to yours. The letter from Daisy's uncle. The photograph of you and Daisy at the pool, and the one of Daisy's — and your — deceased father, Malcolm Church, and his deceased wife, Louise, standing on the chalk down of the White Cliffs of Dover. The spire of Dover Castle hovers over their heads, poking through the fog, as if it knows it will be the last photograph ever taken of Malcolm, and it is trying to lift him toward the light. I scanned it and cropped it before I had it printed, so that only Malcolm and Louise remained.

I haven't brought all those other pages of white paper on which I scrawled my barely legible revision, my plea, my tangled attempt to finally see the past and let it rest. I know now that I wrote it mostly for myself. It's my story those pages contain, not anyone else's, and the only story you need now is your own. So the stack of white paper has been left behind. I've moved it from the hatbox to a safe-deposit box, where the story it tells can't do any more harm.

I stare out the window of the plane. I watch the land shrink behind us, and inside, I feel a sea of emotion. Because in spite of all the words I wrote since the letter arrived from Emme's uncle on Valentine's Day, some part of me must have believed I'd be allowed to keep from you pieces of the truth — namely, the secret of who you are, and who Emme is, and who you are to each other. The secret I'm afraid might really break your heart.

I close my eyes and listen to the white

noise of the airplane's engines. I remember sitting in the car the night we brought you home from the rehab center at Christmas, when your body was healing and your heart was still whole and the house was strung with lights. We listened to that old song from your infancy, and your father cried, and I knew that we were blessed and lucky. I remind myself that we are blessed and lucky again, now that you are found. I remind myself it is the same mother's love I felt that day in the car that is bringing me to you now. And if the news I have to give you breaks your heart, I will tell you I am sorry, and I will trust that your heart will mend. I will trust that your father's will mend, too, in time. I will remember Polly, in bed last summer, touching my face, and my tears, and reminding me what matters.

EPILOGUE

Labor Day weekend, exactly a year since your accident. It was Jonathan's weekend with the girls, but he invited me to come to Gold Hill on Sunday. He said there was a carnival day at the pool. A dunk tank, a water slide, bobbing for apples. Good clean fun, he promised. I didn't know about going back to that pool, given the memories, but I wanted us to be a family, so I went.

The girls were already at the pool. The neighbors next door had walked them up. Jonathan said there was a house for sale down the street. Did I want to come take a look at it?

I didn't ask questions. I didn't want to jinx anything. We walked the block in silence.

The owner showed us around herself, since the house wasn't yet on the market. It was beautiful, with pale walls and pale wood and big windows looking out over an expansive view. There was an elegant contemporary fixture over the kitchen island, a deconstructed chandelier with brilliant glass crystals hanging in a line from a chrome rod, interlaced with strands of tiny rice lights. It made an impression — an entirely new thing shedding light on the ancient slab of granite below.

As we walked back, I asked Jonathan why the woman was selling.

"A divorce," he said.

"That's sad."

"Yes. It is sad."

"It's a beautiful house."

"Yes."

"If Robbie ever decides to tear himself away from Oxfordshire and needs a place for a while, he could have the guesthouse out back."

"Yes," he said. "I thought of that, too."

He reached over and took my hand. The back of my neck began to tingle with — what?

"Let's go for a drive," he said.

So we went for a drive, up a windy road under towering pines to the top of Skyline. We parked at the end of a dirt road where we could see the whole valley and the bay on one side and the Pacific Ocean on the other. He leaned across the center console and kissed me. It was the first kiss in many months, and it reminded me that it was only inside Jonathan's kisses that I had ever felt entirely known.

He opened the door of the Suburban and put the hatch up and the tailgate down. He spread out an old towel and lay on top of it. I lay down next to him. For a minute I didn't know what was going to happen, then he reached his hand under my skirt, and I did know.

"This is not very dignified," I said after it was over.

"Sure it is," he said. "And anyway, there's no one around to see us."

It was three o'clock in the afternoon. The towel beneath us smelled of chlorine and sex. We were naked, stretched out in the back of an SUV, our bare feet and calves extending into the open air. That's all anybody would see of us. His hairy calves, my shaven ones. My unpainted toenails, clipped short. His heels, hacked up with calluses, as if he'd carved pieces out of them with a pocket-knife.

There was a breeze sighing in the trees. The sky was very blue. A formation of geese appeared above us, honking as it moved toward the horizon. How shocking to stumble upon a scene like this, I thought, inside an institution as battered and tenuous as our marriage.

"This is not the kind of thing married people do in the middle of the afternoon in a car," I said.

"We're not really married," he replied.

"We're not?"

"Not properly. We don't live together."

"That's true."

"But we will."

"We will?"

"Sure. Why not? Let's put an offer in on that house."

"Okay. But can we afford it?"

"As a matter of fact, we can."

He told me about the deal he'd struck with a large trade publishing house that planned to purchase a half-share of his business in exchange for exclusive rights to proprietary content he'd acquired from various doctors he'd met at Stanford in the fall. We would have plenty of money for a down payment, even if we didn't immediately sell the house in the city.

"What about school for the girls?"

He'd thought of that. He'd interviewed the principal of the local elementary school. He'd filled out the forms, just in case.

"What do you want to do about the lease on the store?" he said.

"I don't know. It's been so nice spending time with the girls this summer. Maybe I should close the store for good and stay home. Start volunteering, or something."

He looked right at me. "You need your store," he said. "The world needs your store. There's a retail space in Palo Alto coming up for lease. Right downtown, next to an art gallery."

"That beats a lingerie store," I said.

He leaned toward me and kissed me. I laid my head on his chest. He wrapped his arms around me. We seemed not to have recovered what we'd lost, but to have forged something different, something older and heavier, a precious compound neither of us knew could be made from the material of our marriage. I felt a rush of love such as I had not felt in years. But did he feel it, too?

"What would help me now are words," I said.

"What words?"

"I don't know. Words of love, I guess."

He tightened his arms around me. He flung his leg over my legs.

"Why do we need words?" he whispered. "We know the love is there."

ACKNOWLEDGMENTS

I am deeply indebted to my agent, PJ Mark, for his long-standing interest in my work and his brilliant guidance through the labyrinth of publishing, and to my editors at Random House: Anna Pitoniak, for her supreme competence and painstaking editing, and the incomparable Kate Medina, for her wisdom, vision, and graciousness, and for her unfaltering faith in this book.

Gabriele Wilson conceived a beautiful cover, and Paolo Pepe, Robbin Schiff, Susan Turner, and Simon Sullivan tended to the book's aesthetics. Countless others have helped this novel make its way into the world, including my foreign rights agent, Stephanie Koven, and the whole team at Random House, especially Beth Pearson, London King, Poonam Mantha, and Erika Seyfried.

Early readers who offered encouragement and addressed the book's accuracy and authenticity include my good friend Naomi Andrews, as well as Marya Spence, Amy Ridout Silletto, Andi Pearson, Amy Edelman, Maralee Youngs, Barbara Hellett, and Alison Afra. Emma Donoghue, Ann Packer, and Robin Black reached deep and wrote generous endorsements, and Cynthia McReynolds provided superb metaphors and expert advice during difficult times.

Dedicated teachers shared what they knew and helped shaped my nascent writing efforts, including Sister Katherine Jean, Katy Sadler, Nancy Packer, Nona Caspers, Maxine Chernoff, Toni Mirosevich, Antonya Nelson, Charles D'Ambrosio, and especially Alice LaPlante, my first creative writing teacher, who has given me priceless encouragement, mentoring, and friendship.

Many fine organizations provided community and the time and space to write, including Flintridge Sacred Heart Academy, Stanford Continuing Studies, San Francisco State University's MFA program, the Vermont Studio Center, the Breadloaf Writers' Conference, Napa Valley Writers' Conference, Taos Summer Writers' Conference, and the Tin House Summer Writer's Workshop.

Yolanda Lopez cared for my babies with unparalleled love and patience during the early years when I snuck off to write, and Brittney Reiser stepped in and took over with unfailing cheerfulness, efficiency, and grace.

David Susman reminded me to write and believed in this book before I did, and Katherine Maxfield, Veronica Kornberg, Elizabeth Fergason, and Amy Payne have been my steadfast companions in this writing adventure for more than a decade.

Old friends have propped me up and propelled me along: Simone Genatt spirited me to Paris when I was nineteen; Hilary Harris has covered for me since the days I was still bumming beers and bouncing checks; my next-door neighbor, Maryellen McCabe, has graced me with humor, home-baked cookies and the loan of many books; Libby Raab took it upon herself to throw a fabulous party when a story of mine finally made it into print; and Erin Mulligan has been a beacon of excellence in literary taste for thirty years.

My marvelous siblings — Steven, Tosha, and Corwyn Ellison — first taught me the meaning of family and made it possible for me to write a book with that subject at its heart. My wonderful in-laws, the Baszucki and Morris families, and my beloved Elmore and Ellison grandparents, aunts, uncles, and cousins, have been a source of enthusiastic support and much love. My aunt and uncle, Rick and Sandra Krantz, have amazed me with their fortitude in the face of unimaginable grief, as well as their fierce, enduring love for each other and for their son, my late first cousin, Andrew Miles Krantz, in whose memory this book was written. Andrew arrived in this world many months too early and left a lifetime too soon, but he lives on in the hearts of those of us who were lucky enough to know him.

I would not be a writer if my father, Todd Ellison, had not held such unshakable faith in me and in the power of the written word, and this book would have withered in a drawer if my mother, Susan Elmore, had not so often swooped in to run my household while I fled to the mountains to write. I continue to be awed by her unbounded energy, self-sacrifice, generosity, and courage.

Above all, a debt of gratitude belongs to the five people who make words worth writing and life worth living — my four children, Matthew, Claire, Diana, and Charlotte, who are beautiful beyond measure and who remind me, daily, of my undeserved blessings, and my husband, David, whose abiding love, unsurpassed intelligence, wicked wit, loyalty, broadmindedness, and dashing good looks have sustained me for twenty-two years. How lucky I am that he turned up across the dance floor all those years ago and believed, then as now, that we were meant to build a life together.

ABOUT THE AUTHOR

Jan Ellison is a graduate of Stanford and of San Francisco State University's MFA program. She has published award-winning short fiction and was the recipient of a 2007 O. Henry Prize for her first story to appear in print. Her work has also been short-listed for *The Best American Short Stories* and the Pushcart Prize. She lives in Northern California with her husband and their four children. *A Small Indiscretion* is her first book.

The employees of Thorndike Press hope you have enjoyed this Large Print book. All our Thorndike, Wheeler, and Kennebec Large Print titles are designed for easy reading, and all our books are made to last. Other Thorndike Press Large Print books are available at your library, through selected bookstores, or directly from us.

For information about titles, please call:
   (800) 223-1244

or visit our Web site at:
   http://gale.cengage.com/thorndike

To share your comments, please write:
   Publisher
   Thorndike Press
   10 Water St., Suite 310
   Waterville, ME 04901